C

The head of the family is Roger Mallon, immensely distinguished and universally esteemed Irish man of letters, who lives in Dublin on the reputation of six vast books, but who has not written a line for forty-five years. His family, children and grandchildren, live in his house, providing both a burden to encumber it and unpaid servants to run it. To visit them—and presently to visit them daily—comes young Mark Roche, who idolizes Mallon; and an American scholar, Thomas MacLean, who is after some good material for research—and very soon after Mallon's diary, the existence of which is a secret.

Eilís Dillon's story is a story by Mallon that his descendants. It is also concerned with selfishness: the selfishness of the old and flattered, and of the young whose lives are overshadowed by their nearness to a spirit so much stronger than their own. The contents of Mallon's diary, and the reaction of the family to its revelations and to the intervention of Mark and MacLean, are gradually and fully revealed.

The Head of the Family

Born in Galway in 1920, Eilis Dillon has written over forty books, published in several languages including Irish, English, French, Flemish, German, Polish, Czech, Icelandic, Swedish, Hebrew and Italian. Her six novels and many children's books, on a wide variety of subjects, had already won her numerous distinctions and a widespread critical reputation by the time her bestselling historical novel, *Across the Bitter Sea,* was published in 1974. Acclaimed by the *Sunday Times* as 'a quite remarkable novel ... a novel of which Zola might have felt proud', this was followed by *Blood Relations* (1977), *Wild Geese* (1981) and *Citizen Burke* (1984). In 1982 she published *Inside Ireland*, a personal essay about the country, its people, places and history. Eilis Dillon was elected a Fellow of the Royal Society of Literature in 1979.

EILÍS DILLON
The Head of the Family

POOLBEG

First published 1960 by
Faber and Faber Ltd., London

Paperback edition published 1982 by
Ward River Press Limited, Dublin

This edition published 1987 by
Poolbeg Press Limited,
Swords, Co. Dublin, Ireland

Cover painting by Helen Pomphrey
Cover design by Steven Hope
Printed by The Guernsey Press Co. Ltd.,
Vale, Guernsey, Channel Islands.

1

Every evening for six months now, Mark Roche had left the house immediately after dinner to go to the Mallons. He did it furtively, surreptitiously, like an old lady who keeps a secret bottle behind the leather-bound volumes of Dickens in her parlour bookshelves.

He left his mother sitting resentfully at the table and went to put on his hat and coat, watching himself in the huge hall glass as carefully as if he were going to the opera. His father trotted past on his way to the study, brushing cigar-smoke off his black velvet jacket.

"Yes, yes," he said absently. "Do go and enjoy yourself. Don't worry about us. We'll entertain ourselves."

The study door closed on his dry sheep-like chuckle. There he would spend the rest of the evening, savouring the sins of medieval princes, rolling their names on his tongue like old wine to bring out their full flavour, wagging his head from time to time and sighing for that glorious era of scarlet and gold.

Mark opened the front door and stepped silently out into Fitzwilliam Street. He took the first few yards quickly, for once or twice his mother had followed him to the door and called him back on some pretext which was soon disposed of, but which nevertheless had delayed him for a few agonizing minutes. Now his conscience twitched uneasily, but at twenty the conscience is still delightfully pliable and elastic and it did not trouble him for long.

Mark was fond of his mother, in an impatient way which he could not have explained. Her wedgwood blue and grey drawing-room bored him, like a theatre scene that is too long left unchanged. There were little white china figures and soft lamps too dim to read by, shining brass around the fire, even his

9

mother's blue-white hair seemed specially contrived to fit in with a preconceived picture, an idea that she wanted to convey.

He thought now as he hurried along how Roger Mallon would have enjoyed describing that drawing-room, with what delightful, poker-faced irony he would have dissected it, down to the very pile of shiny magazines, hidden under the sofa-cushions from his father's sardonic eye. Still Roger's enormous charity would have ensured that the dissection was not merely cruel. This was only one of the essential reasons why he had succeeded when most of his disciples had failed.

Roger Mallon's reputation was based on six vast books, of which five were novels and the last a volume of short stories. Long before they had met, Mark had been an intense admirer of Mallon's works. He had read them so often and so diligently that he could recognize and place a quotation from any one of them without the smallest difficulty. He was also a connoisseur of the whole jargon and philosophy and cult of Meticulism, the literary movement of which Mallon had been the unwitting founder.

It was impossible to discover now where the name had originated. It had probably come from America, where lectures on Mallon were given and received at all the universities with the awe that in these islands is usually reserved for Shakespeare. Mark did not like the name, for it seemed to him that it placed a misleading emphasis on the least essential aspect of Mallon's work. It was true that by a meticulous recital of detail he was able to build up atmosphere, or tension, or background. There was little that the reader did not know about a Mallon character, from his boot-laces through his waistcoat buttons and all the way up to his hair-oil. In Roger Mallon's hands this device was used to reveal the personality and temperament which set his characters on their inevitable course. In the hands of Mallon's disciples it became a monstrous bore. Most of them lacked his insight and humour, and none of them had as good a story to tell. They did not have his skill in selection, and often where he was delicate they were coarse. Still they laboured on, analysing and labelling, but never, of course, duplicating the elusive genius that animated the whole, and that belonged to Mallon alone. There was a Meticulistic philosophy too, distilled from the books with great skill by the commentators.

It had never occurred to Mark that he might one day meet Roger Mallon. The last of the books had appeared in 1913, forty-five years ago. Mark had assumed that he was dead, like Shakespeare and Chaucer and Chekov and any other great men whose names swim readily into the mind. Vaguely he had felt that without the cachet of being dead, Mallon's prestige could never have grown to such proportions. In any event, from the literary point of view Mallon was indeed dead, for he had not published a line for over forty years, not so much as a letter to the papers about the preservation of Georgian Dublin nor a correction of the sometimes preposterous folk-lore that had accumulated around his name.

Mark knew, of course, that there were several people in Dublin, doctors, lawyers and keepers of public-houses, who were permitted to go about with lifted chin and raised eyebrow because they had been Mallon's close associates in the days of his feverish productivity. One or two of them had written little monographs on him, and had thus become entitled to be considered as literary men themselves. But nowadays they all spoke of him as someone from the remote past. When Mark discovered that Mallon was alive, he questioned his father about him.

"I thought you were only interested in moderns—intellectual working men founding new philosophies—all that sort of thing—O'Casey, Lawrence. Or perhaps they would be thought old fashioned nowadays. When I was young they were all the rage."

"At present," said Mark, "it's literary professors discovering the facts of life."

"Ah, yes," said his father. "Plain, uninhibited speaking. And yet, you know, our old friend sex was always with us, even in my time. In fact I should say more, if less self-consciously with us than now."

"Tell me about Mallon," said Mark patiently. "Why isn't he one of that literary group that spends so much of its time in talking about him? I'm told he doesn't even visit their houses."

"I know the reason for that, all right." His father chuckled. "They were all a good fifteen years older than me, but I saw it happen. When I was growing up, they were all getting married. Yes, and Mallon was married about the same time. They were all

11

married rather late, because of having to make their way in the world first. It looked fine, in the beginning. Each in turn asked the Mallons to dinner and a stimulating evening of intellectual conversation afterwards. But the Mallons never asked them back. As far as I know, it was as simple as that. In those days conventions were more rigid than they are now. It made life dull. Convention without colour is dull."

Mark brought him back to the point, before he could launch himself into a description of medieval ceremonial. Presently his father said: "Yes, the Mallons never asked them back. Other failings would have been passed over, but there was no getting over this one. The men wouldn't have minded. Several of them I know said that they should be asked again, that convention should be pitched to the winds in the case of such an outstanding figure. But they reckoned without their wives. Feet were stamped, I believe, and at least one lady resorted to a kind of Grecian strike with which you would doubtless be unfamiliar." He chuckled and almost rubbed his hands. "Mrs. Mallon made things worse. Indeed I'm sure it was all her doing. I remember her well. Her name was Flora Montgomery before she married Mallon. She was a tall, angular, dramatic figure, always dressed in fluttering draperies. They came down to her heels, and I and my friends sometimes passed an idle ten minutes in wondering how she got in and out of them without hanging herself.

"She used to stride along at a great rate, thrusting aside any passer-by who impeded her. She had enormous eyes, but almost no chin. I never saw her smile. There was a little something in the family." He waved a handful of fingers vaguely. "Her sister was just as bad, but in a quieter way. They were descended from impoverished landowners somewhere in Kilkenny. Never got a decent bite to eat, I'd say, by the look of them.

"Mrs. Mallon had old-fashioned ways, though she was no more than thirty when I saw her first. She would stop in the street and bow in a way that had quite gone out, and of course that attracted a great deal of attention. Mallon's dearest friend, Dr. Finnegan, used to play up to her at first and bow also. Then one day Mrs. Mallon met Mrs. Finnegan in the street and said: 'Ah, Mrs. Finnegan, dear Mrs. Finnegan, it was so nice to have you both in for dinner last night. But I wish that my cook could put up as good a dinner as yours. Do tell me how she makes the brandy sauce and I'll make mine try it next time if it kills her.' All very affable. The snag was that the Finnegans had not been to the Mallons at all; in fact they were anxiously waiting from day to day for an invitation. It was the same with all the others, Mr. Gould and Dr. Kennedy and the Drapers and the Ryans. I could never quite make out whether Mrs. Mallon really thought she had had them in for dinner, or whether it was all an elaborate joke. The only one who didn't seem to mind was Mallon's old professor, Michael Cunningham, but his wife was dead. They remained great friends until he died himself, about fifteen years ago.

"How do I know all this? Dublin shook with it, at the time. Then gradually the Mallons were dismissed as oddities, which indeed they were. Mallon had been a bit of a lad in his day, too, so that some people regarded him as dangerous company. A fashionable doctor living on his wits cannot afford to be mixed up with oddities. Neither can a barrister, fawning for his early briefs. They tried again to make friends when Mrs. Mallon died, but this time Mallon refused outright. No doubt some of the things that were being said about them had been repeated to him. It is my experience that if you speak ill of someone to a friend, that friend immediately hires a cab and speeds off to visit the slandered one and tell him all about it. Especially between relations. Yes, especially between relations. And now, if you don't mind, I have some work to do. I find the present much more fatiguing than the past."

He chuckled with satisfaction at Mark's discomfiture. As he left the study, Mark reflected almost in admiration on the ingenuity of his father's repertoire of snubs, each of which assured him of a good twenty-four hours of peace.

He marvelled at his own sensitivity after a lifetime of this handling. His relations with his father had been happy enough until he had reached the age of eight or nine. Then as he began to read more widely, gradually he came to understand the meaning of those long words and complicated phrases with which his father had been accustomed to insult him ever since he was born. Thus a rift had come between them which could never be bridged. Not that his father had any intention of

13

bridging it. Mark remembered painfully how on the day when he had first shown that he understood, his father had worn a look of triumph, as a man might who sees at last the fruits of many years of labour. On that day the study door had shut with a clash like cymbals and Mark bathed in tears of rage and humiliation had sworn to himself that he would never speak to his father again.

But he had, of course, because his father was too clever for him. Since then he had treated Mark with exaggerated courtesy, armoured here and there with little barbs which made affection impossible, and which kept Mark permanently on the wrong foot. And because Mark was too young to repudiate the natural bond between them, his father's position was made even stronger. Thus they had lived together for many years in a state of tension which Mark found almost intolerable but which his father seemed to view as a sailor who glories in a taut sail and a strong following wind.

Mark's acquaintance with the Mallon family had come when he had just begun to feel within himself the first seeds of a bitterness that would in time, if it were not arrested, far outdo that of his father. Recognizing this he had allowed himself to be swallowed up by the Mallons. He had accepted literally their invitation to visit them every evening. Frances Mallon, who rarely troubled to put people at their ease, had said plainly:

"You're the only one who comes here that we all like."

It had begun in the autumn, at a second-year lecture in history at the University. The professor was Dennis, tall, thin, black-haired, and given to justifiable bouts of fury against the Danes, the Normans, Cromwell, my Lords Grey and Carew, the North Cork Militia, the Famine Queen and indeed anyone who had ever lifted a finger against Ireland. While Mark could not help admiring his patriotic fervour, still he felt that a single outburst at the beginning of the year could well have indicated Dennis's standpoint, and after that perhaps he would have been free to lay bare some of the facts on which he was expected to discourse. Mark himself was a born band-follower. His eyes filled with secret tears at the first notes of any song that told of Ireland's wrongs. He always felt a little guilty therefore when Dennis got going, because the diatribes left him so cold. It was

14

a relief from this embarrassment to notice that the young man next to him was doing a clever portrait of Dennis in the form of a dragon, with scaly wings and tail and with forked fire spouting from his mouth.

Mark chuckled appreciatively. The young man after a moment's thought put a long sword into the dragon's right claw and then very carefully dressed his creation in kilts. Tiring of this he took out a penknife and began to carve his name, John Mallon, with some skill on the back of the bench in front of him. Disgusted, Mark turned his attention to Dennis again. Still he found that he had to watch the progress of his neighbour's work. It was done at great speed, with long smooth strokes of his fine fingers. Clearly he had had plenty of practice. When he had finished, he treated the raw wood first with lead pencil and then with ink dropped from his fountain pen and patted into the grooves with a finger. While he was doing this, Professor Dennis suddenly looked at his watch, stopped in mid-sentence and plunged out of the room.

The other students began to shuffle out. Mark's neighbour said:

"Always pencil and then ink. It looks quite old now, don't you think?"

"Why do you do it?"

"It's an attempt to prove to myself that I really exist. I've done it all over College. I hope that it will be a comfort when I come in here again, to find my name on the bench. It will show that I have been here before. In twenty years' time it will be even more important because by then I shall have begun to despair." He leaned back a little to observe his work impartially. "I'm getting rather good at it."

"Yes. Are you Mallon?"

"You shouldn't ask me that," said Mallon reproachfully. "Don't you understand that my terrible doubt is that I am not Mallon, not *anyone*?"

"I haven't seen you before," said Mark, suddenly pleased with his find.

"No. I don't come often. It wearies me."

They went outside. Mallon did indeed look weary. He was tall and slightly stooped, with thin black hair. His eyes were dark and sunken and his jaws narrow. The jacket of his worn tweed suit hung in languid folds around his thin body. Mark said:

"Come and have coffee."

"No money."

"I have some."

"Then certainly." With long strides he started immediately for St. Stephen's Green, pointing like a gun-dog towards the D.B.C. restaurant. "Big cups they give you there. But money is necessary, I have found. I did once order coffee and buns without money, but fortunately the waitress knew me and asked to be paid in advance, so she was able to take everything away again and no harm done. Do you have money?"

"Usually."

"That's nice."

Mark flushed a little, but in a moment he decided that Mallon had not intended to be sardonic, that he had simply made an honest comment. Full of coffee and buns, Mallon said:

"Please come and visit me at home this evening. It will keep me from fretting."

"Where do you live?"

"Washington Road. Forty-six. It's at Ballsbridge. And you?"

"Fitzwilliam Street."

"Papa is a doctor, perhaps?"

"No."

"Just as well. I don't like doctors. They know too much. I had dealings with them last year. Yes, it will be better if you visit me. I noted the way you said 'Fitzwilliam Street'. Something tells me I wouldn't like it there. You haven't by any chance got a little *pied-à-terre* somewhere else, a little love-nest all done in pink satin?"

"No."

"Pity. No one has nowadays. Well then, you must come to my house."

"Will your people like that?"

"They will become resigned in time. We all have our own visitors. You'll see." Mallon glanced quickly and penetratingly sideways. "Am I right in thinking that I would not enjoy Fitzwilliam Street?"

"Quite right."

16

There had not been a question of inviting Mallon there. Mark never brought his friends home. They walked through Merrion Row. Mallon said:

"In any case I don't care to leave home in the evenings. Come at about eight. I'll watch out for you, if I can. But if someone else opens the door, push your way past and sit down firmly on the hall chair, just like a bailiff. No one will dare to molest you then, until I come along."

Mark had never before received such an invitation. Precisely at eight he was at Mallon's house. It was a solid Victorian house of brick and granite. Wide granite steps led up to the front door from a little gravel sweep, which was being gradually reduced to a single path by the encroachment of weeds and grass. Lights blazed on all three floors from uncurtained windows. To Mark standing outside it seemed that dozens of figures crossed and recrossed restlessly in all of the rooms, sending out rays of energy that penetrated to him through the window glass. He plunged up the steps, taking them two at a time in his anxiety to find out what was going on inside. The front door stood an inch or two open. On the step he was seized with sudden shyness so that his knock was timid. No one came. He pushed the door gently and went into the hall. There was the chair, on which he had been instructed to sit like a bailiff. Then all at once he felt his upper lip curl downward in contempt, whether of himself for being the slave of convention or of Mallon for his disregard of it he was not sure. He hated the chair particularly, and sent it a narrow-eyed look full of loathing.

Then he became conscious of being watched from between the mirror-glass doors at the other end of the hall. A figure had moved there when he came in first, but it had been his own, reflected in the glass, looking so pinkly sheepish and apologetic that he had turned quickly away from it. Now an old man stood there, thin and slightly stooped at the shoulders, with the bearded face of an El Greco gentleman, but hollow-eyed and ascetic. The mouth was firm but not cynical and he looked directly and piercingly at Mark, who could not have failed to observe the extraordinary similarity both of mind and body that existed between this man and John Mallon. Mark's first thought was that here was a satisfactory explanation of Mallon,

17

that he was an old man's son. The weariness, the cultivated calm, the air of never having been surprised—all of the things that had attracted Mark to Mallon might have been the result of living at close quarters all his life with just such a parent as this. The old man opened one eye very wide, with conspiratorial effect, and said, in a hoarse whisper:

"Young fellow! Come over here!"

Mark walked cautiously along the hall.

"Who are you?"

"Mark Roche."

"Friend of?"

"John."

"Ah. Good taste John has. Come upstairs and talk to me."

"But John said he would watch out for me."

"John is probably asleep. Anyway it won't be the first time I've looted one of his friends. He'll know where to look for you."

Meekly Mark followed him up the shabby stairs and across a broad landing to the door of a room which looked out on the front of the house. The old man moved fast. He paused at the door and waited, holding it hospitably wide and looking eagerly at Mark as if he expected to find him good to eat. Hesitantly Mark crossed the threshold and heard the door click shut behind him.

They were in a huge square-shaped room which was furnished as if it often had to accommodate a great number of guests. Little chairs were everywhere. They were quite unrelated to each other in shape or style. Mark loved them instantly for that, and also because they stood wherever they liked and did not follow a rigid pattern. There were piles of dusty books, scraps of paper and literary magazines here and there on the floor. Books and magazines rose to a height of several feet from the three side tables and from the library table that stood in the middle of the floor. There was a wide bed of inlaid rosewood against one wall, covered with an old embroidered silk quilt. A wing-backed arm-chair stood with its back to the three tall windows and its toes to a blazing coal fire in the blackened, brass-mounted grate. Mark looked curiously at the windows and observed that there were faded velvet curtains which the old man could have drawn if he had thought

18

it worth the trouble. He did so now, moving quickly but with accustomed ease between the obstacles that stood in his way. Then he came back and stood beside the wing-backed chair, still looking at Mark with the same wide-eyed delight. He bowed suddenly and said:

"Roger Mallon, your servant, sir!"

Blood rushed to Mark's forehead. It was as if the old man had announced himself as the Prophet Daniel. By the time he had recovered, Mark had managed to put himself sitting in a chair at the opposite side of the fire, without losing his dignity. And then, with the warmth of the fire, a rich glow mounted gradually through his body until it found its way out to his very finger-tips. There sat in front of him one of the giants of Anglo-Irish literature. A momentary shock of doubt as to whether there could be more Roger Mallons than one was soon reassured with the answer to his urgent question:

"Are you the real Roger Mallon?"

The old man nodded solemnly and said:

"None other."

And Mark settled down with a long sigh of pure pleasure to enjoy him. There could have been no happier beginning to their friendship. Roger Mallon was accustomed to postal adulation, which though very comforting could never give him the same degree of satisfaction as a live encounter with an admirer. He glowed, too, therefore, though with more restraint, as he savoured the effect of the announcement of his name on his young visitor. It was thus that John had found them an hour later, held in an almost palpable aura of good-will. He looked quickly from one of them to the other and said:

"Grandpa got you. I thought he would. I fell asleep."

Roger said:

"Who is downstairs?"

"Everyone. And Rosa and Henry too. Mark had better come down and meet them all, if he's going to be coming every evening."

Mark looked cautiously at John, but the last remark had been made quite without emphasis so that he supposed he should take it literally. Roger stood up a little stiffly and said:

"I'll come too."

As they came out on to the landing, from another of the

19

upstairs rooms came a long, high, fluttering trill of flute music, so sudden and clear and unexpected that they all stood still to listen.

"My cousin Teresa," said John. "That means you won't see her this evening. Even Mamma doesn't dare to interrupt her practice."

The music followed them down the stairs, sweet and delicate but with the integral strength and precision of thin steel. For hours the air was bright with the sound of Teresa practising trills so that ever afterwards Mark's memory of that evening was interwoven with it.

The Mallons took no notice, as people who live near railway stations ignore the trains. They were all assembled in the big drawing-room, just underneath the old man's bedroom. They sat or stood in pairs or singly, as unconnected as people in an hotel. An anthracite stove of old-fashioned design gave out a stifling heat. A sallow, middle-aged man in a sand-coloured tweed suit was sitting as close to the stove as a cat. Roger and John led Mark up to this man at once.

"My son Louis," said Roger at Mark's right hand.

"My father," said John at his left.

Louis lifted a tired eyebrow at Mark and said:

"I'll know you again."

The brisk, highly-coloured woman who sat close beside Louis was his wife, Nellie, John's mother. Mark recoiled a little from her, because of the hardness of her eye. It was thus that she looked at all of John's friends, suspecting each one of them of leading him from the path of virtue.

"And here is Henry O'Brien, my son-in-law," said Roger with obvious displeasure in the short, plump, wise-looking man to whom Mark was led next.

"Ah, yes, yes," said Henry, very teachery. "We have met before."

He was standing in his favourite attitude which Mark always found vaguely offensive, with his hands under his coat-tails and his stout stomach protruding shamelessly, lifting himself rhythmically up and down on the balls of his feet. The little perpetual movement seemed to Mark in a subtle way to convey a certain disrespect for his company.

He and Mark looked at each other with caution. They had

20

indeed already met, for Henry was one of the many lecturers in English at the university. The year before, a coolness had come between them, over the poetry of T. S. Eliot, a subject on which they could never agree. Because of the disagreement, Mark had abandoned English Literature for History. It was a cruel shock to find that Henry had had the entrée to Mallon's house for years. His lectures on Mallon were rightly celebrated, as even Mark had to admit. He never missed one of these, when they were given in the evening and open to all students. But Henry usually spoke of Mallon in the past tense, so that Mark's impression that Mallon was dead had been strengthened.

That first evening, too, Henry's wife Rosa was there, Roger's younger daughter. She was tall and gaunt and brooding, with a questing, hungry eye and almost no conversation. She was thinking about hair-ribbons and school uniforms and shepherd's pie, for she wallowed uncomfortably in her domestic life, but to Mark's inexperience she was astonishingly and mysteriously romantic. Roger's other daughter, Julia, seemed to be the reverse. She was short and grey-haired and calm, and though she sat near the other people of her own age, still she had an air of being detached from them in spirit. This impression was increased by the intent way in which she was working at a voluminous piece of peacock-coloured sewing in her lap. She was the only one who welcomed Mark in conventional terms. Though he was enjoying the casual reception that he received from the others, he found that he liked this, as a traveller on an exotic foreign holiday is suddenly pleased to hear a stranger use a word or two of his native language.

"Julia is Teresa's mother," said John softly, as he led him away to the other end of the room. "Now I'm going to show you to all my brethren and then we can let them all go hang and talk about the things that interest us."

And thus Mark made the acquaintance of four more Mallons. There were two loose-jointed, tired-looking men called Roddy and Edward, and two eager, discontented-looking girls. Each of them was entertaining a friend, but it was easy enough to identify the Mallons by their ancient tweeds and hand-knitted jerseys. They gave no sign of having the slightest interest in Mark. One of them, a plain, dark, sulky girl, was whispering with a short-legged, coarse-looking man who held

21

his bowler hat perched on one striped knee. She turned on John when he approached and said snappishly:

"Go away, for God's sake. Can't you see I'm busy?"

"Loving smile from sister kind," said John. "That is Mary. We think that she intends to set up house with the little man. He is called Patrick Mulligan. Hard to believe, isn't it? But it's true. My other sister Frances nearly always brings home girls, bosom friends of the switchboard that they operate. I take that as a bad sign for her. Now we have done our best with them all. Let's go into the window and forget them."

With a satisfied sigh he sank into a vacant sofa which stood in the arc of the bay window, and did indeed appear to forget them. Roger Mallon stood by the sofa for a moment and said, as if he were leaving the house:

"I'll see you tomorrow evening, then."

And he went to sit with Henry O'Brien.

For a while Mark watched them, until he became absorbed in John's discourse. John had been the disciple of many philosophers, and he liked to begin new friendships by explaining how he had fallen in and out of love with each. Girls he had no time for. They would come later, he said, when he would have acquired finally a foothold on life.

"But I work very hard," he explained seriously, "not like those other two." He sent a sneer in the direction of his brothers. "My ambition is to become so important that people can no longer be rude to me."

Mark quoted:

> "When I am grown to man's estate
> I shall be very proud and great,
> And tell the other girls and boys
> Not to meddle with my toys."

"*Exactly.*"

At eleven, Julia brought in a huge pot of cocoa which everyone drank out of old flowered mugs. Until then Mark had always thought that he hated cocoa. He had become convinced at an early age that it was a vulgar drink, and now the spectacle of the great Roger Mallon drinking his so appreciatively meant that a tower of prejudice must fall to the ground. Very soon he noticed that this cocoa had a special flavour

22

which could not be explained, no more than could the flavour of the strawberry jam at the zoological gardens restaurant, on a Sunday afternoon in summer.

Towards midnight people began to go, one by one. Each was accompanied to the door by his own particular host, who did not afterwards return to the drawing-room. For a long time, Mark found himself unable to move, because John was holding him with an ancient mariner's eye. When at last he stood up, John lifted himself painfully upright without breaking off his monologue. He took Mark by the elbow and steered him out of the room, still talking, and on to the front steps. There he let him go, saying:

"Good night. It has been nice talking to you. You'll come again tomorrow evening."

Walking home with his head in the clouds, Mark knew that he should be angry at such handling, that he should be determined not to make himself cheap by coming again tomorrow evening, that he should let at least a day pass. But already he knew that this was no time for pride. Already the first strands of the bond between himself and Roger Mallon had been woven. For the first time in many years, Mark had found someone with whom he could be completely at ease. With Roger there had been no need for the wearisome effort to pose, no need to watch his words, no need to fear traps set and sprung without warning, no trace in Roger of malicious pleasure in Mark's ignorance. There was peace, though Mark had hitherto been convinced that peace was the prerogative of fools.

After the first evening, John Mallon showed himself strongly unwilling to talk about his family, but by careful questions gradually Mark found out more about them all. Several of them did no work. Roddy and Edward appeared to spend all day happily tinkering with their friends' motor-cars. John described his father as an agent.

"It's the only description possible," he said after careful thought. "Sometimes he has been an insurance agent, collecting sixpences a week from expectant widows. Sometimes he was an agent for margarine or tea or jelly. And sometimes they let him work in the Hospitals Sweepstakes office, but never for long. Once he taught a poor little rich boy for a few weeks, but

23

Mamma put a stop to that because he used to come home all covered with bruises. Mamma used to be a nurse. She says work is bad for him, and that he should retire soon. Frances works at a switchboard. Mary works in a wholesale warehouse, which belongs to that little tyke who comes courting her every evening." He wriggled his shoulders. "I don't want to talk about them."

When Mark questioned him cautiously again he said irritably:

"Teresa? She's a divine musician, but personally she's a dog's dinner. She fights like a weasel with her teacher. She makes him cry. Her age? She's nineteen years and two months old. I was just two years old when she was born. They were the most peaceful years of my life." He turned to stare suspiciously at Mark. "I sometimes think you like them better than me. Let me warn you most solemnly that they're all awful, except Roger, and Julia perhaps. Roger pays my College fees, and he pays for Teresa too. Roger pays for nearly everything."

Even if he and Mark had been to the theatre together, afterwards they walked out to Ballsbridge and sat for a while in the midst of the family. John usually took no notice of them, and they ignored him, but nevertheless he seemed to draw some intellectual sustenance from breathing the same air as they did. He always looked around quickly to see that they were all there, before pointedly turning his back on them and devoting himself to Mark.

So it was only by hurrying out immediately after dinner, leaving his mother sitting disconsolately at the table, that Mark was able to reach the Mallons' house early enough every evening to have a little time with Roger alone.

24

2

The spring air always made Roger uneasy. Standing at the open window watching out for Mark, he found himself suddenly and painfully aware of the many scents that floated around him, of the clear green of the young chestnut leaves still crushed from enclosure in their buds like the feathers of newly-hatched chickens, of the late unaccustomed sunshine that bored into his soul and searched out dark, dusty places, where crouched the fear of death. He lifted an eyebrow sardonically at himself as he remembered how when he was young he used to fear that age would dull the edge of this most valuable pain, and that life would lose its meaning then.

He had come to look forward to Mark's evening visits. It was no effort to be kind to this gentle, sensitive young man, for Roger also had very early felt the sympathetic bond between them. Mark was a little late tonight. Roger turned impatiently away from the window and went to sit in his arm-chair with his back to the light. The grate was empty now. There had been a week of warm weather, deluding everyone into the belief that summer had come. Julia had stopped lighting his fire, and somehow once it was stopped it was very hard to start it again. Not that Julia was mean. Indeed she was not. And she was the only one of all the blood-sucking pack of his relations who really gave him the tangible respect due to the head of the family.

"I am the head of the family," thought Roger, striking an attitude as well as he could while still sitting in his chair.

He contemplated the idea without enthusiasm. Far better, he thought, to be the feet or even the tail.

Steps sounded on the gravel. He got up quickly and darted to the window, but it was only that loud-voiced girl who was so thick with Frances just now. Roger wished he could sit on his little balcony, like an Italian, and watch out in comfort. But the architect of the house had known that in this climate the balcony would be too cold for any but the very young, so he had only put a window instead of french doors to get out by. Old men are usually too stiff to climb out through windows.

He went back to his chair and drew a sheet of paper towards him, meaning to write down the thought about the head of the family. But his fountain pen was dry and he lost heart. A little sneaking devil suggested to him that it did not matter whether he wrote it down or not, since the room was full of his former thoughts noted on pieces of paper and never even glanced at again.

Still this evening he could not be despondent for long. Mark would appreciate the news that Roger was bursting to tell him. Julia had been pleased too, but the rest of them had behaved abominably. Those young pups, his grandsons Roddy and Edward, had as good as said that he had faked the whole thing to make himself look important. Roger had answered them without dignity, unfortunately, and the girls except Teresa had said he was a brawling old man. Louis's wife—he could never even think of her by her first name—had made vulgar efforts to restore peace. On the verge of calling her by the only name that suited her, Roger had stamped out of the room. He had spent the whole day upstairs simmering. Now the recollection made him tremble again with anger, so that Mark opening the door was met with a savage, animal glare full of pure hatred.

Roger recovered himself in a moment and called out cheerfully:

"Come in, come in! I've been watching out for you. Look, look at this!"

Before the door was shut he was scrabbling through his papers, finding a letter and handing it to Mark. But he could not leave him to read it. He had to explain at the same time what it was all about so that presently Mark gave up trying to make sense of the letter and listened to Roger instead.

"It's from an American, as you see." Roger suddenly succeeded in affecting an air of calm amusement. "Thomas Davis MacLean. There's a name for you. A nice, new, fresh American, an enthusiast for Meticulism and me. He's doing a book about me. He's here in Dublin, staying in the Shelbourne. He would very much like to come and see me, to talk about my books, to ask me all sorts of not-too-tiring questions. I like that. Americans are so polite—academic Americans, anyway. Altogether he sounds good. So I've asked him to come to dinner tomorrow. And I want you to come too, to support me, just in case he turns out to be a bore. Sometimes these fellows are frightful bores, like that other American who came a few years ago and talked about himself all the time, though he said he had come to talk about me. You will come, won't you?"

"Of course."

"And I'm asking Henry too because he is such a bore, and bores get on very well with each other, I've always found. Besides, Henry always says that he knows more about me than I know myself."

"I must see what John is planning," said Mark quickly, though he could see that there was no escaping dinner with Henry.

"It's all right," said Roger cheerfully. "John will be here. He promised. I wonder what Julia will give us for dinner. Since I told her about it, little boys have been coming to the door on bicycles, with minute bags. How she feeds this huge household on what I give her is a mystery. Lots of spaghetti and bread, cheese, and bits of animals' insides, some of them surely never intended for human consumption—if indeed animals ever were. However, it's better not to think about that in advance, don't you agree? Thinking about food always gives me indigestion."

When John came to take Mark away, Roger did not come downstairs with them.

"Tell them I'm working, if anyone asks," he said.

But he knew no one would believe it. And anyway no one would ask. All the same he filled his pen and took a sheet of paper and looked at it intently, as if he might presently find that it had miraculously covered itself with immortal words. Nothing happened. Nothing ever did, now. The trouble might be that he had been reading too much: Balzac—all Balzac, mind you—and then the commentaries; Rabelais, and then

27

the commentaries; Ibsen, and then the commentaries, over and over, always discovering new, wonderful ideas that generated great thoughts inside him. But the thoughts never came to anything. And then he had to read the moderns as well, though he could only guess at which of them would be the classics of the future. Reading, thought Roger suddenly, is the enemy of creation. Again he reached for his pen and this time he wrote it down:

"Reading maketh a full man—too full for words."

That was a delightful old cliché, "too full for words", rarely met with nowadays. Roger had a collection of these, material enough for a book when he could get around to it. He had a deep and personal resentment of clichés, as he had for people who did not feel within them the kingdom of God. One reason why he had taken the trouble to encourage Thomas Davis MacLean was that his letter had been couched in the purest of classical English. Another reason was that MacLean had flattered him outrageously. Father of a great literary movement, he had called him. It was true, of course, thought Roger complacently, and so much pleasanter than being father and grandfather of a great lazy family.

Later, when Mark was going away, he sneaked down the stairs and called to him softly:

"Mark! Come early tomorrow evening. Dinner is at seven."

Then he scuttled upstairs again just before the drawing-room door opened to let Mary and her admirer out into the hall.

That night he slept calmly, comfortable in the reassurance that the world had not forgotten him.

Throughout the next day, however, tension mounted through the floor of Roger's room, so that he had to keep on running downstairs to Julia, to escape from it. She was usually to be found in the kitchen, standing with a concentrated expression at the ancient gas-stove, stirring tiny strongly-smelling sauce-pans.

"It takes all day to make a good dinner out of nothing," she said.

Roger did not dare to ask what were the little lumps of meat in the sauce. They could have been sweetbreads, or brains, or

28

kidneys. With a shudder he wondered if they might even be hearts. He hated the idea of eating hearts, like Snow White's step-mother.

He wandered away upstairs again and took down a copy of his major work to refresh his memory on it. It was the story of a week in the life of a philosophical commercial traveller called Sebastian Murphy, who went about his business in Dublin all day and at night took the tram home to his house in Rathfarnham and devoted himself to his lunatic sister. He had evolved a philosophy to deal with his appalling difficulties, and he uttered his maxims freely to all his friends and acquaintances in public-houses and restaurants and in the shops where he transacted his business. There was a symbolism in Sebastian's name, for he was bound hand and foot to his narrow life and martyred with many vicious arrows. The only difference was that his face was more cheerful at the end of it than the faces of the dozens of Saint Sebastians that suffer on the walls of all the galleries in Europe. Because he was an Irishman, his sex life was not exciting, but Roger had been well able to make him interesting without this help. Roger felt that he had been lucky with Sebastian. An inch either way and the whole thing would have been a failure. As he stood, Sebastian certainly was a fine character. The Americans and the French adored him. They read meanings and messages into him that Roger was sure he had never intended, and that turned out to be extraordinarily penetrating and clever.

Roger loved this book, but he had handled it so often that it no longer meant anything to him. There was no need to refresh his memory. He put it down restlessly and rambled downstairs again. He liked the house when all those strange young people, who would not have existed but for him, were out of it. This reminded him of his wife Flora.

He did not think of Flora often now, but when he did it was to wonder how he had managed to live so long without her. In all their years together she had stimulated and interested him with her odd point of view. She had been the enemy of continuous thought. She had the mind of a dragon-fly, or a chimpanzee. And she had broken up his whole personality into little chips which he could never fit together again in a coherent pattern. He had had some premonition perhaps that she

29

would leave him alone some day, and that he must not waste any of the time that they had together. Then when she had so hurriedly died he had found himself unable to write any more. Perhaps he could have learned how to do it again, but it hardly seemed worth the trouble, since Flora was not there to read the results. In times of stress and excitement like this he missed her most. She would have listened to him and soothed him.

Or would she? Now he began to remember times when she had brushed him off and made little of him. The recollection made him flush with anger.

And still he was glad she had not been like Rosa who was the one of her children who most resembled her in appearance. Rosa thought that her Henry was wonderful, much cleverer than Roger and not so *odd*. John had told him of this opinion of Rosa's and though he had laughed at the time, it had worried him often since then. He was odd. But so, by God, was Rosa, as odd as two left feet. Still because she looked like Flora, Roger had always made a point of helping her odious little husband, so that Henry had been able to build up a whole reputation with his lectures on Roger. It might have been a good thing for Henry if he were a little more odd and a little less commonplace. He was on to Roger's sources of inspiration now. A fat lot he knew about Roger's sources!

So spluttering and fuming and remembering and hating, Roger passed the afternoon. By the time that Mark arrived at half-past six, the whole house was dense with the odours of cooking dinner.

"Smells good, doesn't it?" said Roger. "Julia can do wonders when she tries."

He looked nervous and a little irritable. Mark thought he was showing his age this evening. He longed to offer Roger some encouragement but he was still a little overawed by him and he could not find suitable words. Roger was saying:

"I hope those brats will behave themselves at dinner. If I had my way they'd have a bowl of soup in the kitchen at six o'clock and keep out of sight afterwards. But their Mamma is always hoping that they'll absorb some culture through their thick hides, since it's plain they can't manage it through the normal channels."

30

He went across to the window and glared out. Mark said soothingly:

"I'm sure it will be all right."

"No," said Roger from the window. "When they were younger they used to make a point of screaming when there was someone in for dinner. Now they laugh. On the whole I find that a little worse."

Even Mark's loyalty to Roger was tested by this. It seemed that an evening of embarrassment stretched before him like a long, muddy road. When John appeared presently in a worn dark suit and tie, and with a face as rigid as an African wood-carving, he knew that he was right.

"Mr. MacLean has arrived," said John. "He's in the drawing-room now. Come down at once before they can start on him."

Still things began rather well. Thomas Davis MacLean was a tall, thin man of thirty, with a humorous eye and the manners of a diplomat. The amount of respect in his greeting to Roger was just right. A little more would have been fulsome; a little less would have been too careless. Then by firmly turning his shoulder to the rest of the company, he succeeded almost at once in isolating himself and Roger.

"Good old MacLean," said John to Mark at the other side of the room. "Roger is loving him."

Presently Henry came in, followed by Rosa trailing. Roger was so happy with MacLean that he forgot himself. He put his hand on Henry's shoulder and said:

"Here is the expert. You must have a long talk with Henry, later."

Immediately Henry straddled and rolled himself up and down and stuck his hands under his coat-tails so that Roger regretted his kindness. But it was too late by then. When Julia came to say dinner was ready Henry was cornering almost half of the conversation for himself.

In the dining-room, the first thing that caught Roger's eye was that there were two litre flagons of Italian wine on the table. He wondered how on earth Julia had risen to them, and he felt a little sudden rush of gratitude towards her. All the time while they were finding their places and sitting down, he watched Louis's wife narrowly in fear that she would make a

31

coarse remark about the wine, but she did not. She was being a perfect lady this evening. He ground his teeth and turned away from her.

Roger was pleased with the dinner. The soup was clear and strong, because bones are free, with bits of spaghetti in it. Then there was a *vol-au-vent*, lots of good pastry and hardly any meat. MacLean ate his unthinkingly in three fearful bites and then laid his knife and fork sadly side by side on his plate as he realized that there was no more to come. He could not help contrasting this meagre hospitality with the painful lavishness of his aunt in Cork, with whom he had spent a week before coming to Dublin. On the whole he preferred the Mallon version. It was easier on the digestion, and besides he could not care a hang how little he was given so long as he had Roger Mallon beside him.

Then he became aware that Edward, the scruffier of the two young men opposite, was staring at him in an odd way.

"Julia," said Edward delicately, "I think Mr. MacLean would like some more to eat."

Julia flushed. Edward laughed with eyebrows raised and twisting mouth. MacLean said smoothly:

"No more for me, thank you. Since I came to Ireland I'm overwhelmed with hospitality. From now on I'm going to retrench."

Edward and his brother looked at each other significantly and laughed again. Watching their heavy-handed and purposeless rudeness, suddenly it occurred to Roger that they might both be a little mad. All the time while he poured wine for MacLean and brought the conversation back to a more civilized level, while he observed with gratitude that MacLean with a quietly discerning eye had placed the two young men and had decided to ignore them, Roger was examining this entirely new idea. There was a "strain" in Flora's family, as the euphemistic Irish phrase had it. They had married into each other several times over. This produced an occasional genius but also an occasional oddity. And himself could not be called entirely normal. Again Rosa's comment slipped into his mind to torment him. If only Louis were not so weakly petulant, his family might have grown up differently. Louis seemed to find his own life such a burden that he would not take the smallest interest in the state of his children. Throughout the rest of the meal, Roger watched Louis's children with a new insight. They were no longer children. Roddy and Edward were vicious, idle men. Neither of them could be induced to work though they were always on the verge of starting something where their great talents would be appreciated. Frances and Mary were like their mother, coarse, self-seeking, ignorant and rather stupid women, apparently capable of very little, but they had the anxious, hungry Mallon eye for all that. And they made some attempt to work, though they spent their miserable earnings on the wrong things. Teresa was wrapped up in herself too. There was no clue to her, because she took after the shadowy man who had been Julia's husband for only a year when he had died of cancer. Julia was the only one who understood Teresa, and Roger was quite content to leave them to it. Teresa was all prickles, like a sea-urchin. John was not like any of them. John had some sort of a conscience. Suddenly Roger felt a great surge of patriarchal sorrow flood right through him so that he wanted to weep and tear his beard and call out lamentations to his God for having abandoned him.

They finished the wine and had soon eaten up Julia's tiny but excellent cold *soufflés*. Roger had taken such a liking to Mac-Lean that he wanted to bring him up to his own room, but this could not be done without inviting Henry also. And he had a principle of never having Henry in his room. Henry always poked about and tried surreptitiously to read bits of notes, like a bad journalist. He had to be watched all the time. If he were there Roger could not possibly relax and be comfortable and talk freely to MacLean as he wanted to do. Besides, on account of the wine, he felt able to handle Henry in the drawing-room this evening.

So Roger led them all into the drawing-room, where they immediately split up into their usual little groups. Mulligan was already there sitting stolidly waiting for Mary. Louis and his wife took up positions by the stove and played cards. Teresa, who had not spoken a word during dinner, came and sat for a while with her mother and then went upstairs to practise on her flute. A short, stout, earnest and prosperous-looking young man arrived with a sheaf of shiny papers advertising motor-cars. He and Roddy and Edward passed these endlessly from

33

hand to hand throughout the evening, never growing tired of the exercise. Frances stamped about and waited, it seemed to Mark, to be asked to join the circle that Roger was forming with some ceremony near the window. Roger never once even glanced at her, and at last she was left distressingly alone to wait for one of her friends to come and rescue her.

"My book is going to be mainly about your sources of inspiration, sir," said MacLean. "That's why I'm going to spend some time in Dublin. Already I've been around in one or two pubs where the talk is very good. If I had a tape-recorder I could make a book of that talk. It doesn't need any ornament."

"But if you had a tape-recorder there would be no talk," said Henry.

"Or there might be too much of the wrong kind," said Roger dryly, irritated at once that Henry had taken it upon himself to answer for him.

"That I can well believe," said MacLean with a delighted grin at Roger.

"You must have observed that Roger's sources are not mere pub-talk," said Henry, with the smallest trace of patronage.

"That is what so much interests me," said MacLean eagerly, firmly addressing Roger. "Sebastian is too real, it seems to me, to be a purely imagined character and yet I can't believe that he is a synthesis of what is to be found in your pubs."

"Of course we know about Sebastian," said Henry carelessly. "He is Dr Finnegan, when he was a student. You must meet Dr. Finnegan, Mr. MacLean. I know no one better able to evoke the atmosphere of Sebastian's period. Michael Draper, the judge, is Sebastian's friend Cronin. And Dr. Kennedy is his employer MacGurk. They are all very amusing people. And quite accustomed to giving the kind of information you want."

Henry had had some wine too. Carefully now he lectured MacLean on Meticulism, how it appeared to make nonsense of the theory that Art is selective, but that in fact it was selection *par excellence*, the very soul and spirit of selection. MacLean began to look bored. Mark noticed that Roger's forehead was slowly turning red. Rosa was looking at Henry with a kind of wondering admiration, like someone listening to a flowing sermon in a foreign language which he has long and unsuccessfully been attempting to learn. John was also gazing at Henry, but with such horror and disgust that it seemed to Mark that Henry must inevitably notice it. Then Roger said suddenly, talking very fast:

"That's all my eye about Matt Finnegan being Sebastian. Yes, yes, I know it has always been the fashionable story and Matt likes it that way. Don't go to Finnegan, Tom. May I call you Tom? It saves time and we can't be saying Thomas Davis every moment."

MacLean nodded, speechless with delight. Roger went on:

"Finnegan is too long handing out that story about Sebastian. It's stale, and misleading too."

Henry, distressed beyond bearing, went too far.

"But it must be Finnegan. That has always been accepted. You can't change that now. How could Sebastian be anyone but Finnegan? You couldn't have invented Sebastian."

"Why shouldn't he be a figment of my imagination, the child of my brain?" said Roger, softly.

Mark and John sat up straight. They had both learned that it was a bad sign when Roger began to quote from his collection of clichés. Now he was glaring at Henry, making fierce and threatening faces at him like a giant trying to frighten the third son in a fairy-tale.

"Fee—faw—fum!" said Roger, thundering. "Why shouldn't Sebastian be in my head? Shakespeare didn't have to use his wicked uncle as a model for Macbeth, did he? Or his landlady for Hamlet's mother, did he? Why shouldn't I have invented Sebastian? Tell me that, you backstairs literary man, you gentleman's gentleman! Answer me that! By the gods, you shall digest the venom of your insinuation though it do split you!"

There was an expectant silence in the room. Julia came over quickly and said:

"Roger, please don't talk to Henry like that. Henry, you know he doesn't mean it."

"Don't I, faith? My tongue is the pen of a scrivener that writeth swiftly. I wish that all the seas were ink, so that I might go on writing for ever what I think of people who say that I couldn't have invented Sebastian."

35

Suddenly he saw Rosa, fluttering and flapping like a terrified hen, and he decided to have done with Henry.

"It's all right, Julia," he said, swallowing his rage in a great indigestible lump. "Henry and I are just having a little discussion. Isn't that so, Henry, my old friend and admirer?"

"Yes," said Henry uncertainly.

Mulligan turned his moon-face back to Mary and whispered eagerly. Julia left Roger's group and went to sit down, and the others all took up their conversations again, their hopes of spilled blood abandoned.

Roger said:

"You're doing a thesis, Tom?"

"Yes, yes," said MacLean eagerly. "And I hope that my father-in-law is going to publish it—he's the President of Hollands Inc. My wife is a Holland. My father-in-law is very keen to have something about you, sir."

Roger beamed. Henry relaxed quietly, for he had quickly decided that even now there was no need to cut himself off from Roger. He had had large intellectual expectations of Rosa when he had married her. She had not disappointed him in any way. He did not understand very well the workings of Roger's real mind, but this was so different from the philosopher of the books that there was no need to make the effort. He was not personally fond of Roger at all, which made him in many ways independent of him. Now, for instance, he was tentatively planning a great American lecture tour for whenever Roger would die. It was not a bit too soon to begin making notes. So he reassumed his habitual non-committal smile and let Roger talk on, while he could.

"If it's a thesis, you must have something original to say. It's no use handing up the same old stuff that has all been said before." Roger passed his hand across his forehead, feeling unaccountably tired. The lively face of the young man opposite pleased him; it was full of the respect of the new world for the old, of the pupil for the master: it was clean and simple and uncomplicated, and yet it plainly expressed a fine intelligence and a sophisticated sense of humour. Now all at once a way occurred to Roger in which he could revenge himself on Henry and at the same time help this most worthy and honest young man.

36

"I can do something for you that no one else can do," he said, speaking directly to MacLean as if the rest of the little circle had vanished. "Tomorrow you must come again, alone. No, not tomorrow. I'll be tired. Come the next day, alone. I kept a diary long ago, all the time while I was writing. I overflowed with words, in those days, and I had no difficulty in writing them down. The diary is a sort of commentary on all of the books. If I were to publish it, there would be no further argument about the order in which they were written. A great many other controversial points would be cleared up too. But controversy is the life of literature, and in any case I don't intend ever to publish it. There are too many personal things there. I think you will find much to interest you, but it's quite long and all in manuscript. Have you plenty of time?"

"Yes, sir," said MacLean in a daze. "Plenty, plenty of time."

"Well, I'll show it to you. I have it upstairs. No one has ever seen it before. I'll go through it with you, and in it you will find proof that Matt Finnegan could not possibly be Sebastian."

Roger sighed deeply, utterly satisfied with the expression on Henry's face. It was so satisfying that his triumph was even a little mixed with pity.

"And while I can feel pity", thought Roger, "I am not completely wicked."

With a soft sigh he leaned back in his chair, gazed unwinkingly from Mark to John and back again, and then began to question MacLean about life in America.

"Life in the *country*, I mean," he said. "Towns are much the same everywhere."

Later MacLean could never remember what he had told Roger about his native land. He knew that he had spoken of beavers and buffaloes and prairie-dogs and chipmunks, but an amused expression on Roger's face at the end of the evening made him suspect that he might not have placed all of these beasts at their proper occupations.

Mark walked with MacLean home to the Shelbourne Hotel, as one might carefully attend a child or a drunk. MacLean was silent for most of the way, except for a series of enormous, isolated chuckles. At last he said in a tone full of wonder:

"Mallon kept a diary that no one has ever seen, and he's

37

going to show it to me. To me! And I always thought I was unlucky. Wait till I tell that to my father-in-law! I'd give anything to see his face. I'll have to write it to him. I couldn't risk a cable. The secret might get out. Why didn't we work out a code before I left home? But he'll hear it in a couple of days, and that will give me time to get used to the idea. He did say he'd show me the diary, didn't he?"

"That's what he said," said Mark.

Suddenly he wearied of MacLean. Such exuberance seemed unsuitable in a man of his years. And at the same moment Mark found that a venomous stream of flat, black jealousy began to course through himself. If he had only been ten years older, it might have been to him that Roger would have shown the diary. MacLean only thought of it as a literary catch. Mark would have appreciated it as the precious key to Mallon's personal genius. And a genius who does not want to be adored is as dangerous as a spinster cat.

Mark's father laughed openly at his glowering face as he came into the hall.

"You didn't enjoy yourself, I see. One so seldom does, nowadays. When I was young, my friends amused me far more than yours appear to do. *Mal de siècle*, perhaps, or the shadow of the atomic bomb. I think you talk of the wrong things."

He waited until Mark was half-way up the stairs before adding with elaborate casualness:

"Roger Mallon telephoned a few minutes ago. He wants you to go out to his house early tomorrow afternoon, to discuss something. I said you would be pleased to go. Your mother will be out shopping. I shall be glad of a free afternoon myself. One never feels so free as in an empty house."

His infuriating titter floated after Mark as he bolted up the stairs.

3

Mark had had a good deal of trouble in deciding at what hour he should arrive at Mallon's. He would have liked to come very early, but on the other hand he did not want to appear too eager. If he waited until four o'clock, which according to his mother was the proper time for an afternoon visit, Roger might have become impatient and might even have gone out. Half-past three would be rather dangerous. Half-past two would look as if he were planning to go on somewhere else afterwards. At last he fixed on three o'clock, a comfortable-looking, round figure and a safe, conservative hour. Walking through Mallon's gateway then, he had no idea that he was being spotted from every window.

In her bedroom on the top floor, Teresa was brushing her heavy, black hair with great, long, murderous strokes. Not until she had completely subdued it could she begin to practise, not until every maddening little strand was utterly flattened and held back with a broad ribbon. Then the small, bare room must be tidied still further. A piece of thread, shown up by the beam of sunlight on the carpet, made her want to scream. But she would wait until her hair was finished, and then she would leap upon and seize the thread, and crush it up and throw it out of the window. Her lungs felt tight and empty, and there was a prickling inside her forehead that meant there was a headache coming if she were not careful. Not now, but when her hair was done, she would open the window wide in one long, precise, restrained movement. She never wasted the smallest scrap of energy. Everything she did was exact, directed by a painful tension which was beginning to show in a narrowing of her eyes, and a tightening, down-drawn muscle at either side of her mouth.

She looked towards the window, half-consciously planning where she would place her fingers on the window-frame so as to keep a perfect balance as she lifted it. There was Mark Roche coming in, his overcoat buttoned tidily even on such a warm day, his shoes polished, his trousers creased. He was even wearing a hat. They had maids at home to polish the shoes and so on, John had told her. Teresa's lovely, dark-blue eyes became dreamy at the thought of the maids. They would do every single damned thing that had to be done. She could hardly imagine it. If Julia only had a few of them chained by the leg in the kitchen—but you couldn't have them here. They would starve. They would freeze in winter, poor things, unless they slept in the drawing-room where the stove was, as Teresa sometimes did, creeping downstairs when everyone had gone to bed. It was only then that the wretched Louis and his pussy-cat wife Nellie moved away from the stove so that someone else could get near it. Wrapped in two blankets on the floor, Teresa always got warm and happy, and then she wished that she could have her flute with her to play very softly. But it was out of the question. Roger in the room above would wake up, and it would hurt him to find out that she had come down to get warm.

Roger liked to pretend that they were all contented and happy, though it must be quite clear to him that they were a nest of vipers. All those cousins and aunts and uncles and things could not possibly be happy under one roof. Each of them had at least one thing to hate about every one of the others. Teresa knew that they had several things to hate about her, all right. First, that there was only one of her. Second, that her father had died before they could find out anything about him, and so they could not pick out the bad spots in her character and blame them on him. Third, her good looks. She was the best-looking of them all, which was not difficult, and Julia saw to it that she was always properly dressed. Fourth, her music. They hated and despised that so much that she wanted to go around and blow outside all of their doors, into their ears, until they screamed and went mad. Sometimes she hated her music herself, indeed, but she knew that she could not live without it. Roger and Mark and John liked it, and sometimes she played for them in Roger's room. Mark had thanked her for it so politely that she had wanted to cry.

Really if she had not got Aldo, she might have had a try for Mark. He would be very nice to his wife, one could easily see. But Teresa knew that she would probably be very nasty to him. He would look so hurt, and he would never answer back. There would be too much satisfaction in it, at first, and then she would feel sorry for him, and of all things, Teresa could not bear to feel sorry for people. Her feeling of pity had become completely exhausted, used up, many years ago. That was one of the reasons why she loved Aldo so very, very much that the pain of it was almost unpleasant. Aldo was secure and certain and calm. Teresa thought he must have been like that even when he was a small boy, always calm and humorous and able to make his own decisions. He knew exactly how to behave, and how to dress. He said that Italians are the best-dressed men in the world, but he was not boasting. It was just the truth. When she was with him, Teresa stopped grinding her teeth, and twisting up her mouth. She sat still, and looked at him as she would look some day at God.

Yesterday, oh, yesterday! They had sat on the grass in Phoenix Park after having walked and walked in the People's Gardens until the scent of the flowers was heavy in her head and she felt quite drowsy. Aldo had just put his arm around her so that she could smell the fine foreign smell of the cloth on his sleeve. She wanted to sit there for ever and not to think of anything. She wished that she could not hear the sound of the traffic at all, but there was an unending high-pitched drone that never stopped. She leaned one ear against Aldo's shoulder so that the sound was reduced by half. Then he told her that he had written to his parents in Rome, but the post was slow and it would be a few days before he would know what they thought. He had explained to them that she was Roger Mallon's grand-daughter, because Italians have a great sense of family and they like to know something about future members. Especially with the nobility this was so, said Aldo, and he told her some very amusing things about the conditions under which brides used to be accepted in aristocratic Italian families in former times. The married sons lived in flats with their wives on the upper floors while the parents had the ground-floor rooms and the big reception rooms for themselves. The whole tribe ate together in a huge dining-room. The bride had a sort of contract whereby she was to get two new dresses every year, and a fixed number of meals with meat every day. Anything extra was noted down by the major-domo and it had to come out of her dowry. Teresa snorted and said that that would leave her dependent on the fixed meals. Things were not like that now, Aldo had said. It was just as well. The other thing sounded mighty like Mallon's house as it was today, except that there were no dowries in Mallon's and not many meals with meat either. Aldo and Teresa would have half of a *palazzo* to live in, by themselves. That had been arranged when he was fifteen, ten years ago, though it had been assumed then that his wife would be Italian. Teresa sighed with pleasure at the idea of only two people being under the roof as well as the maids. She would not even have a cat at first, until she would have got used to the feeling of the empty *palazzo*. Then they would have lots of children—at least six—and Teresa would always see to it that no one tormented them. Italians are fond of children, Aldo said, and they know how to treat them. They never take advantage of them because they are small, nor expect them to be able to do things that are beyond their capacity, and that is why Italian children are the most polite and the handsomest in the world. Aldo was not boasting. He was simply stating a fact. Teresa giggled at the notion that all of her sons would be Counts—lots of them, all six feet tall, with Aldo's magnificent Roman head, and all animated with the hot blood of the O'Neills, kings of Ulster, provided by Teresa herself, and inherited by her from her father. There would be a mixture! She could hardly wait to see them.

She said all this to Aldo, of course, every word of it, because she never made secrets, and he laughed and stretched his arms wide so that she fell back on the grass, and then he got up suddenly, though she had thought he was going to pounce on her, and he said they had better have the wedding as soon as possible.

So she would really have to have a talk with her mother this evening. Julia knew Aldo, because he had come to the house lots of times to take Teresa out. He liked Julia. He had brought the bottles of wine for last night's dinner-party, to please her. Though if he had brought a charge of dynamite it would not have been more devastating, judging from Julia's account of the effect of the wine on Roger. Teresa was sorry she had missed seeing Henry being chased up a tree by Roger.

Julia would not think it unreasonable that Teresa should be married at nineteen. She had been married at thirty herself and she had more than once told Teresa that it was much too late.

Aldo never would sit in the drawing-room for more than a few minutes. His own manners were so good that he could not bear the way that the Mallons walked in and out without appearing even to see him, though he stood up for all the female ones. Teresa never encouraged him to stay, because she knew that on any day now Louis's wife Nellie might let him see that she thought all Italians, except the Pope, were ice-cream merchants or tailors.

She finished her hair, and opened the windows, and threw out the thread, which fluttered in again twice in the most annoying way. But she got the better of it, and then she stood erect in front of the open window and breathed deeply, rhythmically fifty times, clean, fresh air, as recommended by Signor Rossi, the stinking little cur who was her teacher. One of the great pleasures of leaving Dublin would be in leaving Rossi behind. It would be a pleasure to him, too, she knew, though he told her through grinding dentures that he had never had a pupil as good as her. He had grown visibly old in the last year, but so had Teresa, so she could not feel an atom of pity for him. His bitter, poisonous tongue was poisoning himself as well as her. And still they clung to each other. He was a magnificent teacher, except that hardly anyone wanted to play the flute, and Teresa was a teacher's dream. He had plans for her, marvellous tours all over the world. He would certainly get a drop when she would tell him that she was going to marry an Italian Count who preferred that she should not play at public concerts. A Count of any other nationality could have been dismissed as a probable fraud, but Rossi would have to swallow Aldo. The notion made her laugh aloud, so that she was in good humour as she arranged her music and picked up her flute to begin.

But just then Frances edged in. If it had been anyone else, Teresa would have shot them out again with a few stinging insults. But she could not be too rough with Frances though

43

God alone knew how much she despised her. Frances had
nothing. Nothing at all. Her hair and her figure unfortunately
had been inherited from Nellie's side of the family, the one
mouse-coloured and lank, the other squat and square with
thick ankles and feet that did funny things when they walked.
Her skin was sallow and oily, not in the smooth Spanish way
but like a piece of wet newspaper. Only her hands were beautiful, delicate Mallon hands with long tapering fingers and easy-
flowing movements. Frances valued her hands painfully high.
She used them often to cover her face, and this had developed
into a fairly successful gesture. Because of it, when Teresa sat
in company she kept her hands perfectly still in her lap as if
they were paralysed.

Teresa knew at once why Frances had come. She had seen
Mark too. She was in love with Mark, horribly, hopelessly,
pathetically, miserably, obviously, and she had to talk about it
to anyone who would listen. Every day Teresa warned her not
to tell her brothers, not to tell her mother, not to tell Mrs.
Murphy, the charwoman who had been coming once a week
since Frances was a child. Frances knew that these were sensible warnings, but the result was that there was no one of the
family left but Teresa in whom she could confide at any length.
She had a half-holiday today, or she would have been telling it
to that big, managing, noisy girl named Carole who was her
best friend at the moment and who sat beside her all day at the
switchboard, giving her bad advice in the intervals of plugging
in.

Teresa let her flute dangle and looked opaquely at Frances
who began immediately:

"Did you see Mark coming in? I was sitting at my window
mending vests and I looked up and there he was. I got such a
wonderful surprise, I stuck the needle right through my finger
but I didn't mind a bit. I was thinking of him, of course, and
seeing him suddenly like that was a sort of miracle."

She rambled over to the window and looked out as if she
hoped that he would materialize again. She picked a thread off
the sleeve of her ungainly hand-knitted jumper and dropped it
on the floor. Teresa slid across and took it up at once and
ground it between her fingers. Frances was saying:

"It's dreadful, what's happening to me. I can hardly bear it.

44

I've been meeting Mark every evening for the last four days."

"You've been meeting him?"

This was something of a shock.

"Yes. I've found out that he gets the half-past seven bus from Merrion Row and I wait there until he comes. I pretend that I don't see him. I get in first. Then he comes and sits beside me and pays my fare and talks to me, until we get to the end of the road."

"But you haven't been coming in together."

"No, because then I tell him to walk on, that I must go into the shop for messages. I can't help it, Teresa. It's the only way that I can see him alone and have him to myself. The moment he gets here he goes up to Roger's room, and afterwards in the drawing-room he stays with John. I tried being in Roger's room when he came but Roger doesn't like me and he just told me to go away."

"And you have been waiting two hours for Mark every evening," said Teresa. "You shouldn't do that."

"It feels like two minutes because I'm thinking of him, all the time. And he doesn't know that I'm waiting. I told him that I'm working late."

"But you never work late."

"He doesn't know that."

"Supposing he passes earlier than half-past seven, for some reason, and sees you there waiting."

The very thought of this made Teresa squirm for Frances.

"I'd see him miles away, and I'd get into a doorway."

"You're mad."

"I know. I never thought that one could feel so utterly and completely miserable. Last night I hardly slept at all. I wish I could die. Oh, Teresa, what can I do? I must tell him about it. And Carole says I must tell him."

Teresa turned away, suddenly amused. Though she was so fond of Mark, the vision of his reaction if Frances were to tell him her guilty secret was really too funny for words. He would scrabble backwards into the nearest burrow and never come out again. When she turned back to Frances again she said sharply:

"You'll do no such thing. He'd stop coming here. John would be furious with you. Carole only wants to get things

45

moving, to see what would happen. And you'll have to give up waiting for him. If he notices what you're at, he'll be completely frightened off."

It took a quarter of an hour to persuade Frances out of her new plan, and then Teresa had to listen to a long discourse on Mark's psychology. Some of it was very penetrating indeed. Frances had spotted, for instance, that Mark was not much interested in women, and that any girl who wanted to marry him would have to take the lead.

"Though I know he would never think of marrying me," said Frances, in tears now and looking quite revolting, "but I'd be satisfied with anything."

Teresa blew a long, high note on her flute to express surprise and said:

"You would, would you? Is that what you're thinking of all day at the switchboard?"

"Yes," Frances wailed, and threw herself on Teresa's bed, so that the quilt became quite wrinkled and twisted.

Teresa's eyes narrowed with rage, but she was able to control her tongue. That was one thing she had learned from her association with Rossi, though he would have been more than surprised to hear that she thought so.

Teresa was suddenly very much interested in what Frances had to say. Not until this moment had it occurred to her that they could ever have anything in common. Then immediately she found the association distasteful and she wanted to get Frances out of the room as quickly as possible. But Frances had seen the sympathetic look in her eye, and she knew about Aldo. So she lay on her back in an abandoned attitude and invited Teresa to compare notes about their feelings. As soon as this began, Teresa's soul shrivelled up and became small and dry like a head-hunter's trophy. She had been weak in showing her interest, so now she had to listen while Frances let off steam. Frances had gone very far in her dream. She mourned the fact that the moral reputation of Irish girls stood so high, because this would prevent Mark from making her an offer. But surely, she said resentfully, Roger's presence in the house gave them all a right to be treated like Bohemians. This from Frances was the limit, and Teresa brusquely ordered her off to recover in her own room and clean herself up.

46

When she had gone, Teresa had to do her breathing exercises all over again, because in spite of her intellectual detachment, she found that other people's emotional displays excited her. Long after Frances had gone, the air was foul with her feelings. But gradually Teresa's scales cleared them out, long, cool, flowing, unhurried scales, as impersonally purifying as a highly efficient electric ventilator.

From the dining-room window, Nellie saw Mark come in. "There's John's rich friend," she said speculatively, thinking of Frances. "Louis, do look at him. He's not like a young man at all."

But Louis would not look. He never looked outwards if he could help it. Nellie was there to tell him what was happening and that was good enough for Louis. The light hurt his eyes, in any case, and besides if he looked out he might want to go out, and he knew that this would be dangerous for him. He had learned the hard way that you could never trust a spring day. Rheumatism, bronchitis, catarrh, influenza, pneumonia and death lurked under that unhealthy-looking sun, and Louis was not going to be caught out by any of them.

Besides, if he had turned his head he would have seen Mary. It was quite bad enough to hear her talking, talking endlessly to her mother about the plans for her wedding, using an odd, half-whispering tone of voice as if the room were full of servants who must not hear, or as if the subject were obscene. There was indeed something a little obscene in her determination to marry that queer little man, called incongruously Paddy and wearing a bowler hat perpetually. Louis almost wished he could arouse himself sufficiently to protest even once, but his conscience did not quite demand it. After all, Mary must be at least twenty-three, and that surely made him independent of her problems.

Taking everything into account, thought Louis meanly, Nellie had been a mistake. As a nurse she had had training in practical things. She had given him grisly details of what it had been like, getting up at six in the morning and doing revoltingly intimate things for all sorts of strangers of both sexes. But now when she should have been doing something positive about Mary and her impossible fiancé, putting down her foot, instead she was rationalizing her agreement to the marriage because

47

he was wealthy by Mallon standards. There was no other possible explanation of her toleration of the prospect of admitting Paddy to the family. Usually Nellie hated little short-legged men in bowler hats.

All these children were a mistake too, thought Louis. It was because of them that he had to share Roger's house. And they were dull children, mouse-grey inside and out, quite without value. Except John. He seemed to be better than the others. If it had not been for the children, Nellie would have had more time to give to Louis. She was able and willing to work. They could have had a house of their own, and Nellie could have taken in a few chronic patients. He wanted to tell her now about the new pain in his head, which only came on in the evenings, about the time when Roger came down to the drawing-room. It was so bad that Louis was thinking seriously of going to bed every evening at eight, for the next few months. Or perhaps he should stay there altogether. He felt safer in bed. He would get well if he were to rest more. There were too many people in the house, as anyone could see, though somehow he did not object to the visitors half as much as he did to the members of the family. For a second this thought made him feel uneasy, but then with the very idea of bed he relaxed a little so that he knew it was the right place for him. Even Nellie was more considerate there.

Just as he was beginning to feel almost happy, he heard Mary mention money. At once a little shudder went right through him, out to the tips of his fingers and toes and up to the top of his head so that his light hair tickled on his scalp. She would need money, Mary was saying, for her wedding dress, for some clothes so that she need not be ashamed before Paddy, for hair-cuts for the boys so that they could come to the wedding, for new clothes for them too, flannel trousers and tweed jackets.

"Common!" said Nellie. "Gaberdine, perhaps, but not flannel."

Suits would be better, Mary was saying, or else they would have to stay away. And she must have a proper wedding breakfast in an hotel, because Paddy was conventional about these things and he would have less respect for her if she did not have a conventional wedding. His family must be asked, and a

48

proper number of hers to balance. They would get nothing under fifty pounds, she said firmly.

Louis trembled, and his thin blood began to mount to his head. Now Mary was saying that Roger would have to be warned to behave himself. Paddy had been shocked last night when Roger had shouted at Henry. Paddy never shouted. His manner to her had changed after the incident. He had seemed to be watching her, perhaps looking for some trace of hereditary bad temper, from Roger. Paddy distrusted the queer way that the Mallons lived, said Mary. He had asked a lot of questions last night, about the family history, and especially about her grandmother, Roger's wife. Mary had not been able to tell him much, and he had seemed to think that she was hiding something, or perhaps it was that he had heard gossip. Suddenly she was in tears, and inarticulate, but presently it became clear that she feared that Paddy might refuse to marry her now, and that she would never escape from Roger's house.

At this suggestion Louis blew up. Living with Roger was a privilege, an education, he said. Anyone who could not appreciate Roger was a fool. Roger was one of the biggest names in Anglo-Irish literature and they should all be proud to have his blood in their veins. Besides, if Mary could not be civil to Roger how could she expect him to pay for her wedding? No one else could do it, that was certain. It was no use asking Louis for money, because he had none to give, not a penny.

When he had said this, Louis felt suddenly calm. Now the position was clear. Now they all knew where they stood. Louis stood up to his full height and lifted his long, slender hands to his narrow head in a tired gesture. He let his delicate eyelids droop so that he looked withdrawn and absorbed. Then he started with long, precise steps for the door, prepared to turn and shriek shrill hysterical protestations at Nellie if she attempted to stop him. She did not. Outside the door he sighed shortly, once, and then darted up the stairs as light and quick as a weasel.

Roger in his room glanced out of the window for the fiftieth time and saw Mark coming through the gateway. He had placed a chair so that he could see out, because as he had predicted, he was tired today. On the table before him was the heap of untidy worn papers which he called the diary. Its only

49

title to the name was in the fact that each entry was dated, beginning in early June, 1905. That had been a momentous day for him, a day of revolution, of decision, of instant and immediate action, the impetus of which had carried him forward for eight years. On that day he had met Flora, by September they had been married and by the following June the first of the books had been completed. He had been writing for years before, small stuff, mostly for the College magazine and for the entertainment of his friends. Matt Finnegan had been his favourite of these, but he had gone unaccountably stuffy later. Michael Draper was another, but when he was made a judge he put on a judge's mask and became uninteresting. By the time that this had happened, Roger had already gone soaring into the upper air and had left them far behind. With calm detachment he had observed their pettiness and their lack of staying power, and compared it with his own exuberance and vitality and intelligence. It was all in the diary, every word of it, and there was also, side by side with this and intermixed with it, an analysis and a record of the slow development and maturing of his own style in writing and of the building up of his characters.

Since the diary was never intended for publication, there had been no need for false modesty. Roger had found that the exercise of putting his true feelings down on paper had helped him to deepen the characters on whose creation he was expending so much of his energies. So shamelessly he congratulated himself when he had done well, or commented scathingly on the self-seeking hypocrisy of his friends as they made their way in the world, or expressed his burning pain when it became clear that they did not value him as highly as they should, or even patronized him, after his books had been published. Most painful of all had been the suggestion of some of the more righteous of them that his books were obscene. Roger wanted to howl aloud that they were no more obscene than daily life, but he knew it would be no use. He could see that anyone who thought his books were obscene had simply not understood them at all. It was as if he had been mouthing behind a wall of glass.

All of this was recorded in impeccable English. Roger felt sure that Thomas Davis MacLean would appreciate that.

50

What made him uneasy was a different thing. It was the fear that MacLean would fail to understand the necessary egotism which had possessed Roger at the time when he was writing his books, and without which he could never have done the work. And also there was the story of Flora.

Flora and her story ran through the diary like a flame which could not be extinguished. Every day's entry was in some way concerned with her, so that it was impossible while reading the diary ever to forget her. And a strange thing was that in treating of her, Roger had adopted a special style, simple and intense, through which his love for her glowed, magnified as in a burning glass. Especially towards the end, when it had become obvious that he could not save her, his living agony was transmitted to the reader with unbearably painful force.

Once he had promised to show MacLean the diary Roger had no intention of withdrawing. But before alien eyes would rest on it, he had felt the need of showing it to someone who was sure to be friendly. This was why he had telephoned to Mark last night. Especially because he was young, Mark would understand his difficulties. He would see how important it was that Flora's feelings should not be hurt, though she was dead for forty-five years.

When Mark came into the room he saw at once that Roger was excited. Usually Roger shook his hand ceremoniously as if they had not met for a month, but today he hardly glanced up from his table before saying:

"I wanted you to see the diary, Mark. I have it here. We'll go over it together and see how we can direct MacLean in his researches." Roger's fingers whitened on the table's edge. "He must read it all, of course. It's no use thinking we can block off sections that he's not to see."

"Are you sure that you want to show it at all?"

"How very perspicacious of you. I do not want to show it. But last night I promised in the light and heat of Henry's presence. It serves me right for losing my temper. I liked MacLean for being so innocent and childlike, and now he must be given the careful treatment that one gives to a child. This will be a great catch for him. It would be criminal to disappoint him."

Mark wondered if he would tell Roger that MacLean would

51

already have notified his father-in-law of the existence of the diary. Distrustful as he was of older people, he could not predict Roger's reaction. It even occurred to him that it might in some way be directed against himself, but to be fair to Mark, he cared less for that than for the fact that he could not bear to see Roger angry. Once or twice he had been present when Roger had walked trembling up and down his room, pouring out his rage against one or other member of his family, on the heads of John and Mark. There was something large and spacious about it, like seeing Jove in fury scattering thunderbolts but it was also a little undignified. It was this that Mark had hated.

Without a word he sat at the table and began to read the beginning of the diary. Behind him Roger was quite motionless, watching him lift the pages carefully one by one and lay them face downwards in a neat pile. At first Mark was as uneasy as an artist sitting sketching in a field, trying to ignore the soft, warm breathing of an interested bull on the back of his neck. But after he had read several pages he became utterly absorbed in the material before him. It was not like anything of Roger's that he had ever read before.

It began with a trumpet-call:

"I have met her, at last."

Flora flashed into being with those words. Soon she became a living woman, so real that Mark felt as if himself had known her once, long ago. He remembered his father's description of her, as an oddity in mind and body. Roger's picture was of a goddess, majestic in appearance and brilliant in wit, and a daily inspiration to Roger in the creation of his books. She seemed to have had the effect of illuminating Roger's mind, so that when he was with her he remembered things that he thought he had long forgotten, scents and sounds from early childhood, scenes viewed from below, as a child sees them, with awful clarity.

"This is marvellous, this is wonderful," Mark burst out, stammering. "This should have been published long ago. It will make a sensation, just as it is."

"It certainly would," said Roger dryly. He stood up to glance at the number of the page that was open. "Read on," he said, sitting down heavily.

52

Feeling as if he had been in some way tactless, Mark settled down to read again. But first he flicked back a page or two to savour once more Roger's outpoured delight in Flora's promise to marry him. On the same day, the first page of the first book had been written. Mark would have liked to stroke the page of the diary at that place, as pilgrims to Mecca stroke the holy stones.

Now began the commentary on the books, that Roger had promised MacLean. There were long notes on Sebastian, accounts of conversations with Flora, analyses of Sebastian's secret resentments and grievances, discussions as to whether or not Sebastian should become resigned to his fate or should fight against it. And most interesting of all was Roger's assessment of his own powers as a writer. The arrogance, the assurance of this were colossal, but somehow they did not appear to Mark in the least presumptuous. This was a man talking to himself, valuing himself exactly as he was, knowing his own worth as no outsider could possibly do. It was true that he only mentioned his virtues, but as Mark read on it seemed to him that Roger was surely immune from ordinary failings. The miracle was that he had put it all on paper. In justice to Roger it must be published exactly as it stood, said Mark to himself. It showed Roger in such an intimate light that it would give to all those unfortunate people who did not have the privilege of knowing him a true picture of his endearing personality.

Then, still quivering with the excitement of this idea, Mark came upon something that he did not understand. He turned quickly to look at Roger, and spoke with a kind of irritation at the delay:

"Here it says: 'Today I went to see Sybil and the children for the first time since my marriage.' Who was Sybil? You could put in her other name there, to make it clear."

"Read on," said Roger. "It will be clear enough in a moment."

Mark turned back to the diary and skimmed quickly over the rest of the page. He went back and read it again. Then he became aware of Roger's presence behind him as something huge and terrible, but pathetic too, like a cobra in captivity.

"Are you shocked?" Roger asked softly.

Mark would not admit it.

"No. Just surprised," he said.

"You see how we must direct MacLean so carefully. He'll be like Cinderella picking peas out of the ashes. He must sieve and screen out of the diary every reference to my wife and to my other family. and leave only what concerns my books."

"That will be difficult."

"Of course. You don't get a Ph.D. for nothing. He must work at it."

Still Mark could not look at Roger as he said:

"I meant that it will be difficult for MacLean to resist leaving in the personal story. His interest is not purely academic. He said his father-in-law was going to publish his thesis. Do you want to keep this secret?"

"What is a secret?" said Roger impatiently. "The best way to keep a secret is to tell half of it. It was well known long ago that I had an association with a lady who lived in Harcourt Street. She was described as a widow, which she was not. I doubt it anyone knew that her children were mine. She moved to Harcourt Street after the youngest child was born."

"How many children?"

"Three of them," said Roger gloomily, but still Mark thought with a good measure of satisfaction too. "I would have married her. I told her so, I urged her many a time, but she would not."

"Why?"

"Three hundred pounds a year," said Roger, who was now marching heavily up and down the room. "That was her price. Her father had left her an annuity of that amount. If she had married she would have lost it. She was hard-headed for a young woman. And she had no such scruples as I had about getting the blessing of the Church on our union. My constant fear in those days was that she would leave me. I shall never forget the agony of this fear, that I should come along some day and find the flat empty. I used to spring up the stairs, two at a time, with my heart in my mouth, and pound on the door until she would open it. It was nothing to the pain I suffered later when I met Flora. Then I prayed for what I had feared before. But Sybil was quite comfortable there in her flat in Harcourt Street, and she never even thought of moving, much

54

less of leaving Dublin. Why should she, after all? Never, never get yourself into those difficulties, Mark. They're damnable. It's all there in the diary. Flora hated it."

He was silent then, and Mark could not find a single word to say. The confusion of thoughts that rushed through his mind, like a mountain river in flood, washed away even the most banal and awkward platitudes that he might have used. Then Roger went on savagely:

"I made a terrible mistake. I had not enough courage. Flora lifted me on to a higher plane, but I was always weakly missing the comfortable, cosy, mediocrity of my former state. I was always sneaking back to visit Sybil, though I hadn't much respect for her, to sit in her warm room and hear the feminine gossip of Dublin. *Now* you are shocked. You never thought that of me. I'll tell you more. When I married Flora, Sybil had a baby, Edgar, just two months old. That was why I visited her at first, to make sure that she was not in difficulties. I told myself that you can't desert a poor woman with three small children. But I found her quite content and living in better style than I was myself. It was she who suggested that I should continue to visit her. There was no need to drop old friends just because I had made new ones, she said. Then when I began to write seriously, I found her company a relief. Especially when Sebastian was suffering I had to get away. I couldn't bear it. And Flora reminded me of him, every time I looked at her. We had talked about him so much. We knew every turn of his mind. We had made him together. It would have been well for me if Flora had been as real to me as Sebastian was. She found out about Sybil, presently, just about the time that Rosa was born. Old bitch from Rathgar called with a jacket that would have fitted a baby elephant. Friend of Flora's mother. Little gift for the baby. Such a sweet little baby. Such a pity about Papa's morals. She's frying in Hell by now, I have no doubt."

"And what happened?"

Mark could not restrain the swift question. Roger turned to stare at him as if he were an impertinent stranger and said furiously:

"Why don't you read on? Read on, man!"

"I'd rather hear it from you," said Mark.

"She began to drink," said Roger. "She began to take

morphine. I tried to help her. I tried every way. But it was no use. She died at last, of a dirty hypodermic needle."

Then he sat down slowly in the wing-backed chair by the empty fireplace and wept, the slow, cold tears of an old man.

4

Mark's pity for Roger was almost immediately shadowed by
the intensity of his pleasure in such a proof of Roger's confidence in him. Instantly he was ashamed of this, but nevertheless it remained the strongest of his reactions as he waited for
Roger to recover himself. He found that he had developed a
slight distaste for the diary, as if it were a living person who
had meanly disclosed old secrets. It was indeed true that
Mark's opinion of Roger was slightly lowered since he had
learned of his early weakness. Suddenly angry at this, he even
wished that the diary had never been written. Far from insist-
ing that it should be published, he would now have liked to pile
it all into the empty grate and send it spinning up the chimney
in smoke. But his new knowledge of Roger told him that this
would never be done. The fact that Roger had for so long
preserved a written record of his very real pain was proof
enough of that. Mark was no artist himself, and he was a little
disgusted at this capacity of artists, which he had noticed before,
for turning their private emotions to account. He could understand that a musician might give the best performance of his
life on the day of his wife's funeral, but it seemed indecent that
he should then be eager for the resultant applause. He had no
understanding of the parallel personalities that inhabit every
artist, nor of the manner in which each of these personalities
can on occasion help the other. In fact Roger loved the diary
because it set a limit to his pain. As soon as the story had been
written down, it had become unalterable, and had gradually
hardened with age. Only sometimes, when he was taken unawares, did his emotions let him down. Tomorrow with Mac-
Lean he would be different. He would be nonchalant and
detached but yet watchful. He might have practised this on

57

Mark, but after having given him a glimpse of his real feelings it would have been unfair to have pulled down a blind against him. Therefore he said softly:

"Do you think it strange that Flora was so put out? I can see that you have no idea of the impact of such a situation in real life. It's quite horrible, and not in the least dramatic. First there is dawning suspicion, followed by remorse of conscience and self-disgust at the idea of entertaining such vile thoughts. Then there is renewed suspicion, then deadly, sickening certainty, then despair. I saw it all on Flora's face. People lived innocently in those days. Oh, we knew how to be wicked all right but there was always a great front of respectability. Flora had lived in the country all her life, sheltered from ever hearing that such things could happen. Their house was very hard to reach—roads like rivers in winter, like Saharas in summer, and then when you got to the gate, a mile and half of driveway with rotten trees falling across it just behind your heels, so that your nerves were shattered by the time you came to the top. This was probably why the family had survived at all. They were Catholic gentry, and it should have been someone's business to go and smoke them out. I have a theory that the conqueror was discouraged by that avenue. I met Flora in Dublin and, of course, she insisted that I go to stay with her mother. The house was in a shocking state. Palladian doorway coated with moss, looked as if it had been struck by lightning. Mushrooms in the hall. Beds like bogs. The stair shook when you walked on it. A biscuit-tin on top of the kitchen fire was the only oven. Rats ate off your coat-buttons while you were asleep. There were slinking dogs everywhere, and a mad aunt in the attic prophesying disaster at the top of her voice in the middle of the night. Flora's mother was charming, but it was a terrible place for a girl to grow up. So naturally Flora trusted me completely. I had got her out of that house. I had brought her here to live. My father had just died and left me this place. I had a little money too, that lasted until the books began to pay. She was delighted with everything here. There was a gas-stove in the kitchen. There was enough to eat. There was not a single dog. She hated dogs. I let her down badly."

Mark asked abruptly:

"What about Sybil? When did she die?"

"She didn't die," said Roger. "Catch her to die. She's still living in Harcourt Street. I have to see her once in a while, about money." He glanced penetratingly at Mark and away again. "I am beginning to think that I should never have told you all this. You'll never forgive me. It was a stupid thing to do."

He stood up abruptly and went to the window. With his back to the room he went on in a tone full of cold offence:

"As I told you, I felt that I could discuss with you how much of the diary MacLean should be allowed to use."

"You can. Please do," said Mark, quivering with embarrassment at his own transparency.

Roger had evidently seen quite clearly that Mark blamed him, not so much for his early association, as he called it, with Sybil as for causing such intense suffering to Flora that she had virtually taken her own life. And Roger was entitled to resent any form of blame as an impertinence, not only from such a young man but especially from one who need never have known the story if Roger had not confided it to him. Mark was actually wondering whether he should leave the house at once without another word when Roger turned suddenly from the window and said:

"Thank you, I shall be glad to." With the same clear-sightedness he seemed to have taken Mark's wretched bleat for the apology that it was. Quite briskly he went on:

"I certainly can't discuss it with my family. Louis and Julia know about Sybil, by the way, but Rosa doesn't, so we may hope that Henry doesn't either. That is a comfort, at least. Louis has always resented the fact that so much of my income must go to the other family."

This was unfair, but Roger felt the need of being unfair to someone, so he did not withdraw it. He pulled up a chair and sat beside Mark in front of the diary, and together they began from the beginning to note the pages which contained references to Roger's complicated private life. Gradually Mark came to understand that nothing need change between them, and that Roger was prepared to behave as if Mark had always known his history.

When John yawning widely came into the room at five o'clock, they paused for the first time.

"Tantrums downstairs," said John. "Couldn't get a wink of sleep. Didn't you hear?"

"Not a sound," said Roger. "Who is it?"

"Mary. It seems that it costs money to get married. I never knew that. Did you?"

"Yes," said Roger.

"Well, Mary knows all about it. There's her own clothes, to begin with. There's an immovable tradition about that—one suit, one overcoat, two dresses. It goes on and on. Very *bourgeois*. I came down to see what the racket was about and I got it all. And it doesn't stop at clothes. You'd hardly believe—it's the bride's business or duty to buy the bedroom suite, whatever that may be, and the linen, and the things for the kitchen. And she must pay for the wedding breakfast, and she must even pay the officiating priest. Isn't it fascinating? I had no idea that this was going on all around me. It appears that Mary will be shamed for ever in the eyes of the girls if she doesn't carry out the tribal customs to the letter. I pointed out that she would have the laugh on them since she would have Paddy, but the mention of him only seemed to make her crosser. My other suggestion was ill received too, that she should elope with Paddy, clutching the bare necessities in a paper bag. Damn it, you just can't carry a bedroom suite and a whole lot of pots and pans down a ladder in the middle of the night. She wouldn't even consider that. Mamma is in a fair taking too."

"Why?" Roger asked. "I thought she was rather pleased at the idea."

"She is. But it seems that Mary mentioned money to Father."

"Oh."

"Yes, and he's gone upstairs, which is a bad sign. She's afraid he's going to be ill again. He's been complaining of a pain in his head."

"The headache", said Roger, "is man's greatest invention. No one can see it, yet no one can flatly deny its existence. There is the happy victim, blandly announcing that he is afflicted, and there's no more to be said. If he looks cheerful, it's because his courage keeps his chin up. If he looks glum, it's because he is in agonizing pain. And the cures are pleasantly various and suited to all tastes. You may lie in bed, or take a walk, or listen to soft music, or have complete silence, or drink tea or whisky. The only thing you must not do is work. All sufferers are agreed on that point."

"All the same I don't think Father looks well."

Roger snorted.

"Which of us looks well?" he said. "Louis needs exercise. A brisk walk to work every day would put him right in no time."

The same thought occurred to Mark and John together, that Roger had never briskly walked to work in his life. Perhaps he thought of this too, because he said in a more sympathetic tone:

"Do you really think that Louis has no money at all?"

"It's impossible to know for certain," said John. "But he hasn't worked for months."

"Perhaps I could have a talk with Paddy and explain the situation?"

"I should think that if you do Mary will poison your tea. Don't interfere at all, if you can help it. I just thought you should know what's going on, so that you won't be taken unawares."

"Thank you. That was considerate of you."

John bowed ceremoniously and then asked:

"What are you two doing here, with your heads together? Is that the diary? May I see it?"

"No. I've had enough of it for today."

Roger shuffled the pages together, affecting boredom, and placed them on a high shelf between the windows. "Are you staying for supper, Mark?"

"No," said John. "He's going to eat in Roberts's tonight with me, and then we're going on to *Macbeth* at the Gate. Supper at home and *Macbeth* on the same evening would be too much for me. We'll see you afterwards." He chuckled, a rare sound from him. "When the hurly-burly's done, when the battle's lost or won."

"That will be at set of sun," said Roger politely.

When John had swept Mark out, Roger wished he had said he would go with them, to supper and *Macbeth*. He wondered if they would have welcomed the suggestion. The idea that they might not hurt, but not so much as the prospect of spending the evening in his room, alone with the shades of Sybil and

61

Flora. He thought as he had often thought before of what bad value Sybil had been. He wondered if he would have felt differently about her if her children had not been so dull. To Roger one of the greatest mysteries of his life was in the fact that all of his children, except Julia, were dull. Some of it was his own fault, he supposed; certainly Louis need not have been dull. He had only become so at the age of seven when his mother died. But Sybil's children did not even know that Roger was their father, so he could not possibly be blamed for them. George, the second one, often seemed to treat Roger as if he were some kind of a dependant of Sybil's, instead of the reverse. George was a barrister, which gave him a right to lay down the law. He was making money now, Roger suspected, but still he figured occasionally on Sybil's list of expenses.

Grimly Roger remembered exactly when Sybil had become expensive. To himself, but to no one else, not even to the diary, he could admit that one of her attractions long ago had always been that she did not cost him a farthing. Roger had always had a good head for business. Otherwise he could never have gone through his whole life balanced as on the rim of a bad penny. It was dangerous at times but he never quite fell off. He never ran bills. That was his strength. He spent very little on himself, and he divided fairly what money he had between those of his dependants who needed it. When they had spent what he gave them, they knew that it was no use asking for more until the next reckoning day. He had trained them to that so successfully that he had very little trouble except from Sybil.

Thinking of expensive women reminded him of Mary, and now Roger noticed that he was experiencing a protective urge towards her and a feeling of annoyance with Paddy. This meant, surely, that he was at least a little fond of Mary. Or perhaps it was only that he had a sense of responsibility to her because she lived in his house. In any case the sentiment did him some credit, but not much, for he felt no desire to warn Mary against marrying Paddy. In fact he rather hoped she would do so and thus dispose of herself as a problem for Roger. After all, he understood that girls feel cheated if they don't get married, and she would probably be contented enough with her bargain. She would not expect much—a

Mallon child or two, for she was gratifyingly proud of her relationship with Roger, reasonably good food and clothes, which Paddy could well afford to give her, and an occasional kindness. So she would reap the main advantage of her stark upbringing—that of being easily pleased.

This notion that young people should be given as little as possible had been one of Roger's favourite principles. He had sometimes wondered if Flora would have agreed with it, if she had lived. She had shown signs of spoiling Louis, before she had lost interest in him, and Roger thought that in doing this she had injured him immeasurably. If she had treated him with less consideration, he would not have become so dependent on her, and he would perhaps not have been so distressed when she had deserted him. Louis, with the clear-sighted eye of childhood, had blamed Roger for his mother's death, even before he had discovered the exact cause of it. Roger had never, since then, been able to achieve friendly relations with him. Louis's frightened look was an insult in itself. His constant readiness against attack made Roger long to attack him, as it were to complete the action.

There was no doubt, thought Roger, that women had a special capacity for coming to terms with children. It was not for nothing that they were always bracketed together—women and children. They made a solid, united, unbreakable front against the men. Sybil and her children were as thick as thieves. He smiled with wry appreciation at the justice of this expression, remembering how much they had thieved from him. Sybil had broken her undefined contract with him. When she had urged him to continue to visit her, she had seemed to understand that their former relationship was at an end. Roger had even innocently believed that she would be pleased; he thought that she had moved into the second or domestic stage of a woman's life, wherein the man like the male spider has outlived his usefulness, and wisely removes himself to a safe distance lest he be eaten up. But he had been wrong. If she had not resented his withdrawal, why had she begun to make him pay in cash, always with the little pussy-cat smile which he had once found so attractive? The complications of sin are endless, he thought, remembering how she had actually invited him, when Flora was dead, to make an honest woman of her. His answering "No, by God!" had come like a pistol-shot, and she had never forgiven him for it.

She had arrived at Washington Road dressed in black—he snorted even now to think of it—to commiserate with him. Her offer had been unpremeditated, he could swear, until she had seen the house. Naturally it was her first visit there. Her measuring eye had trotted over the furniture like an inquisitive little mouse. One could almost see her think it out. The children had come in uninvited, Louis already looking hurt and cheated, Julia already gone silent, and Rosa earnest and conscientious at the age of three as she was today. Sybil had quickly decided that they were not an insurmountable disadvantage. She had made her offer, having first asked him to put the children out of the room. Roger had rejected the offer, but she had stayed for tea as if nothing nasty had happened, chatting and gossiping with an artificial brightness unsuited to the occasion. But her eye had been bright too with the prospects of revenge, and soon afterwards she had begun to send Roger bills.

She had judged his paying capacity to a nicety. Clearly her aim had been to bend but not to break him. He was a gander laying valuable eggs, and it would have been foolish indeed to have wrung his neck. At first he had thought that she was either in league with the devil or with his bank manager. Else how could she so exactly have absorbed all temporary increases in his income, and have held her hand when he was suffering a setback? But later he became convinced that she had employed a press-cutting agency to keep her posted about the variations in his fortunes, and that she studied the cuttings as people betting on horses study form. He had never courted publicity in Ireland, so that her information must certainly have come from outside.

In the beginning he had only had to pay for clothes. Then there were school fees and university fees for George, and presently there was Philomena's wedding. Roger had been pleased at that, imagining that Philomena would now have to fend for herself. He had even bought a gramophone in expectation of saving a little on her. It was the last time he had ever done such a thing.

Philomena had married a teacher from Dingle and had gone

64

to live there with him. But in no time at all she was back in Dublin, finding work for her husband, buying a house, having a thousand-and-one children. Every vicissitude of Philomena's cost Roger money. Her husband—a small, hairy, alert man—took to the drink and had to be reformed at great expense. The effect of this was that he was no longer alert, so that he had to retire from work at fifty. That was ten years ago. Philomena, Roger calculated, was now fifty-seven. He had baulked at educating her children. He had learned his lesson there. No more education for anyone, except John. He did not count Teresa's music as education. Music was like food to Teresa. Without it she would have starved to death. That could not be allowed to happen to any member of Roger's household. Philomena's children were dotted around Dublin in shops and offices, leading dull but reasonably worthy lives.

George, the second of Sybil's children, was only a year younger than Philomena, but he tended himself so well that he looked no more than forty. He had dug himself in with a firm of old-fashioned lawyers who seemed to find him useful. He cultivated dark suits and a wise look, and was well thought of for his heavy honesty. But impelled by the presence of Roger's blood in him, he had the impertinence to write, slow, inconclusive short stories whose deadly significant ideas impressed themselves embarrassingly like hanging underwear. He only did it about four times a year, but still Roger resented it mightily, as young girls resent the presence of a middle-aged spinster at a ball. George was married to a pleasant, hard-working woman who devoted her free time to good works. Sybil hated her, and made no secret of her hatred. She courted George with presents paid for by Roger, in unsuccessful attempts to divert him from his own home to hers.

Sybil's younger son Edgar had gone early into the insurance business. Happily he was somewhat secretive about his affairs, even with his mother, so that she was not so open-handed with him. He was the one of her children who would best have been able to support her, and he had indeed pressed her more than once to come and live with him. But Sybil at eighty would never move from Harcourt Street again. White-haired but still coy, she continued to live in her own way. Age had given her a gratuitous dignity, so that when people spoke of the early

65

scandal that echoed a little to the present day, they saw her as a romantic *femme fatale*, never in the least ridiculous.

Handling the diary had made Roger fall into the unaccustomed error of reflecting on these exasperatingly second-rate people. Father Morrissey, the Jesuit from Gardiner Street who had helped to straighten out his conscience some forty years ago, had warned him against thinking about them. He had decided that it was not necessary for Roger to atone for his crime by listening to Sybil's chatter for the rest of his life. Besides, Father Morrissey pointed out, if he were to marry Sybil, she would have gained by Flora's death for which she was partly to blame, and this would not do. Roger was mightily relieved to hear it. He had long outgrown Sybil, and he would as soon have married her as he would have sought out his old nurse and put her in charge of himself and his household.

Nevertheless he could not but feel responsible for Sybil's children, and sometimes he was even stirred by inconvenient paternal feelings for them which had nothing to do with good sense. When the children were younger these had been more pronounced, and often on dull, overcast autumn or spring days he had felt gloomily impelled to visit them, hoping that seeing them afresh in each new stage of development, some day he would find that one or all of them had improved. But this never happened. They were predictable and that to Roger meant that they could have no interest for him.

Even now, as he thought of them, his face took on the expression of irritated contempt which reflected his feelings. An unpleasant thumping grew and swelled in his chest, so that he knew he must relax and think kinder thoughts about all humanity if he were not to make himself ill.

Then, in her room two doors away, he heard Teresa play the scale of C major. A moment later she began on the Mozart Concerto for flute and harp. Roger got up carefully from his chair and walked to the door. He opened it in practised silence and stood listening, trying to gauge Teresa's mood from the quality of the music. With his head cocked on one side he decided that it was calmer than usual. But was it the calmness of desperation? He rather thought it was, and he was in no mood for calm desperation this evening.

He closed the door again, feeling pleased with himself.

66

Teresa's music would not have had a soothing effect at all. He did feel soothed, however. His satisfaction at his own cleverness had done him quite as much good as if he had got her into his room to play for him. The effect was quicker, and besides he did not have to burden himself with the enigma of Teresa. Wherever she went, a ghostly aura of tension went with her. Roger found himself compelled continually to stamp down a feeling of pity for her. He had no idea why he pitied her, and he had made a firm resolution never to find out. He gave her the essential things that she seemed to need and that was quite enough. In his experience, young people pleased themselves, and it was better to leave them as much as possible to look after their own affairs.

There was one thing that he might do for Teresa, though. Later on, when all this excitement about the diary would be over, he might try to put the idea into Mark's head that he should marry her. That would keep Mark in the family, without having him fall into the clutches of the wretched Frances who was making ludicrous cows' eyes at him for the last couple of months. Later her approach might become more practical, more dangerous. As Roger himself knew to his cost, a determined female is full of wiles and Mark in his simplicity might be as easy a catch as Roger had once been. Far better for him to have Teresa. Her toughness would be good for him. And Mark would be rich enough to buy all those bedroom suites and things so that Roger would not have to worry about them. His affection for Mark deepened perceptibly at this thought and an expansively magnanimous glow spread through him.

When Julia's gong sounded in the hall, announcing supper, he was quite himself again. Moving without caution now, he went directly to Teresa's room, waited at the open door until she finished a phrase, and then took her with him down to the dining-room.

5

On the evening that he was to visit Roger, Thomas Davis MacLean was as nervous as he had been on his wedding day. He had an extra bath to calm himself, and while he was soaking in it he was delighted to hear two housemaids in conversation about him outside the door.

"He's in the bath again," said one.

"Them Americans is always having baths," said the other. "They must be a terrible dirty crowd."

This was Ireland, all right, he chuckled to himself as he dressed. Or had the voices been raised specially for his benefit? He could not be sure, but he was long enough in Ireland to know that the possibility existed.

MacLean would not have been disappointed if Roger had been a stage-literary-Irishman. He had been geared, ready for that. It was his habit when he visited a country for the first time to clear his mind as far as possible of prejudice, but he had not quite succeeded in eradicating the conventional vision of the shouting, bragging, ballad-singing, verse-reciting ignoramus who was blessedly rare in real life. So little was known about Mallon's person that anything was possible.

It had been a special joy, then, to have found a quiet, cultivated, rather sad-faced old gentleman, who only allowed the smouldering spark that distinguished him to flash into momentary fire. The shabby faded old house had been the right setting for Roger. Nevertheless this shabbiness had been the inspiration of the plan which MacLean with the generosity of his race had already formulated and communicated to his father-in-law.

Old Holland was making millions a year. He lived on coffee and stomach-pills. He was as bald as an ostrich-egg and he went to bed at eight-thirty every night. He didn't do many good works. He said he had no imagination to think them up with. But MacLean had observed that he had imagination in plenty if there were some dollars to be made out of his works, good or bad. Therefore he would be likely to respond at once to MacLean's suggestion. This had, after all, been contained in a cable. MacLean would have died in the night if he had not sent that cable. "Can get you original Mallon diary for advance of 20,000 dollars find of century," it said. Twenty-thousand dollars would be a flea-bite to Holland, but still MacLean guessed that the old spider would cut it down to fifteen on principle. Well, if he did, on principle MacLean would fight him for the other five. At this distance he would not be able to hear the old man thumping the table-top and kicking its legs in temper. Already MacLean was planning cable after cable, including a beauty which would say: "Sorry Mallon won't sell under twenty." He glowed at the thought of the new dresses the girls would be able to buy, and the relief that it would be to Julia to have more money for the housekeeping.

And for himself, the utter joy of having the diary in his possession would be reward enough. He didn't have to see it or handle it to know that. In the few words that Roger had used to describe it, there had been a vision of bliss. MacLean felt like a sculptor who sees a leaping salmon in a curling wave, held in a block of grained marble. All he needs to do is to release it. And Roger, saltily tough and sardonic, would be at his elbow to help him, if there were any need. MacLean could see the book already. They would use Augustus John's portrait of Mallon as a frontispiece. Far more dignified than a photograph.

The approach to the book could be handled in different ways. That would all become clear when he would have read the diary. Perhaps he could divide it into sections, with a commentary by himself on each one.

Half-bewildered at the change in his life, he thought back to the day when he had arrived in Dublin, and to the project that had then filled his mind. He had intended to bob around the perimeter of Roger's magic circle, like a brown mouse bobbing round and round the oatmeal chest, hoping that a grain would fall from time to time so that he could snap it up. He was to have met people who had known Mallon long ago, Draper and

Finnegan and others. He shook his head in astonishment now to think of it. What had inspired him to go straight to the top? He did not know. Old Holland had suggested it. He always asked for the managing director, even if he only wanted to buy a packet of pins. But MacLean rarely took Holland's advice. He certainly intended to visit Draper and Finnegan and the rest of them when he would have read the diary, but what a strong position he would be in then! And of course he would not despise anything that he could get from Henry O'Brien.

He smiled shyly, happily at his reflection in the glass, as a lovely girl does when she is dressed for a ball. He was newly shaved and wearing a clean silk shirt. It was all he could do. He would have liked to burn incense.

Like a Biblical lamb he skipped down the stairs. Sure enough, a cable had just arrived from Holland the horny-handed crowing over the find but limiting MacLean to fifteen thousand dollars. Now the battle was engaged and Holland had fired the first shot. The wolf rose up in MacLean's breast and ousted the lamb. He slavered at the mental jowls, savouring in anticipation the running, living blood of his father-in-law.

He was a little put out when he reached Mallon's house to find Mark Roche settled immovably, in the attitude of an observer, in a chair by the window. Roger made it clear at once that he was to stay.

"Mark knows all about me," he said. "He has been reading the diary. He started yesterday and came back to finish it to-day, but he hasn't quite come to the end of it. I have asked him to advise me."

MacLean looked at Mark with sharp hatred, but presently he allowed himself to be placed in a chair in front of the table on which the diary lay open, waiting for him. Mark was amused to watch his reactions follow exactly on the pattern of his own. First there was dedication, devotion and the mystical intensity of a man in prayer. Then there was restless excitement as the picture of Flora began to take form and as the measure of her influence on Roger's work was shown. When Sybil appeared in the story, MacLean went perfectly still. Mark watched him read on and then turn back a page or two as he had done. It seemed to him that MacLean swelled up visibly,

70

with the effort to contain his unbearable exaltation. His ears and his very hair appeared to twitch. He stopped. He read another piece. He stopped again. He laid his hands helplessly on the table and said faintly, as if he had just swum a river in flood:

"No. No. I can't. It's too much. After this evening I'll never sleep again. I'll get ulcers, like Holland." He looked across at Roger with a mixture of love and accusation:

"Mr. Mallon, I'm sorry. It's killing me. I just can't understand why I should be the man to have this." He stroked the diary like a beloved cat. He swallowed then, and sat up straighter, and drew in his stomach, and took his hands off the table, down on to his lap where no one could see their antics. He almost succeeded in imitating the loud tone of a determined American buying a piece of European culture dirt cheap as he said:

"I am authorized by my father-in-law Oscar Holland of Hollands Inc. to offer you a twenty-thousand dollars advance on this diary. He says fifteen but he means twenty. We'll work out details later, but the advance is the important thing for you. When I tell you that, I'm your best friend. We'll publish it word for word, just as it stands. We won't even Americanize it. Students will have to fix that for themselves. I'll do the commentary, under your personal supervision. You won't have any complaints. This will make your fortune," he finished reverently and his voice broke. "It has everything. Every single thing."

Then he had to be told that the diary in its entire state was not for sale at all, and that Roger wanted no fee for the part of it that MacLean would use for his thesis. Roger explained the philosophy of this. Since he could not let MacLean have the whole diary, he felt that he was doing him an injury for which he could only compensate by letting him have half of it for nothing.

"But it's not my money," MacLean pleaded. "It's Holland's money. No one passes up a chance of taking some of Holland's money from him."

"Money doesn't come into it at all, really," said Roger patiently. "You're not getting what you want, so why should you pay? As for me, I don't want money."

71

"Perhaps your family could do with some," said MacLean tentatively.

Roger was not offended.

"No," he said. "I think this family is about to break up. One of the girls is getting married soon, and when one goes they'll all go. In any case, I should feel mean if I were to take a fee from you. Research workers should never have to pay for these amenities. And it would take all the value for me out of my offer of showing you the diary. No, no, young man. You must learn to receive a favour sometimes without paying for it. I have always found it harder to receive than to give."

Whether this kindly misunderstanding were deliberate or not, MacLean could never discover. One thing was certain, that Roger had coolly and effortlessly reversed the balance of the situation so that now not only was Roger on top but it almost began to seem as if MacLean's offer had been in bad taste. And yet how could it be in bad taste to offer a man a large sum of money for a book which had been written so many years before?

Gradually now, as he watched Roger's unperturbed expression MacLean began to feel the horror of his loss. So might a mother, informed of the death of her child, at first disbelieve it and then slowly without any conscious movement of her reasoning powers at last come to know its truth, as if that truth had become part of her being. MacLean groaned aloud in his agony. Knowing quite well the futility of a last protest he said in earnest tones:

"Mr. Mallon, twenty thousand dollars is a lot of money."

"That's all right, old chap," said Roger easily, conciliatingly. "I don't need the money. That makes my decision simpler. You just take what you want from the diary and we'll all be satisfied."

The discussion could have gone all night, if MacLean had said:

"But I want it all!"

He could see that it would be no use. He was reminded of the kind of song that goes round and round, never ending, until someone screams with the boredom of it. In any case he could not discuss it any further just then because while he had last been speaking, Roger's grandson John had come into the

72

room. It had seemed indecent enough to have spoken of Holland's offer in the presence of Mark. With John there as well it would have been quite impossible.

John said in his tired voice:

"Yum-yum! Who's talking about twenty thousand dollars?"

"An academic discussion merely," said Roger.

Now that he had put his foot down, he was feeling powerful and benevolent. He liked MacLean's attitude about the diary on the whole. It had been wonderful watching him come gradually under the spell of the old maestro. This was a pleasure not usually given to novelists. A good dramatist can sit in the back row of the theatre and watch his words squeeze the tears out of a fascinated audience. For this alone, Roger would himself have ventured into the business of writing plays if he had not been clever enough to see that his word-spinning would never have done for the theatre. Yeats had urged him, implored him to write a play for the Abbey Theatre and had offered to help with construction and cutting. Naturally Roger had refused. He appreciated his friendship with Yeats. Anyone attempting to cut Roger could never be a friend of his again.

This was another good thing in MacLean. Quite obviously he could not bear the thought of blotting a line of the diary. Every word had been valued, rightly, far above any gold of Holland's. It was clear from MacLean's expression as he made his offer that he understood how impossible it was to estimate the diary by the standard of money. And yet Roger would show him that cuts made by himself would still leave in it a thing of priceless worth. The offer of money had not fluttered a feather of his determination to cut out all references to Sybil and her effect on Flora. But it had pleased him above all to see how MacLean had found life in his two women, after all these years. All the better that it had been only a kind of literary life. He had seen them as characters in a novel rather than as real, tragic people. Else he would have been apologetic about urging the publication of such a personal story. Instead of feeling disappointed at this, Roger was gratified. It proved to him that the diary was a work of art, that he had unconsciously made it so even in the midst of his pain. For a split second he wondered if he had the right to keep it from the world. Then he re-awoke to common sense and decency and a number of other

73

bourgeois virtues and standards, and he pushed the idea aside with little difficulty, reflecting thankfully on the providence of God in not permitting the thoughts of man to be plain for all to see.

"I came to get Mark," said John. "Do you want him?"

"Not this evening, I think," said Roger kindly, as if he were lending his bicycle. "Tom will have to read the diary right through before we can get on to editing it."

He frowned in vexation at himself. He must be excited, after all, as old men become when anything outside of their usual routine is going on. He had not intended to let John know too much. It was not that he had anything against him, but a special instinct always warned Roger not to confide in any of his blood relations. Patriarchs and other persons in high places often feel like that about their near associates. However, he had not really given anything away, and in any case it was not his habit to include John with his brethren for any purpose.

It seemed extraordinary that Nellie should have been his mother. They disliked each other, and they seemed to agree that their pre-natal association had given them quite enough experience of each other's company. As soon as John had learned to walk, he had used his new power to walk up the stairs to Roger's room. Nellie had made no objection, and Roger first taught him to read and had then entertained all of his youthful years with his wonderful collection of children's books. These included Louis Wain's moon-faced cats engaged in human activities, and many volumes of an American children's magazine called *Saint Nicholas*, and Heath Robinson's fantasy, "Bill the Minder", and Harry Clarke's *Hans Andersen*: great heavy volumes whose contents lived up to the promise of their covers and illustrations. With care and foresight Roger had led him through stage after stage: *The Heroes*, and Shakespeare and Stevenson at seven, Dickens at nine and anything he fancied from ten onwards. And poetry at all ages. The result had been magnificent. John had every appearance of shaping into that old-fashioned product, a scholar and a gentleman. And Roger loved him, though he had sworn secretly and venomously never to love anyone again. If John's name had not been Mallon he might have trusted him also.

It seemed now, however, that no harm had been done, that

74

John had hardly heard Roger. He was leading Mark out of the room, bowing ceremoniously to MacLean and closing the door as if it were the door of a hospital ward full of moribund patients. Outside on the landing he said:

"The man who can control his emotions is king over those who can't. *What* was that about twenty thousand dollars?"

"MacLean offered Roger that amount for the diary."

"I thought so. And Roger refused?"

"As you heard."

"Why?"

"He said he doesn't need the money."

"That can't be the reason. He never thought of the money when he was writing, but he was always glad to see it when it came. He often told me so, and I think it was true. What's in the diary?"

"You heard him describe it. It's a commentary on the books, and an account of their progress and so on, just as he said."

" 'You heard, you heard,' " said John thoughtfully. "You are hedging, my dear friend. There's something else in the diary too, as sure as my Auntie Minnie's modesty vest. Yield up your story."

"No. I promised Roger not to."

All at once John was alert and watchful. He peered at Mark in the semi-darkness of the landing, as if he could easily see into the depths of his soul. It was not an unfriendly scrutiny, but rather the detached curiosity of a man who peers over a fellow-passenger's shoulder to read his newspaper. Still it made Mark uncomfortable, and it stiffened his determination not to allow Roger's confidences to be drawn from him. John took his arm after a moment and began to lead him downstairs.

"I'm not going to assail your virtue," he said. "You have nothing to fear from me, my proud beauty. Your discretion does you credit. In any case I bet I know what's in that diary. What makes an American or a Turk, for that matter, quiver with the desire to give the world the benefit of a certain piece of writing? What makes him urge old gentlemen to accept large sums of money? There is only one answer. That diary contains the story of Roger's heart." He shot a glance at Mark and then looked away again, affecting a *blasé* manner which was belied by the uneven tone of his voice. "Just as I thought. A hideous

75

secret. I must admire Roger for his resolution. As Mr. Mac-Lean says so justly, twenty thousand dollars is a lot of money. I don't mind telling you that at half of that price all of my hideous secrets would be his for the asking. But mine would perhaps not be so interesting as Roger's."

There was a little appeal in his sidewards glance this time, but Mark made no reply. John sighed and said:

"Ah, well. I promised I wouldn't twist your ears until you tell, and I won't. There's more ways of killing a cat than choking him with butter." As they left the house he said reflectively: "Who would have thought the old man to have had so much blood in him?"

He took Mark's chuckle of appreciation as confirmation that he had been right in his guess.

"The lecture tonight is by Henry," he said as they walked towards the College. "On the subject of Roger's philosophy."

Mark stopped and said:

"I had forgotten. Must we?"

"Positively yes. And laugh ha-ha at all of his jokes. He'll be on the watch for insubordination, especially from our side of the house. So no frown and wrinkled lip and sneer of cold common sense, if you please."

"I find him rather good," said Mark mildly. "It's just that I felt a momentary wish for a change of subject. I'd like time to think."

"Henry talks great bosh on the subject of Roger."

"You think so because you know them both too well," said Mark, determined not to be bullied.

"That is exactly why I am in a position to know that Henry is deceiving the public," said John. "When you know Roger as well as I do, perhaps you will agree with me."

The room upstairs where the lecture was to be held was already crowded when they arrived. It was an attentive and reverent audience. Henry's stock stood high, but apart from that it was well known that he had a way of noticing who was missing, even among spotty first-years whom no one else could tell apart. And if he noticed who was missing, he also noticed who was present, and observed the effect of his words upon them. Weeks or even months later he would make known his displeasure at a lifted eyebrow or a snort of disagreement. The

76

amateur psychologists among the students had no trouble in detecting Henry's underlying sense of insecurity. Nothing could ever satisfy him except whole-hearted unqualified praise, they said, not only from the simple but also from the thoughtful and intellectual. Since this was not possible, clearly he was doomed to a life of misery.

One advantage of his uneasiness was that he prepared his discourses with great care and delivered them with nicely calculated effects, so that to an outsider his manner might have seemed almost too well assured for one who was, after all, engaged in offering critical opinions. This evening was no exception. Every gesture, every inflexion had been planned. He supported his conclusions as to Roger's message with many well-chosen excerpts from his writings. Nevertheless Mark found that it all sounded a little hollow now. He blamed John for this, at first. Never before had he doubted Henry's capacity to illuminate aspects of Roger's mind. As time went on, the doubt grew like a tumour, withering all around it what had seemed healthy before. He edged a little away from John in a subconscious attempt to reduce his influence, but there was no improvement. He knew that the spell was irrevocably broken, even before John leaned towards him and whispered sharply into his ear:

"Is there a cold, wet devil riding on your neck? Is there? *Is* there?"

"Yes. Shut *up*."

"That's Henry."

Satisfied, John returned smirking to his former position. Henry had seen them of course, and was already rolling up and down on the balls of his feet as he always did before biting a hole in an unappreciative member of the student body. Mark squirmed, for he hated to be the subject of anyone's attention in public. Now Henry was placing his hands under his coattails, an abominable habit and another bad sign. But nothing came of it. Instead he got on with the rest of his lecture rather faster than was his custom, though without omitting any of his usual mannerisms. It was like hearing a gramophone record played too fast, coming out on a higher note and with a slightly mad feel about it. Mark reflected that it was hard on Henry having John in the audience. Really he deserved great

77

credit for never having suggested to him that he might stay away, since he knew so much about Roger at first hand. Even now, when Henry might have had the pleasure of rebuking John and Mark for their bad manners, he had most nobly restrained himself.

Mark's sympathy with Henry was an offshoot of his new insight into the tricks of Henry's trade. Once you have been behind the scenes, the play is never the same again. You see the dust on the knees of the actor's hose, the rust on their tin crowns, miraculously invisible before. Now watching Henry strut and fret, a memory swam into Mark's mind. It was of a puppet-show, to which he had gone when he was eleven, nine years ago. The tiny stage peopled with proportionately sized figures had been very real until a huge, hairy human hand, the hand of a monster, had appeared from below, clutching the legs of the miniature heroine, reducing her suddenly to nothing. A moment before she had had life, personality, charm. Then all at once she was just a couple of pegs draped with tawdry cloth. Mark had felt quite ill, and he had had to leave the theatre soon afterwards. He wished he could have done the same now, but somewhere in adolescence he had lost the capacity for slipping out of ugly situations. The loss represented one of the bonds of maturity. How marvellous it would be to be able to return to that state of innocence in which he could gape with rustic awe in wonder that Henry's fat head could carry all he knew.

When the lecture was over, the audience applauded without reserve. They always did. After a stiff, unsmiling bow of acknowledgement, Henry gathered up his papers and trotted into the back room. Mark and John delayed to give him time to get away, but when they came out on to the steps he was there, waiting for them. John prepared to walk limply past him, but Henry said casually:

"I'm going to have some coffee. Would you like to come?"

"Certainly. Of course. To be sure," said John, suddenly and forcefully revived. "Where shall we gang and dine today?"

"I'm afraid I must go home," said Mark.

"Nonsense. You never go home at this time. Come along and help to celebrate Henry's triumph. Well, Henry, old cock, old stock, old stick-in-the-mud, we're waiting. Lead on."

Henry looked slightly put out at this enthusiasm, as well he might. John's voice was pitched low, but it had a vibrant, carrying quality at times which sang out like the note of the oboe in an orchestra. In a sudden flash of insight, Mark saw what John would be like in middle age, if something were not done about him. He wished it were possible to let John have a look at his father, who would surely prove to be a useful warning, since the main delight of both of them was to embarrass those around him. Still it was partly for his oddity that Mark liked John. How different would he be if he were taught to be conventional, or if a reaction to his present mode of behaviour were to set in? How much would be left, he wondered.

Certainly Henry would be pleased with any change. Now he and John were arguing as to which café they would patronize. John favoured an *espresso* bar off Grafton Street but Henry was at least intelligent enough not to be caught out like that. It would be crammed with a mixture of his own students and those of Trinity College, and John would never be able to resist the temptation to humiliate Henry in front of them all.

"We'll go to Roberts," said Henry firmly. "It's quieter, and I want to talk to you both."

He was rolling up and down again, jingling the money in his pockets as if to point out that he could choose the café since he would pay the bill. He and John measured each other and then John said with a sigh of resignation:

"Roberts for us, then. Upright, respectable Roberts."

"Shades of the prison-house," said Henry genially.

Mark chuckled, surprised and pleased. John glared at him and dug him in the ribs with his elbow rather obviously, so that all three of them walked to Grafton Street in angry silence. Things improved over the coffee, however. Henry watched benevolently while John rapidly consumed the four best buns. Then he lit a small, inferior cheroot and said in confidential man-to-man tones:

"I'm worried about Roger's diary. I wonder if either of you could persuade him to let me see it."

"Why don't you get Rosa to ask him?" said John cagily. "Roger is very fond of her."

Henry's colour deepened, but whether from the coffee, or the cheroot, or with annoyance at having to discuss such a vital matter with John, Mark could not decide.

79

"It's a question of finding the right person," said Henry. "Rosa admires Roger tremendously, but she has never really read his books properly. If she were to say the wrong thing, by any chance, the door might be closed altogether."

"You could ask him yourself. I've often heard him give you material for your lectures. Why should he refuse you now?"

A look of utter misery came over Henry's face, so that the two young men were shocked into stares of surprise.

"I have no idea." His fingers picked and pinched at the cheroot. "I always thought he liked me, and trusted me. He helped me to build up a considerable reputation for lectures on himself and his Meticulism. Now it looks as if he has led me astray, deliberately, for the pleasure of making a fool of me with this diary."

"Oh, not deliberately," said John faintly. "Not to make a fool of you."

"Why did he do it, then? *He* has always known what is in the diary, since he wrote it himself. Why did he give me a wrong picture all these years, and then turn on me suddenly in public, and call me an ass for having accepted it? Every critic is a 'backstairs literary man'." Clearly these words were burned into Henry's brain. But they found it hard to sympathize with him for long because his tone became stuffy and righteous: "It is morally wrong of Roger to withdraw now. He has obligations to me. He would not have had, if he had not been so kind to me all these years, but now he has an obligation to give me the first rights in anything new about himself."

"Obligations your granny," said John warmly. "Roger is a free man."

"I'm sure he doesn't mean you any harm," said Mark, feeling silly at not being able to say more.

He knew, none better, that Roger meant neither harm nor good to Henry, who was without importance for him except in his capacity as Rosa's husband, provider of her food and generator of her children. Roger would have hooted with fury at the notion that Henry could pronounce on the ethics of his behaviour. But Mark found himself agreeing with Henry that patrons have a moral obligation towards their protégés. It seemed to him that Roger had treated Henry badly, not so

80

much in withholding the diary from him now as in giving him his confidence over all the years, when he had such a low opinion of him. No doubt Henry and Rosa had pressed Roger intolerably for these confidences, but Roger should have seen that the day would come when he would be unable to conceal any longer his contempt for Henry. What worried Mark most was the suspicion that Roger had always intended to let Henry down, that he had subconsciously planned an unspecified revenge for all the unintentional *bêtises* that Henry, like any critic, had necessarily committed in relation to his work. Henry's mistake was criminal in its stupidity, of course. He should have known better than to pick a live author as his speciality. Roger would have had to be a man of stone to have stood up to Henry's searchings, to have watched unmoved while the workings of his mind were lopsidedly exposed in an endless series of articles. It was all very distressing, as only a family disagreement can be. Mark felt only a little mean in wishing momentarily that he were not involved in it.

Henry was saying:

"All that stuff I give out I got from himself. It was he who told me that Dr. Finnegan was the model for Sebastian and that Michael Draper was Cronin and so on. Or rather, he said they were the originators or suggesters of the characters—he used some strange word for it. If he was telling the truth then, he's a liar now. He can't have it both ways." He saw how John's eyes narrowed with anger at this. "It was all lies," said Henry forcefully. "It's no use trying to cover that." He stopped suddenly, with a look of shock. "Is it possible that Roger was telling the truth then and that now he told lies to MacLean? That is possible, isn't it? Perhaps there is nothing new in the diary?" He looked sharply from one to the other, like a man measuring a way of escape from a flooding cave. "You have both read it, I suppose?"

"Mark has," said John calmly. "I have not."

Henry turned to gaze at Mark, and in a moment he had recovered himself. Mark was a stranger. Even though he were to sit with Roger night after night for the rest of his days, he would never become a Mallon; he would not lose even an ounce of his own separateness, much less become one of those fluid, temperamental, easily-bullied oddities who inhabited

81

Roger's house. With them Henry always felt superior. There were so many things, ordinary things, that they did not know, and they would ask about these so naïvely that one always gave a condensed, childish explanation, as if they would not be able to understand a more complicated one. And the reward was usually a derisive comment on some extraneous point, showing that nothing had been learned. Henry did not have to be very shrewd to see that Mark was not like them. Mark had to be reckoned with. He was clever. He was well-read. His mind worked logically. There had been that business about the poetry of Eliot, in which Henry had been chased up a tree. There was no denying that. Indeed Henry would have admitted it, for he was well aware of his own limitations, if Mark had not been so young, and especially if he had not been a student. He was always extra wary with students.

"You have read the diary?" said Henry.

"Yes," said Mark uneasily.

"And perhaps there was nothing new in it?"

But it was clear from Mark's expression that this was the wrong line. Henry tried again, more cautiously:

"It won't be a secret when MacLean publishes it."

Then he was struck dumb for a full minute as he imagined the effect of its publication in America, where Henry's own stock stood high at the universities. Roger cared nothing for that. Old men are childishly absorbed in themselves, he thought bitterly. Worried by the silence, Mark said uncomfortably:

"You heard Roger say there were new things to be learned from the diary."

"If I had even the smallest idea of what is in it," said Henry meditatively, "I could give a hint in my next articles that there is something coming soon which will cast a new light, and so on——"

But it was no use. There they sat, John satiated with buns and coffee, half-asleep like a cannibal king after a feast, and Mark politely upright but clearly on his guard, somewhat bored, and not going to give anything away. Henry might have made yet another try, but just then a tall, thin student called Sullivan, an abominable would-be literary type with side-whiskers and an Aran jersey, walked across from the other side of the café and stood by John. They were friends, Henry knew,

82

and practical admirers of each other in that they both practised a long, lounging gait and a tired manner.

"Sorry I didn't see you sooner," said Sullivan. "We could
have celebrated together."

"What are you celebrating?" Henry asked acidly.

"Just a little story of mine, going to be published," said
Sullivan carelessly, his eye alight with the loving devotion of a
parent at a dancing-class.

John heaved himself slowly upright, fixed a long brown eye
on Sullivan and said:

" 'I bit my arm, I sucked the blood,
And cried: "A sale a sale!" ' "

"Jealousy," said Sullivan casually, but he looked displeased.

John settled down again as if he intended to sleep.

"The wise man does nothing," he said. "Your story is a
drop in the ocean. One week after it appears, it will be
forgotten."

"Not by me," said Sullivan.

He sat down swiftly at the table, obviously eager to discuss
it. But Henry stood up and flicked a finger for his bill, and
walked out into the street. For quite two minutes after he had
gone, Mark worried about whether he should have followed
him and thanked him for the coffee. Then he forgot him and
became absorbed in the more interesting subject of the merits
of Sullivan's writings.

6

It was three days before Mark could bring himself to visit Mallon's again. He would not have thought of staying away, for he formed habits easily, if his father had not stopped him in the hall next evening just as he was going out, and said:

"Would you be so kind as to come into my study? I want to give you some advice. Yes, that is my duty, my privilege and my right."

Too well Mark recognized the anticipatory chuckle with which his father opened the study door. Inside, he set a chair ceremoniously by the desk and said:

"It won't take me long to say my say, but sit down all the same. You may put your hat on the desk, avoiding the prints, if you please."

The last words shot out venomously, but then came the little chuckle again, ingratiating but by no means apologetic. Mark placed his hat on the desk and his hands folded on his knees as if he were being interviewed for a position which he had no hope of getting. His father did not sit down. He was a small man, and the stoop which he affected made him seem smaller. Therefore it was his custom to dominate the room from the fender, where he benefited by being raised an inch or two above the floor.

"How difficult it is to give advice," he said. His eyes behind his rimless glasses sparked with amusement. "One has to know a great deal about the subject before one may dare interfere. It has never been my wish to know very much about you. Your mother has always been quite competent to deal with the more sordid aspects of your life. I continue to feed and house you free of charge, though you came into your uncle's money when you reached the age of twenty-one. Stop! I do not mean to suggest that you should live somewhere else. In fact I value your presence here. It amuses your mother, for one thing. And the maids give better service where there is a young person in the house than they would do for two old people. Better food especially. No, it's not that I want you to go."

Mark made no move, though he knew his father was watching him to discover if he had stirred him up sufficiently. He always waited until he could produce his plum with the maximum effect. After a moment he went on:

"No, I don't want you to go. At least not for the present. But while you are here I feel that you are entitled to the benefit of my advice."

Now Mark gloated internally, for his father did not usually repeat himself. It was surely a sign of weakness, or at least of Mark's strength. He redoubled his defences against showing emotion as his father continued:

"It seems to me that you are engaged in the dangerous practice of cabin-hunting."

"Cabin-hunting?" Mark asked woodenly.

"An expressive term," his father said. "I learned it from my old nurse. She had the greatest contempt for people who allowed their children to go cabin-hunting. It means that they visit the same or different houses too often, without invitation, and take meals with the family, and are either too insensitive or too careless to know when they are not wanted. You go to Mallon's every evening?"

"To visit Roger."

"What of the other people in the house? Do they love to see you come? Must they not reckon that you will consume some food which I suspect they could do with themselves?"

"I don't take a meal there, only cocoa, late at night."

"*Cocoa!* And *late at night!* Well, that's their affair. Then there are girls in the house. You would be the type to appeal to young girls, especially young girls in poor circumstances. Has it occurred to you that you may have raised a hope in one or all of their virgin breasts? You look surprised. What an innocent creature you are, to be sure, not at all as we used to be long ago. Those were the points I wished to make, and I can see that I have made them. You were on your way out, I think? Don't let me delay you any longer."

So it was impossible for Mark to go to Mallon's that night. In a state of acute agony, he rambled about the streets until his head and his feet ached. All of his former uneasiness now returned to torment him. He remembered the embarrassment that he had endured on the first extraordinary evening, when John and Roger had placed him so firmly and with such ceremony in the bosom of their family, how he had squirmed and suffered in fear that he was unwelcome. But his fears had been quieted so well that they had almost died, until now his father had brought them to hideous life again.

So thin was the bond between them that Mark was quite at a loss to discover his father's motives. Not for one moment did he consider that they might be disinterested. Jealousy, an active dislike for the simple emotions of friendship, a devilish pleasure in spreading despondency and mischief—any of these he thought might be the reasons why the old man could not bear to have let him alone.

Mark wondered for how long his father had been considering making his attack. In his first discourse on Roger, he had made no mention of the grandchildren nor of the present state of Roger's household. Indeed it had seemed that he took it for granted that the most interesting part of Roger's life was over. How had he found out about the girls, for instance? Had some old hen called to warn him about the danger to Mark of associating too much with them? With wry amusement, Mark imagined himself trying to wrest Mary from the arms of Paddy Mulligan. And surely all Dublin knew about Teresa and Aldo. That left only Frances, and no one would call poor Frances a danger. The whole thing was fantastic, stupid, malicious, but it snatched Mark's peace of mind from him so completely that he could scarcely remember that he had ever been happy.

With weighted feet he walked across O'Connell Bridge, past the huge monuments that adorned O'Connell Street, peering into the crammed restaurants whose lights became more brilliant as their prices went lower. They shone green, red and yellow, adding an unearthly brightness to the colours of the customers' clothes. There were girls like flowers, in red and blue and yellow and with heels like four-inch nails on their shiny pointed shoes. Their faces were painted skilfully in colours to match their clothes. The boys had bright jerseys and socks and ties, and knowing faces. Drinking coffee alone at the bar of one of these restaurants, Mark became aware that many of the young people were watching him. He could see them in the shining mirror behind the counter and he could see them out of the corners of his eyes. The row of waitresses in glittering white coats with glittering blonde hair watched him too, so that at last he had to get up and pay his bill and go out. They did not want him there. He knew that, though several of the girls made appreciative noises at him and invited him back as he hurried outside. For a moment he tried to imagine himself dressed in black jeans and soft-soled shoes and a red jersey. That would give his father something to think about. If only he could bring himself to do it perhaps he could mix unnoticed in that crowd. But he thought that his face might look wrong. Seen in the glass behind the counter a few minutes ago, it had been the face of a little nun. It would take him years to cultivate the slack jaw and glazed eye, and then it would be time for him to learn his way back to his present state. What a problem it all was, and how absolutely insoluble! It seemed that one must dress either like an overgrown boy or an undersized man, and either way one looked ridiculous. There was one thing he could do, though. Crossing the bridge again, he removed his hat, leaned over the parapet and dropped the hat carefully into the mottled water. Immediately it disappeared under the bridge. Mark moved his head from side to side, feeling as delightfully free as if he had discarded a medieval helmet instead of a few ounces of felt. Without a hat he almost felt that he might go back some other evening and try his luck at the same restaurant again.

Slowly he walked home, head down, first past rhythmically flashing neon signs and then past closed shops and humming pubs where hulking shadows gloomed suddenly behind frosted glass. At his own door he paused and looked up with a little spurt of hatred at the elegant fanlight, like a bland, confident, patronizing, half-closed eye above him. Quietly he took out his key and let himself into the hall. By the grandfather clock it was only half-past nine. He crept upstairs like a thief listening with stretched ears for his father's chirping little titter. Heaven knew he had nothing to conceal. He had not felt the smallest desire to bring home one of the young women from the restaurant and secrete her in his bedroom, not only on principle but also because he had inherited his father's fastidiousness.

It was astonishing to think that at his age, Roger Mallon had already made his arrangement with Sybil, and was soon to negotiate marriage with Flora. Mark did not in the least envy him this inconvenient vitality. Then it occurred to him to wonder who had had charge of Roger's upbringing. Perhaps the reason was to be found there, rather than in any extra vitality. Roger's disregard for law and order had landed him into plenty of trouble, thought Mark prudently, and yet himself was possessed for a moment by a little tingle of excitement at the idea of breaking all the laws that were ever made. This very evening he had done a daring thing, in throwing his hat over the bridge. He remembered with pleasure the little ping! that had occurred inside him at that moment, as if a tight elastic band which had been constricting his vitals had suddenly broken. A satisfactory aspect of this sensation was that it proved by roundabout means that he had vitals. But if he had, why was he so easily influenced by his father for whom after all he had small respect indeed?

So all evening long he argued with himself, padding soft-footed around the cradle of his soul as if in fear of waking it from sleep. During that first evening a wicked little thought, carelessly dropped by his father, began weakly to germinate into an idea.

The next day, he could not decide to risk meeting John Mallon at the College, so he stayed at home altogether. At lunch-time his father commented on it.

"You didn't go out this morning?"

"No."

"Ah. I thought not. I always feel it when someone in my household is neglecting his duty. My sense of responsibility reacts and disturbs me, so that I can't get on with my own work. I couldn't write a line this morning for thinking about you. And I had promised an article to the Academy's journal for the end of the week. Were there not lectures today?"

"Yes."

"And are you so well-informed that you have no need to go to them? As the person who pays your fees I feel entitled to make any inquiries which will show whether value is being received for the money."

The idea in Mark's mind put forth a pale and weakly branch.

"Please don't talk like that at meals, Michael," said his mother, looking resentfully at Mark as the cause of the unpleasantness.

So he went out after lunch, and wandered about in mean streets where he had never been before, until he found himself back in the civilized neighbourhood of Grafton Street again. Then he felt justified in sitting in a café for an hour. Unaccustomed to walking on hard pavements, his feet were again painfully tired, and every muscle in his body relaxed in sympathy with them. This had the curious effect of clearing his brain of inessentials, so that he saw quite plainly at last that his relations with his father would never improve. It was easy enough to reach this conclusion when he realized that the fault did not lie with himself. At lunch-time, and last night, Mark had felt his body cringe shamefully in his father's presence, though his soul had stood more or less erect. But if they lived much longer together, he could see that the day would inevitably come when he would begin to subordinate his judgment to the convenience or terror of the moment. With his new knowledge, he need waste no more time in speculating as to why his father hated and despised him so. Those were the two words that occurred to him, and they made him shiver, for he was not yet by any means sufficiently detached.

It still hurt him to remember how even his magnificent examination results had failed to produce more than a curled sardonic lip. Mark's own lips curled now with pain and embarrassment as he recalled how he had gambolled home with the news, as if he had expected a pat on the back for his reward. It was true that he had hoped for some good effect, however slight, and naturally his disappointment had been increased when it had not come. Yet he knew that in the same circumstances he would act the same way again, because he ordered all of his relationships with people on principle. A son owed an inexorable duty to his father, a duty of obedience, of charity, of patience, and toleration, but mainly a duty of love. Mark loved his father with all the power of his intellect. A thin, cold voice inside him now advised him to confine that love to the intellect, to force it bitterly away from the emotional level, where it might ruin him. With his arms dropped slackly over the back of the hard café chair, he submitted for a moment to a wave of helpless pity for himself and for everyone else in his situation. For it seemed to him that this problem of his must be a common one, and that all around him were tortured young people wrestling miserably with over-life-sized devils whose daily, wily business it was to destroy the peace of their souls.

Then, suddenly, there was Teresa sitting in front of him. From her shocked expression he knew at once that his distressed state of mind was plainly to be seen. Slowly he pulled himself upright and tried to replace section by section his usual expression of controlled calm. But Teresa spoiled it all by seizing one of his hands in both of hers and saying:

"Mark! For God's sake tell me what has happened to you!"

A long shudder went through him and to his astonishment two enormous tears fell and splashed on to the table. This had not happened since he was ten years old. He lifted his free hand and covered the tears with it, and then he turned his hand palm upwards as if to see whether it were really wet. Teresa said angrily:

"Where have you been? Why didn't you come to us when this happened, whatever it is? Don't you know how to use your friends? It's like—it's like seeing a *policeman* cry. I can't stand it."

This made him smile, and at once the horrible unaccustomed tide of emotion began to recede. Looking at Teresa he felt that himself belonged to a decadent stock. Every part of her was alive, springing with vitality: her curling black shining hair, her glittering snow-white forehead, her flashing, sparkling, dark-blue eyes, her lips like holly-berries, her strong clean long-fingered hands at rest now on the table. Her strength and determination gave off almost tangible emanations which touched him like healing rays so that he began to be able to judge right from wrong again, and to see his own position in the midst of the cold confusion in which he lived.

"Where's your hat?" Teresa asked suddenly.

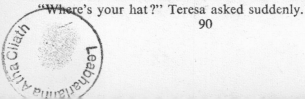

"I threw it away."

"Good. Now don't go buying another. What age are you, Mark?"

"Twenty-one. Since January."

"Since January? Did you have a party?"

"No. I never have a party."

"We'd have had one for you if we'd known. Why didn't you tell us?"

"I didn't think of it."

"Oh, Mark, you have a lot to learn. Even Frances had a party when she was twenty-one."

She stopped suddenly, remembering Frances. Mark was looking amused.

"How old are you?" he asked her.

"Nineteen," said Teresa, "unfortunately."

"There's nothing unfortunate about you," said Mark.

"Isn't there? I'll be telling you about it, soon. You haven't told me why you were crying."

At this bald description of his state, Mark blushed with embarrassment, but Teresa went on unconcerned:

"You must come back to see Roger. He wants you."

"Is anything wrong with Roger?" Mark asked in sudden panic.

"No, no. He's having a lovely time with his American. But he wants you to share it with him. You didn't have a fight with him, by any chance?"

"No. But I did have one with my father, if you could call it a fight. It was one-sided. I never argue with him."

"Why not?"

"It would be like arguing with a corpse," said Mark savagely. "My father is as cold as Nelson's Pillar. He's hollow inside too, now that I come to think of it. Those articles he writes never have anything new in them. They're all derivative, all syntheses of other people's work. But he's as proud as Lucifer of them. He thinks their creation justifies him in shutting himself away in his study day after day for years, attacking and insulting everyone who interrupts him, even if it's only the fact of their existence that interrupts his thoughts, even if they're not physically present with him or have no wish to be. That's the way it is between him and me. The voice of con-

91

science can't be entirely stifled. I'm on his conscience, and he hates me for it." Mark looked at Teresa in astonishment. "I never understood this before, until I began to tell you about it. Isn't that extraordinary?"

"It's a common experience," said Teresa casually. "What does your old man do for a living?"

"Nothing. I thought you knew that he is the Roche of Roche and Wallis, the builders' suppliers. I have a lot of shares in the business myself. My uncle left me his a few months ago. I've never had the nerve to go there. Wallis and the manager do the work. They pay Roche to keep out, because he's so unpleasant with the men. So it's not only because he does no real work that he's ugly. He was ugly first. Wait! I see more. At sixteen he was apprenticed to the firm. His father had a theory that education unfits people for business. He wanted to go to the university. I'm having the things he never had, which is an additional reason for his hatred of me. Could it be as simple as that?"

"No," said Teresa, "but it will do for him. Pick any old label you like. Why should you bother about him? Perhaps he's just sour by nature, or perhaps he saw something nasty in the woodshed."

"There wouldn't be anything nastier than himself in the woodshed," said Mark.

"And stop saying he hates you," said Teresa. "That's an unlikely sentiment between father and son."

"I shouldn't have said it," said Mark. "I never have talked about him like this before."

"It seems to me that a father is a mixed blessing," said Teresa detachedly. "Look at Louis. He's a dead loss too. He's hinting now that he's going to go sick again, which will mean more work for my mother. He hasn't been out of bed for two days. When Louis stays in bed he has to have the best of everything, no twice-cooked food nor second-quality stuff. That part of it is a bit funny because all the food in our house is cooked twice, if not three times."

"Doesn't Nellie look after him at all?" Mark asked, fascinated as always by the details of the workings of Roger's household.

"Nellie doesn't work," said Teresa. "She sits around being

92

ill-used. She has a way of saying: 'Pass the ash-tray' that makes people get up and cross the room and get an ash-tray to placate her. She used to make a thing of having babies, Julia said, sitting and sitting and sitting as if she were hatching them. Having Louis to show, she had rights, whereas Julia being a widow had none. Julia was to be grateful to be allowed to live in Roger's house, doing the work, waiting on Nellie, even minding Nellie's babies when they were small, though fortunately Nellie was a bit possessive about them. And besides they were an alibi for more sitting."

"But didn't Roger see all this? He could have stopped it."

"No. Roger looks the other way. He wouldn't interfere. In fact he was pleased that things worked out the way they did, because he doesn't like Nellie, and he wouldn't like to have to endure her housekeeping. He prefers Julia's. Anyway that will all be changed soon. Can you come and see Roger now? It's tea and buns for supper, if you'll stay for that."

Holding his elbow she brought him out of the café. They walked along Chatham Street behind two shuffling old men with stubbly, resentful faces. As they passed by a butcher's shop one of them suddenly knocked sharply on the glass behind which were artistically displayed rows of chops and steaks and joints.

"As long as that's there, I'm going to have enough to eat," said the old man loudly. "I'll go in and help myself. Man has equal rights. The worst thing is to starve, so it is. Where would we all be without the bite of food? And I'll tell you something: a lot of so-called Christians is really only bastards in disguise. That's what they are: bastards in disguise. Living on the fat of the land. The day will come when they'll all be done away with."

People were turning to stare as the voice rose higher and higher. Mothers hurried their children away as the naughty words struck the air. Swiftly Mark felt in his pocket for two half-crowns. He leaned forward and tapped the old man on the shoulder, showing the silver almost simultaneously in the heel of his hand as he said:

"Would this be any use to you?"

"Would a duck swim?"

Without a glance at Mark, he seized the money, touched the

front of his cap once, casually, and then trotted briskly across the road followed by his silent but appreciative friend. Mark and Teresa stood still and watched them slip into "The Heart Bowed Down" on the corner of Balfe Street. Then Teresa said delightedly:

"That was lovely. But they might have abused you for listening to them."

"I hadn't time to think."

Comfortably they walked along St. Stephen's Green. They were in Baggott Street, well on the way to Washington Road, when Mark suddenly remembered Henry O'Brien. Though he said nothing, Teresa with her artist's antennae sensed immediately a new unwillingness in him.

"What's the matter *now*?" she asked.

"Has Henry O'Brien been in your house in the last day or two?"

"Yes, of course. Every day. But no one minds Henry. He's madly jealous of MacLean as anyone can see, but Roger won't let him into his room. Really, Mark, I have no patience with you. Why should you be afraid?"

"I'm not afraid," said Mark indignantly.

But he was afraid, and now he was suddenly drawn to Teresa for the directness of her mind, for her clear unclouded vision. He had never known anyone like her before for expressing her opinions exactly: and yet she was not crude. He wondered if Aldo appreciated this aspect of her as much as he should.

At Mallon's house, everything looked a little unfamiliar to Mark as if he had been away for three months instead of three days. In the bright daylight the garden looked shamefully out of trim. The fast-growing grass lay in heavy loops and had encroached still farther on the trodden path so that the whole thing was like a badly-parted head of hair.

"Disgusting, isn't it?" said Teresa impartially, following his glance. "If I were Roger I would attach Roddy and Edward by a long chain to the leg, one in each corner, and force them to clean it up. But Roger would never make the effort, and he has practice in not seeing what he doesn't want to see."

When Mark came into his room, Roger looked up in affected surprise, but Mark guessed that his step on the stairs

94

had been recognized. MacLean was there, sitting in front of the diary. He had lost the look of dazed wonder that he had had when Mark had last seen him. Now he looked confident and businesslike, and rather like a well-trained greyhound. He had several piles of paper on the table. Roger came hurrying across to seize Mark's arm and lead him over to look at these. MacLean looked a little displeased, but he leaned back in his chair without comment and allowed Mark to bend over the papers.

"Clever, isn't it?" said Roger. "Look, one is headed: 'Meticulism, growth of.' Here is one called: 'Sources of characters.' Here's one about Sebastian's family life. Isn't it marvellous? These are for a long preface that will go into every aspect of Meticulism as revealed by the diary. That will be the original work for which Tom will undoubtedly be awarded his Ph.D., and after that will come the diary itself, edited and shortened, of course, which will prove up to the hilt everything that is said in the preface."

MacLean shifted in his chair and bent his head, tightening his mouth as if to prevent himself from speaking. Roger seemed unaware of the presence of any strain in the atmosphere. He smiled down on MacLean's head in the most benevolent, fatherly way and said:

"I love the way Americans go to work on this kind of thing. They take it so seriously, so objectively. Now, an Irishman would be at a disadvantage from the start, because he would have a fixed conviction that he could have written all of my works far better than I did, given my opportunities. That is one of the things that is wrong with Henry."

"No, no," said Mark, remembering Henry's misery in the café. "Henry has a real reverence for you. I'm sure his main anxiety is to interpret you properly, to do you justice. He knows well that he is not capable of creating anything new."

He stopped suddenly, because Roger was directing on him a look full of venom. Now the likeness to John showed itself clearly in a long, flat, brown stare, impersonal, ruthless, and yet full of a kind of pure, dedicated idealism which made Mark feel small and ignorant and a little mean, and which absolved Roger from any possible charge of self-interest. The shock of this look was such that Roger's words penetrated with difficulty into his consciousness:

"What the hell do you know about Henry or what goes on in Henry's head? Have you been discussing me with Henry?"

"No," said Mark sharply, stung by the memory of his last conversation with Henry.

"Well, don't do it," said Roger after a short pause. "He'll be after you to know what is in the diary. He has a way of worming things out of people, has Henry. He's done it to me. That's how I know. And I'm a tough old bird. I should have been able for him. I liked having a Boswell around, which was a weakness. Henry sees a weakness a mile away. He knew I wanted to please Rosa, too, and he made use of that approach. She's been asking me to show him the diary, but I won't. I told her that. Don't you make the mistake of underestimating Henry."

"I'll be careful," said Mark.

Somewhere in the middle of Roger's babble of words, he had forgiven him for his attack. Roger was old, Roger was excited, Roger was his friend, on equal terms in spite of the difference in their ages. Friends feel free to be rude to each other sometimes, he suggested to himself tentatively, but he had to abandon that line because he knew it was false. Anyway, Roger was marvellous, and Mark had just had a taste of what life would be without him. So he would ignore that ugly little interlude which had already begun to seem as if it had never happened at all. Roger said now, with a complete change of tone:

"Where have you been these last three days? I've been wishing you were here. Were you ill?"

"I had a cold," said Mark weakly, conscious of the limp form of MacLean between them, making their conversation slightly ridiculous.

"I can see it wasn't a bad one," said Roger carelessly. "You shouldn't stay indoors with a cold."

"And I had a falling-out with my father," said Mark loudly, wanting desperately to affirm the existence for himself of some kind of private life. "I needed a couple of days to think it over."

"It was three days," said Roger severely. "I don't believe I ever gave my father as much as half a day's thought. Let him fend for himself. He doesn't care a hang about you."

"How can I be sure?"

"He never cared about anyone but himself," said Roger. "I know him well. Small man with a face like a sheep. Writes a lot of rubbish about domestic conditions in medieval times, mostly cribbed out of other people's stuff. Michael Cunningham was always complaining about him. Of course your father was never at the university. Cunningham always said he might have made something of him if he had had him as a student. Cunningham was able to get blood out of turnips, so he might have. We'll never know, and it's no use speculating about such tiresome people. And I remember now that he was one of the people who was rude about Flora. I hated him for that, once, though I know Flora provoked people. She used to laugh her head off afterwards at the jokes she played on them. Don't bother your barney about your father. Why don't you go and live somewhere else? From what I hear, you could afford to."

"That is what I have been thinking of for the last three days," said Mark.

Suddenly he was shaken with a great tremor of joy at having said it, at having heard his devilish father summed up and knocked off in a few simple, half-formed sentences which contained within them the mandate of his own freedom.

"Adam had no father," said Roger, "but I bet he grovelled in the slime of the earth that he came out of. I'm a father myself, and I can tell you fathers don't want their children hanging on to them all their lives. They like to see them independent. People are individuals, not appendages of each other. You must learn to be detached. That is the whole secret of sane living."

How immensely clever Roger was, thought Mark, delighted beyond measure with all of this as he felt his own balance return to normal.

Later when he came down to supper of tea and buns with Roger and MacLean, Teresa saw at once that he was relaxed and happy. He even reached for a bun without waiting to be offered it, an unprecedented occurrence. That evening it seemed to her that Roger's arched eyebrows and slender features gave him the appearance of an elderly devil disguised as a snake. For an hour she sat silently in the drawing-room, as was her habit, watching them all. Frances was there, adoring Mark first from a distance but edging closer and closer as time went on. Her devotion was the most painful thing that Teresa had ever seen. For three days Frances had been dead. Now she was suddenly restored to agonizing life. Every nerve in her wretched, wretched body was pulled to breaking point. If only God had seen fit to encase her soul in a different body, thought Teresa, Frances might now be glowing with a heavenly beauty which would have affected everyone in the room, making them smile on her thankfully for giving them such a vision of young love. If she had been beautiful, Mark would have been at least conscious of her. At least he would have thrown her one glance of recognition when he had come into the room. But God had done the dirt on Frances in giving her that face. Shocked at herself for this thought, Teresa paused to examine it. There was no doubt that in her present state Frances's sentiments sat ridiculously on her, like the ambitions of a mongrel kitchen dog trying to achieve the drawing-room. But watching her impartially through narrowed eyes, Teresa came to the conclusion that God was not to blame. From her earliest years and with her own co-operation, Frances had always been made to look as ugly as possible, one would almost have said deliberately. Mentally Teresa stripped her to the skin and began again. The hair: a permanent wave. The clothes: into the fire and try for the love of Mike to get her something that *fitted* instead of those baggy, County, home-made jobs that you couldn't get away with unless you had a title, or had canoed up the Amazon, or had some smashing intellectual achievement to do you instead of elegance. The figure: careful dieting and no nibbling between meals. Then there was the undoubted fact that Frances didn't wash enough.

At this point Teresa gave her up. Care and money could do a lot for the outside of Frances. If Julia had been her mother she would have been dressed differently. Teresa preened the peacock-blue dress which she was now wearing. But the inside of Frances was another matter. It was that that gave her the expression on her face and the awkward, inept movements. Her head had so little in it that the few thoughts that were there rattled audibly for all the world to hear. It would be a sin and a shame to waste Mark on her. The mere fact that she wanted him gave her no right to him.

And now Teresa found that she could not stand another minute of Frances. With her eyes blank and glazed with fury, she got up and went out of the room. Bach was the cure— clean, unhurried Bach: calm, sophisticated Bach. All the way up the stairs she prayed for the soul of Bach without whom she would long, long ago have gone out of her mind.

7

Since the arrival of MacLean, Roger had been sleeping well. This was why he had taken to getting up early again, and prowling about the house before anyone else except Julia was downstairs. He was shocked to find how late they all got up. He went into the kitchen and bothered Julia about it.

"No one downstairs except you and me and Teresa," he said. "How long has this been going on?"

"Years," said Julia calmly, making toast at the gas-stove.

"Why didn't you tell me about it? Why don't you do something about it?"

"I call them at eight when I'm on my way downstairs. Teresa is usually down five minutes later."

"But the others! The others! What about the others?"

"Don't shout, if you please. The others are not my responsibility. They're not my children."

"That's mean of you, Julia. They're all our children, yours and mine and everyone's."

"Not mine," said Julia firmly. "Move aside, please. I want to put the tray there."

"No one is to get breakfast in bed. I'm seventy-nine years old and I don't have breakfast in bed. Who is that for?"

"That is for brother Louis, who is undoubtedly one of your children. And I said please don't shout. Louis has not only breakfast but dinner and supper in bed, didn't you know?"

Roger knew, and it silenced him for a while. He went across and turned the gas low under the kettle. Julia immediately and without comment turned it up again.

"Where are the boys?" Roger asked. "Why aren't they downstairs?"

"Because: one, they have nothing to get up for; and two,

they stay up too late at night. And my pious hope is that they won't come down until I and Teresa have finished breakfast. The sight of them gives me indigestion."

"Julia, you sound bitter," said Roger in a solemn tone.

"Never mind," said Julia. "Lots of people are bitter before breakfast. Afterwards they get strength to face the day. Come along and have breakfast with us. We'll give you some of our toast."

Roger was pleased with the invitation. Seeing him through the open dining-room door, Mary and Frances elected to breakfast in the kitchen. They were always late, and they left the house hurriedly together, shutting the door with a tremendous crash and quarrelling all the way out to the gate. Frances's coat had a tear in the back. Julia looked across at Teresa, as neat as a new pin and already drumming her fingers on the table-edge as she planned her morning's practice. Julia thought how interesting it had been to watch Nellie, in her anxiety to do the right thing by her children, making every possible mistake in relation to them. Even cleanliness and order had been forbidden to them because these were conventional virtues. In rearing them like a decadent aristocracy, Nellie had not reckoned with the fact that they would one day have to earn their living. Nor had she appeared to notice that the heirs to the decadent aristocracy often take care to marry the clean, fresh, wealthy daughters of successful American business men. But of course Julia knew that Nellie never really reckoned at all. Though she hated Roger, she was impressed with the fact that she had married his son, and she was always hoping that Roger by a miracle would some day touch her own graceless lumps of sons and turn them into gentlemen.

It was true that Julia gave very little thought to Nellie's children. Teresa was hers, and quite enough. She was the very image and likeness of her father, who had only seen her once. She had inherited her music from him, and she was at least as hard to handle. But like her father she was never dull. Every day of Julia's single year of married life was imprinted indelibly on her brain. Sometimes she wondered if Aldo knew that he was catching a Tartar in Teresa. From her nineteen years in Roger's house, Julia had learned not to interfere with people, and she had no intention of interfering with Teresa now. If Teresa married Aldo a number of problems would be solved and a number of new ones created. And that in Julia's experience was what happened with every new move that people make. Only a fool tries to swim against the stream, hold back the avalanche, change the course of history. Julia could never decide whether this fatalism stemmed from an incurable bitterness or from religious resignation. She would have to wait until she was dead to find out.

During the morning, John came prowling around Roger's room. Though neither of them would admit it, their relationship had changed with the arrival of MacLean. It seemed to John that Roger had become unaccountably suspicious of him, watching him all the time as if he distrusted him. This new attitude was a good example of Roger's principle of detachment in operation, thought John bitterly. Detachment was a better word than selfishness. It comforted the ego. Roger was busy with MacLean and John could wait.

In his resentment, John almost contemplated visiting Louis in bed, but he knew he would never do it. Nellie had been urging him to go.

"Why don't you go to see your father? Go on up and see your father."

"Why?"

"Because he's not well."

"Would a visit from me improve him?"

"Holy God, the child talks exactly like Roger. It's your duty to visit your father."

"It's too far up for me."

"Next door to your own room. You're well able to visit Roger."

"And Louis didn't visit me when I was ill."

"That's different."

"It surely is. I was really ill. Louis is malingering."

"Impertinence. Do you think I don't know illness when I see it? Wasn't it my profession to know?"

"No. It was your profession to attend upon those who knew. But your confidence in yourself makes it easier for Louis to deceive you."

"You're an unnatural son," said Nellie. "I don't know where we got you at all."

102

"An enviable state of innocence, considering," said John, and got out rapidly lest his mother might assault him.

But she had learned long ago not to do that. For an hour she sat motionless, raging, exclaiming to herself at intervals:

"Well! Well!"

Then gradually she forgot why she had been so angry and she went all the way down to the kitchen to pester Julia about Louis's dinner.

John went upstairs to tell Roger about his conversation with Nellie. They had often laughed at Nellie together but this time Roger said meanly:

"It's no use cultivating the wider intelligence if you don't try to learn one or two simple virtues as well. A young man should not speak of his mother as you do."

John was cut to the heart, but he only lifted an eyebrow. He went across to look out of the window, so as not to seem to be scuttling out of the room. Roger behind him rattled papers busily and said:

"Tom MacLean is coming at eleven. You needn't be here then."

"I'm going to College."

"Give them all my love."

Nellie would have been pleased if she had known how soon John was reduced to her own state of helpless rage. As he walked too fast towards the College his blood boiled with fury at Roger's disloyalty, at the disloyalty of every Mallon to every other Mallon, including himself. He had long gone past the stage of wishing he had been brought up in a working-class family, living in a cottage with a polished knocker and a front garden full of flowers, and a kindly fat, aproned mother, and a father whose reading never took him beyond the *Evening Mail*. Now he just wished he could be like Mark Roche with lots of money and not a brother nor a sister to his name. But Mark was by no means as free a man as John would have been in his circumstances. He was burdened almost to breaking point with a weight of principles of all sizes and shapes which inhibited his every move, and which would never, never allow him to do what John was contemplating now. And Mark was going to be useful to him. Indeed without him he could never carry out his plan. John was specially amused at

103

the notion of Mark unwittingly co-operating in dishonesty.

John, of course, intended to read the diary. The idea that he should not was laughable. The whole house was humming with it while he was kept in the dark. Since his early childhood he had cosseted Roger, allowed himself to be directed by him in all his reading, kept him company and received his confidences. Roger's ingratitude was shocking, but John was well able to rise above mere personal considerations. Roger had done a dangerous thing in allowing two strangers, Mark and MacLean, to read the diary while keeping it secret from John who was really the only one who would properly understand its value. John would not allow Roger to injure himself in this fashion. He would read the diary in spite of him, and so be in a position to protect the old man if necessary.

He tried out this point of view from different angles, and found it sound enough except for one thing, that John's own record was not above reproach. There had been one or two nasty incidents. The one about the picture books, for instance, might be held against him. Roger had shown them to John with some ceremony mentioning that they were worth twenty pounds each. There were two of them, small mild-looking books of Japanese drawings, of sprays of flowers and birds. John had not been particularly impressed by them, and yet it was a curious thing that he had never forgotten them. During the following winter, when there was not enough coal for the stove and they were sitting in their overcoats in the drawing-room, John had got tired of it and had told Julia about the books. That was four years ago, in the winter in which Teresa had had pneumonia, which was probably why Julia badgered Roger until he had sold the books for fifty pounds, not forty. There was plenty of coal then, but Roger had been depressed for a long time afterwards. John had been very careful with him for a while, but Roger had not seemed to blame him for telling Julia. John was only a schoolboy and had to be excused, no doubt.

The second affair had not yet been discovered by Roger so far as John knew. Still, on any day it might come up without warning and have to be attended to. It had happened only last year. John had contracted debts with a certain bookmaker who became impatient enough to threaten to visit the house

104

unless he were paid. Roger would have been shocked and humiliated, too, before the rest of the family. He had just been boasting about his skill as the educator of John who was the only one of them all who was fit to follow a course at the university. Roger had looked around the dinner table and described them all, except John, as an idle, ignorant lot. How they would have gloated if they had found out that John was in debt to a bookmaker! Roger had to be protected from that at all costs. So John had taken a five-stone diamond ring that Roger kept put away in a drawer, and had sold it to a shady pawnbroker for seventeen pounds. The pawnbroker was so shady that John knew the ring must have been worth a lot more. But Roger never looked at this ring—John had found it quite by accident—so in justice to everyone it was better to sell it. Seven pounds had gone to the bookmaker, from whom naturally John had at once withdrawn his custom. The other ten pounds had made it possible for him to eat his midday meal in peace in a café for almost two months. At home he had said that a rich friend was paying for the meal. Just when the time had come when the rich friend should be produced, along had come Mark most opportunely, and had unwittingly supplied the missing part of John's alibi. He smirked at the recollection of the triumphal progress on which he had brought Mark around the drawing-room that first evening. Roger had not missed the ring yet, and the excitement of showing the diary to MacLean would probably postpone still further his thinking of it. Besides he was old, thought John vaguely and perhaps he would never remember that he had a ring at all.

Apart from his duty to protect Roger, John told himself that as the only thinking member of the family he must read his grandfather's diary for the family's sake. That sounded well. Heaven alone knew what horrid secrets that diary might contain. Supposing John wanted to marry Teresa, for instance, it would be important to know something about his own ancestry and hers. Supposing Roger and his wife were first cousins, John and Teresa's children might be soft in the head. Or supposing Teresa's father and mother had never been married at all—that's the sort of thing that might be in the diary! He imagined a whole long sequence in Roger's style, lamenting over Julia and her shameful bundle. Altogether it seemed to John that he had better not consider marrying Teresa at all. She was bad news, whatever way you looked at her. And she was much too clever. She would tie knots in him. When John was ready to consider marriage, he intended to go for a more docile type.

But there was plenty of time to think about Teresa. He recalled himself to his argument. Then all at once he remembered MacLean all a-quiver with excitement and offers of dollars, and his curiosity to know what was in the diary filled him with a huge and intolerable pain, so that he knew he did not need a reason for reading it at all. Roger was himself always preaching detachment and the cutting away of sentimental considerations. Only when man was left magnificently alone, said Roger, could he begin on the work that was designed for him in the world. It was not until he was alone that he could even discover what this work was. These were not Roger's words, of course, but as far as John could understand him they conveyed what he meant. John hardly ever dared to ask questions, for Roger was impatient of anyone who did not understand him at once, and it was in self-protection that John had developed his tired, all-knowing expression.

Lately he had noticed to his shame that himself was becoming attached to Mark. It was not only that he felt at ease with him, that he profited from discussion with him. It was something much stronger than that. When he was with Mark, he experienced a feeling of solidarity and confidence of which he was incapable when he was alone. In fact, alone he was only half a man. He blamed Mark in this, for being so reliable, so clever, so charitable, so ready to adjust his mood to John's. There was no getting away from the fact that Mark was a *friend*. And a man who needs a friend, according to Roger, is still far below the ideal state of independence in which he can live alone with God. It was clear that John was still weakly trying to escape from this aloneness, and was thereby putting himself irretrievably into the power of Mark. His present plan of using Mark cynically for his own purposes would be a help in detaching himself from him, and also in proving that it was John who was the powerful one of the two.

106

Mark was waiting for him in the main hall of the College, looking exalted and nervous.

"Come along with me at once," he said. "I want to show you something."

With a most unusual determination, he marched out into the street, so that John could do nothing but follow.

"It's my new flat," said Mark reverently. "I'm moving in at the end of the week."

"Leaving home?"

"Yes. I should have done it long ago. It was Roger, of course, who made it all clear to me. There's no earthly reason why I should stay with my father when we have such a dislike of each other."

"Have you told him yet?" John asked nastily, and had the pleasure of seeing Mark deflate visibly while a look of terror flitted for a second across his face. But John's satisfaction was soon dissipated as he realized that Mark living alone would necessarily develop in independence. Even now, Mark gathered himself up again almost at once and said:

"No, not yet. I have no idea how he'll take it. Roger seemed to think he would be pleased."

"Could happen. I'm *not* a connoisseur of fathers."

The flat was in a great new block of service flats, with a uniformed janitor at the door, a lift service and central heating. There was a bedroom and a sitting-room, and a small kitchen. The bathroom had a shower. The furniture tended towards pink and grey in the matter of upholstery and carpets. Walking around in his unbuttoned, shabby overcoat, whistling softly, John looked like a plumber or a furniture remover.

Mark watched him for a few minutes, and at last he had to ask:

"How do you like it?"

"A little *bourgeois*," said John judicially. "It will suit you."

"Let me tell you that the *bourgeoisie* knows how to do this sort of thing," said Mark warmly, and without a trace of apology.

John was displeased. He lay back in one of the arm-chairs and looked up at Mark through narrowed eyelids.

"I'm glad you like it," he said without expression. "Can you afford it?"

107

"Easily. I wish you could be here with me, but there's only one bedroom."

This thought had occurred to John also, and he had noticed the absence of a second bed. It seemed to him most unfair that John should have this heavenly retreat while himself had to live in the Mallon menagerie. Mark actually *liked* company. John thought he would even miss his mother, who was a dim-witted soul as far as one could judge from his occasional references to her.

John let his eye fall, surreptitiously, with pure delight on the clean, ordinary fittings and furniture. Their soft, unstartling colours pleased him immeasurably, for all his protest against them. They were subdued to their proper place, as such things should be, instead of obtruding themselves as if they had a right to exist apart from their usefulness. Roger's house had been furnished in Victorian times, with triangular chairs and brassy tables and fearful black corner whatnots decorated with china. There were brass bedsteads and marble-topped washstands and great massive obscene ewers and basins, with blue flowers on them. All of these things seemed to affirm the fact that man is kept in bondage by his domestic appliances. Their sordid little histories were the histories of the people who had used them. One felt that they should have been buried with their owners. As long as John remembered, no new piece of furniture or equipment had been bought for Roger's house. Even the china had hardly changed, because Julia always washed it herself and Julia was incapable of dropping anything.

And then, with beautiful simplicity, John's major problem was solved.

"You must bring Roger here to see this, at once, tomorrow," he said earnestly, sitting up straight. "Then he'll understand that you have really broken away at last."

"But Roger is too busy. He spends all day with MacLean. He never leaves his room until the evening, and by then he is too tired to come out."

"I know all that. I've been wanting to get him out of that room for days. He's enjoying himself immensely, of course, but still it's not good for him. The tension should be relaxed in some way, whether he wants it or not. After all, he is seventy-nine years old." John noticed how Mark shrank a little at this. He pressed his advantage. "An old man like that might even have a heart attack. We should take his mind off the diary, if only for a few hours."

Mark could not resist the note of real longing and anxiety in this. He agreed to ask Roger to come and see the flat.

"You must put everything you know into it," said John. "You must be intensely grateful to him for having pointed you to the right way, and excited and nervous about the momentous change in your life and therefore anxious to have your decision ratified by a visit from him. That will fetch him, if you can manage it."

"There will be no difficulty in managing it," said Mark mildly, "since those are my true feelings. Don't be so cynical."

For an awful moment John was afraid that he might have gone too far, but Mark's manner had not changed at all as he went on:

"I could suggest too that MacLean must be longing for a rest. Roger would never admit that he would like a rest himself, but he might have sympathy for MacLean. And there is another thing." He fidgeted with a reading-lamp on the mantel-shelf. "Would you mind very much if Roger were to come here alone? I mean, if you didn't come as well?"

"Of course. Just let me know when you're taking Roger out and I'll disappear. I'm good at disappearing. You're quite right. It will be far more restful for Roger if I'm not here. And keep him out as long as possible, because he may not agree to take another break. How soon did you say you are moving in?"

"I said at the end of the week, but there's no reason why it shouldn't be tomorrow. Yes, why shouldn't it be tomorrow? I didn't want to seem to be in a hurry, but I am in a hurry. I must get used to pleasing myself. I'll tell you something: one of the hardest things in the world is to be completely honest. By the way, you'd better get out of that chair. You're not really entitled to sit in it until I've paid some rent."

John heaved himself out of the chair, chuckling. Good, honest, *useful* Mark! Would anyone else have thought of that one about the chair? And this very innocence was the quality that John most needed in him now. Mark was saying:

"We can have a party here when I move in. It's all sound-proofed, more or less. I've never had a party in my life."

"We'll bring Sullivan, and Hennessy with his guitar," said John. "They're the ones to get a party going. Only Sullivan must be warned not to read his poems."

"I'm all in favour of letting him read his poems, if he wants to," said Mark. "Why shouldn't he? There are too many people being stopped from doing what they want to do."

"You are quite right, of course," said John, suddenly weary. "But still an exception should be made with Sullivan. The trouble is that he doesn't want to do ordinary things."

"All the better!"

"He likes to heat up his stout with a red-hot poker. Some-times that makes the stout shoot out on to the hearthrug. He likes to bring his bicycle into the drawing-room where he can keep an eye on it. He finds that if he comes to a party in his pyjamas he is more likely to be offered a bed at the end of the evening. It's in the nature of a hint, and it saves him the trouble of going home. Also, when he is enjoying himself he doesn't like to feel that other people under the same roof are asleep and out of the fun. So he knocks them all up irrespective of age, sex and relationship with his host, and invites them to join in. It would be a long job knocking at all the doors in this block of flats, but Sullivan has a big heart. He wouldn't grudge the time."

"Perhaps we had better not have a party at all," said Mark.

"That's the coward's way out," said John. "It would be much better to have a party and make Sullivan behave."

"Is that possible?"

"Certainly. But you must take a firm line. I'll take charge of him, if you like."

"I would like."

All the way back to the College, John chuckled with appre-ciation of himself. Imagination and resourcefulness, it seemed to him, were the two most necessary requirements for self-protection. By attributing to Sullivan the peculiarities he had described, John had protected himself perfectly against the agony of having to listen to Sullivan's poems. It was most unlikely that Mark would attempt to check on the details of the story, but even if he did, Sullivan's appearance, and the

110

fact that he wrote poems and short stories, combined to give him a reputation for oddity among his acquaintances. They would be more likely to embroider John's story than to contradict it. And Sullivan himself valued this reputation rather highly. Therefore himself would be the last person to deny yarns which might with encouragement grow into a firm tradition. The prospects were excellent, in every way. It was not often that John felt a glow of well-being. He felt it now, a real glow of triumph as he played Mark like a violin, or like the poor fish that he was.

Mark was reliable. He went home with John presently and stayed for supper. Then he sat patiently beside Roger until Henry engaged MacLean's attention, and he had an opportunity for talking to Roger privately. While affecting to be listening to Henry and MacLean, John watched the other two approvingly. He observed that he felt no stirrings of compunction. He had not been born without a conscience, but he had succeeded rather well in showing it its place. All that play-the-game stuff was *bourgeois*, very convenient for the authorities in schools. *Sauve qui peut* was John's motto. Necessity knows no law.

Roger was listening to Mark attentively. John closed his eyes the better to hear their conversation, but it was impossible with Henry guffawing ingratiatingly to MacLean at his other side.

Henry was having difficulty in making conversation with MacLean, and still he could not let him alone. He seemed to be observing MacLean's head carefully, first from one side and then from the other as if he hoped to be able to see right inside to the knowledge that it contained. He was asking him the most asinine questions: "How do you like our climate?" "Do you find the Shelbourne as good as an American hotel?" It was quite clear from his shifting unhappy eyes that what he wanted to ask was: "Is there something good in the diary? Is there? Is there? *What* is there?"

John smirked at Henry's discomfort, at Henry's restless tail-end rubbing the last of the pile off the horrible blue plush arm-chair in which he was sitting, at Henry getting at last, at long, long last, what was coming to him. He was like a house-bound dog standing ridiculously on his hind legs at a window,

111

ears cocked, tail quivering, watching ten cats making hay in the garden while he was helpless to scatter them. Henry would give anything to get a look at that diary. John reflected on the strangely civilizing effect of age. Or perhaps Henry had never had much courage. Even at John's age, perhaps he had not been capable of the bold stroke of walking into Roger's room and reading the diary, as John intended to do. Or perhaps he only lacked the gift for organization, a gift which simplified a great many difficulties.

Then, for the second time in one day, inspiration visited John. He was so overawed that he felt physically weak. The economy, the dovetailing, the artistic completeness of it was a wonder even to contemplate. Whether it were going to work out or not, to have conceived it as an idea was a work of art in itself. For the first time he understood the meaning of the Greek dramatist who wrote that he had planned every detail of his play, and added: "Now all that remains is to write the verses."

John opened his eyes and looked affectionately at Henry. It was going to be very important to understand all aspects of Henry, and above all not to underestimate him. The approach must be subtle in the extreme, else Henry would reverse the situation and in two shakes have John in his power. Henry's paying capacity must be judged too. Rosa was a bad manager. Julia could knock spots off her in making a single penny to do the work of two. Rosa economized stupidly until her family was hungry and then she felt she had to make it up to them by buying buns and cakes. This was one reason why Henry was so chubby. Another reason was that he was always nipping into cafés for buns and glasses of milk to keep himself alive, poor devil. Still John thought that Henry would find the money for a thing he really wanted.

He indulged himself with a minute's wandering into detail. There was something to be said for taking his money by the week, but the idea of visiting Henry weekly to collect it made John feel ill. It would be better if he could get a lump sum. The size of it could be decided later. Perhaps it would be as much as fifty pounds. John had always liked the sound of that word "fifty", it was so brisk and it rhymed with "nifty" and "thrifty". It also rhymed with "shifty", ha-ha.

The last point to be considered was the use that Henry would make of the knowledge that John would give him. But here John got tired, and he decided to leave that to chance. There was always the possibility that there would be nothing of special interest in the diary after all, though. Mark's and MacLean's reactions pointed strongly to a likelihood that there was. Since they had read the diary both of them had the look of egg-bound hens. Mere literary value could never have produced that look. Such must have been the expression on the face of the barber who discovered that Lowry Luirc had horse's ears, and who suffered agony until he whispered it into a hole in the ground. And there, of course, was the solution to the last piece of John's problem. He would never have to suffer the burden of Roger's secret. He would immediately if not sooner pass it on to Henry, thus easing himself of it and moreover having the satisfaction of being paid for it.

Now John felt really, terrifyingly exhausted. His head sang painfully and he was suddenly cold. He stood up unsteadily, though it was no more than ten o'clock, and announced that he was going to bed.

"You look like death," said Roger sharply. "What have you been doing?"

"Thinking."

Nellie, by the stove, sniffed and said loudly:

"It's a judgement on you. You'll be in bed tomorrow. I know by the look of you. And you needn't think I'll be up to visit you, after you wouldn't do as much for your own father!"

"Let us be thankful for small mercies," said John, and bowed to her as he went out.

Mark followed him into the hall to tell him that Roger had agreed to take the very next afternoon off, and Mark was to come for him as soon as possible after lunch. But John found that this news made him feel worse instead of better. He had difficulty in reaching his room. Once there he lay down and shivered for half an hour before he could bring himself to get into bed. As usual, he soothed himself into a fit state for sleep with a children's book from the shelf beside his bed. Tonight it was the limericks of Edward Lear. Presently he succeeded in composing a limerick himself, which he would later use to

113

annoy those students who belonged to the Total Abstinence Association:

> There was a young man from Athlunkard,
> A nasty, unsociable drunkard.
> But he put up our pin
> And gave up the gin
> And now he's the Mayor of Athlunkard.

Reciting this, with deep chuckles, at last he fell asleep.

8

Roger was secretly pleased at getting a day off from MacLean. It was not that the admiration palled. In fact he found that the deeper he drank of it, the more his soul longed and fainted after it. He was accustomed to being treated with the reverence due to a great man, but he was always quickly irritated by the poverty of his admirers' knowledge of his works. They broke down after the first few remarks into amateurish mumblings which showed that their proper reading was *Home Notes* or *Peg's Paper*. Admiration from a connoisseur was so much more satisfying. With MacLean and Mark he no longer felt like an actor performing in the dark. They supplied the last, necessary part, the part of the intelligent audience, and while he wished that they could be multiplied a thousandfold still he knew that he was luckier than many of his kind in having them at all.

The main trouble was that MacLean was making Roger work, and Roger had not worked for forty years. He was well aware that this was why he felt spent and ill used. It was not for nothing that he was the author of Meticulism. In the deep, dark nooks and crannies of his soul, he could see the little devils sitting about endlessly on wet stones reciting to each other in a weak whining chant philosophical maxims and conclusions which never made their way outwards to the light of day. Roger knew the face and name of each of those devils as well as he knew his own: Lust, Pride, Cruelty, Selfishness, Temper, Sloth, these were only some of them. Everything about them was faint and weak, but in this very weakness lay their strength. Under attack they made no attempt to fight back: they just slithered around corners until the storm was over, and then reappeared, not strengthened but more malignant. Roger knew that a bold stroke would clear them out at any time, and they even turned this knowledge to profit. No one takes a sledge-hammer to drive a tack, they seemed to say. Such small, weak creatures could not be capable of much harm. Look at the stout, healthy devils that some people keep! When Roger suffered a particular revulsion against them, he sometimes thought of going to live in a monastery. When this happened, his little enemies sat as still as death, silent, not cowering but turned to stone. Roger would imagine himself getting up for early prayers with the monks, strolling in the monastery garden, sitting in the aesthetically satisfying refectory eating simple, humble food, possibly from a wooden platter, while a pious monk read aloud from the works of the Scholastics. This last notion always put the whole soothing picture to flight. Roger knew that the pious monk would some day choose to read from a book which would be more pious than scholastic, and then Roger would have to leap to his feet and denounce him, disrupting the holy silence and shocking the simpler of his companions. At this stage in his imaginings, out would stroll the first little devil, looking refreshed, and Roger would go down to the drawing-room and blow the ears off one of his dependants.

There was no doubt that the close reading of the diary, which was necessary in order to screen it for MacLean, had given Roger an entirely new view of his own history. The repeated action of cutting out parts of the story had given those parts a guilty look. Not for a moment did MacLean's attitude suggest that he saw the thing in this way. He had apparently decided to remain neutral, and he never made a comment, nor a protest. Nevertheless tensions were slowly mounting in Roger's brain. He had dreamed of Flora, several times lately. She had not appeared accusing or complaining. She had simply been there, pleasantly and comfortably as she had never been in her life-time. But Roger was a little frightened by the fact that he was softening. And that was the one thing he could not afford to do, surrounded as he was by thieves and rogues of all descriptions. The first sign of impending disintegration in him would bring them out into the open with their various mean little plots. The only safe course for himself was to remain the head of the family. They would lock him in the box-room, some of them, if they got the chance.

So he decided to spend the morning in reviewing the running of the household generally and in visiting Louis and John in bed.

Louis did not answer Roger's knock on his bedroom door, but Roger pushed it open and went in just the same.

Louis lay perfectly still, experiencing with interest but no enjoyment a tingling sensation which possessed his head and his hands. Since his childhood this had been happening. In spite of its intrinsic ugliness, it fascinated him with its strange combination of mental and physical effects. First there was the head: the feeling there was confined to one patch over his left eye, about the size of the black patch that sometimes occurs over the eye of a smooth fox-terrier. Under that patch, a persistent buzzing went on, rising and falling in volume, not rhythmically but still following a repeated pattern. It was not personally painful, but rather was it painful at one remove, like the pain one suffers when someone else's teeth are being drilled. And the marvellous thing was that his hands responded almost exactly in sympathy. There the buzzing began at the palms and travelled in a long, widening, dotted line out to the very ends of his fingers. When he withdrew his hands cautiously from under the bedclothes, he was almost surprised to find that they looked quite normal, rather whiter than usual, if anything. It would have been satisfying to have found his fingers and especially his thumbs fattening at the tips like slowly squeezed balloons, and covered with black spots varying very slightly in size.

At the loudest point, the buzzing in his head always became a roar, and then, though he knew that he was lying safely in bed, Louis had a frightening sensation of falling backwards. A moment later he seemed to recover his equilibrium, and the relief was so pleasant as to make the preceding terror well worth while. At once, then, the whole pattern started again, mounting to its climax and dying away with a long grinding drag, like the drag of a huge, slow wave on a pebbly beach.

Louis was lying on his back, and his bed faced the window. The light strained his eyes, but he had a vague feeling that it also brought the strange, marvellous black spots without which the thing never started properly. Then, of course, Roger

117

came in and spoiled it all. Louis turned petulantly on one side and the vision vanished.

"How are you?" Roger was asking.

Louis opened one eye and said tiredly:

"Terrible."

"What's the matter?"

"I don't know. And there's no point in finding out, since no one would be in the least interested."

"What about yourself? And Nellie? She'd be interested."

"No. She pretends to know more than any doctor," said Louis with fearful shrewdness, "but she really doesn't know anything at all. When I tell her about the buzzing in my head, she says it's my liver. When I tell her about my hands, she says it's my liver too."

"What's wrong with your hands?"

"Buzzing. They buzz and buzz."

"Sounds like bad circulation. Perhaps it would be better if you got up."

"That's the only cure that has been suggested so far. They've all said it, Nellie and Julia and Rosa and even Teresa, though no one asked *her*. I've told her she's not to practise while I'm in bed, by the way. Toot-toot-toot all day long, like a mad steam-engine. While I'm in bed that must stop, I said to her. She says she won't stop, that it's her livelihood. Why can't she go and work in a shop or something, like everyone else? I don't see her making any money out of her tooting. And she hardly ever plays the tune all through. She stops and goes back, and she repeats little bits five hundred times, like a broken gramophone record. That's the most maddening thing of all. I have rights here, though this is not my house."

"How long do you think you'll be in bed?" Roger asked after a pause.

"Maybe a month, maybe a year," said Louis peevishly. "How do I know?"

"The *luí fada*," Roger murmured.

"What's that?"

"A Connemara custom whereby a youngish man, not necessarily in bad health, retires to bed for a year and a day. Sometimes it's because he's crossed in love, but there can be other reasons too. The curious thing is that the relations don't

118

worry too much about it. They just leave him until he feels like getting up again."

"I'm not much interested in folk-lore," said Louis.

Though his tone was mild, the little inner tongue inside him which hardly ever spoke aloud was shrieking at Roger that he was an old fraud, that he might cheat the general public but not his immediate family who could see behind that façade of geniality to his self-absorption, his smugness. But here Louis stopped, for he knew throughout the depths of his being, as certainly as he knew when the sun was shining and when it was not, that Roger was the most wonderful person who had ever been created. Ever since he was a small boy he had known it. When inwardly he tried to make little of Roger, he knew that his bitterness was only a measure of his own inferiority. He knew this because Roger even at his kindest could not disguise his contempt for Louis. And such a truly great man as Roger was very likely to be right. If Louis could have become resigned to his inferiority he might have been happy, he thought. Look at Nellie, who almost wallowed in her ordinariness. She was actually *proud* of having been a nurse! Not that Louis held her profession against her. Roger's principle had always been that one person was as good as another, and accidents of trade and education must not be counted against them. Yet he had lifted his eyebrows at Nellie and her trade when Louis had brought her home and announced that they had been married a week before. Perhaps *that* had been a mistake, but he had done it that way in order to please Roger, who had always said that he liked decisive, rapid action. And anyway, if Louis were as stupid as Roger thought him, then he was not to be blamed for mistakes.

"Have you enough to read?" Roger was asking.

Always trying to educate me, thought Louis, and he almost said it aloud, which would have been fatal. Frightened at this he said pettishly:

"I don't want any books. My eyes are hurting."

"Then can I do nothing for you?"

In that question was the warning that he would go away in a moment, that he would not sit on Louis's bed and talk to him about his books as he talked often to that young blackguard John. Louis knew that this would never happen now, and

119

indeed he was no longer capable of being disappointed. He would hardly have known how to respond at this stage. He thought of the old man in the French poem who complained with such bitterness and regret that he had never been to Carcassonne.

Sure enough, Roger was turning towards the door. Louis murmured:

> "*Mon filleul a vu Perpignan*
> *Et je n'ai pas vu Carcassonne.*"

He saw Roger half-turn in astonishment, but he did not come back. For quite an hour afterwards Louis felt almost adequate.

Roger stood on the landing outside Louis's door for a few minutes before going in to visit John. Sometimes he wondered uneasily if he had underestimated Louis, if Louis's short-comings were perhaps due to defective education. If this were so, then Roger himself was to blame. But he had never been satisfied with Louis, who had been dreamy and unhealthily withdrawn since the beginning of his life. If he had been any good, he should have proved it before now. Lots of people were able to rise above ill health and a lack of understanding on the part of their parents in their youth. Indeed many philo-sophers contend that these drawbacks are often turned to advantage, so that the end result is a far greater character development than would have occurred if there had been indulgence and justice at all times. Therefore Louis was weak. He never read enough. He wouldn't even read Dickens, mar-vellous, exuberant Dickens, because he said the details dis-gusted him. Weakness again! And it could not be hyper-sensitivity. That was proved up to the hilt by the very fact of his having married that awful wife. And a further sign of weakness had been the way in which he had introduced her to Roger's household as a *fait accompli*, because he could not face a discussion about her first.

Now as he thought about him, Roger felt his brain cloud with fury. This always happened, so that no matter how good his intentions he could never reason clearly about Louis at all. John was more satisfactory in every way. Roger believed that it is always easier to understand one's grandchildren than one's

120

children. John was so straightforward, so honest and direct that he was almost like a contemporary. He did not see the difference in their ages as a barrier between them, and therefore it ceased from being a barrier. And the fact that he made very little effort to conceal his shortcomings rather endeared him to Roger than the reverse. He was quite, quite different from Louis in this, and also in the fact that though he was far less healthy than Louis he had a tough streak of courage somewhere which kept him active long after Louis would have given in.

He was fast asleep now, though Roger had made quite a rattle in opening the door. He looked so pale and exhausted that it occurred to Roger that he might be tubercular, until he remembered that everyone nowadays was vaccinated. Wryly he remembered Nellie's painfully scientific questions when the vaccination was going on. But since he could not be tubercular Roger felt a little irritated with him for not being awake. With MacLean missing today, Roger had been looking forward to having someone to talk to. He shuffled around the room for a while, not bothering to be quiet about it, but John did not stir. Racine's *Athalie* was on the floor. He picked it up and read a piece, but Athalie's troubles seemed a little remote today. He put the book down on the table and went out shutting the door loudly, and went down to the kitchen.

But Mrs. Murphy was there, telling Julia about her daughter's little disappointment, who had grown up such a nice girl, domesticated and useful about the house. Not that Mrs. Murphy held with that class of conduct, far from it, but who knows, she said, what we'd all be doing if we got the chance? Clearly there was no place for Roger in this. Julia warned him very firmly with her eye not to start criticizing her methods in the presence of her staff, so he said nothing about the gas being unnecessarily high, nor about too much skin being peeled off the carrots, as a child could see by one glance into the sink. Instead he just gave one general snort and went off upstairs again to his own room. And there, standing in the dimness on the landing, in the act of tapping on his door, was Flora.

He staggered back against the newel-post with a little shriek. Then he saw, of course, that it was not Flora at all but Rosa.

Henry was with her, concealed in the dimness of the angle of the doorway. He bounced forward now and took Roger by the arm and led him into the room, and made him sit down. And then they sat down too, and looked as if they meant to stay.

So it was all a trap, thought Roger, watching them balefully through narrowed eyelids. He knew what they were after, all right, though in decency they had to wait until he had recovered himself before beginning on it. Henry looking very concerned said:

"What happened? Why did you call out?"

"I thought you were someone else," said Roger.

He was surprised at the weakness of his voice and the effort it cost him to bring out the words at all. The trouble seemed to be in his breathing. Henry was looking at him sympathetically and saying:

"I'm afraid you have been working too hard."

"I'm taking a day off today."

"One day off is not enough."

"I can't keep MacLean hanging on in Dublin for ever," said Roger angrily.

"Why don't you let me help you? I have time just now. Lectures have finished."

"Yes, do let Henry help you," said Rosa. "He could do so much for you. And he's so anxious to read the diary, it's a shame not to let him. He's not eating for worrying about it." Rosa looked upset at the very thought of Henry's not eating, as if a week of less than his usual diet would finish him. "And he's lying awake at night too. I know it, though he denies it. The diary can't be such a secret if you're letting that strange American read it."

"And why should Henry lie awake at night worrying about my diary?"

Roger had no trouble with his breathing now. Henry had flushed a little, and was sending Rosa warning looks, as well he might. But she did not seem to see them. She was twining her long fingers in and out through each other, in the very replica of Flora's way, watching them intently as she answered:

"But, Father, Henry must know all about you, all about everything you ever wrote, and that includes the diary. Henry

122

has done so much for you, in keeping your name before the public."

She was the only one who called him "Father". In one way he liked it and in another way he did not. Her voice had a soft, singing, unemphatic quality which made these direct remarks of hers far more powerful than they would otherwise have been. But Roger knew she was excited because the movement of her fingers quickened, as Flora's used to do especially towards the end of her life. Henry said:

"Rosa, please leave this to me."

"She's nothing if not honest," said Roger dryly, as if to himself. "Though her view is somewhat subjective. I suggest that the public would have remembered me, all right, without Henry's help."

"Rosa insisted that I should appeal to you to let me see the diary," said Henry. "Whether I have helped you by my lectures is beside the point. I have no doubts as to how much you have helped me. But I think I have a legitimate complaint. The standard interpretation of your works came directly from me, and I got it directly from you. Now you say you are going to prove it was all nonsense, go back on what you told me. If you don't want to show me the diary for personal reasons, surely you needn't show it to the first stranger that comes along."

"MacLean is not a stranger now. He and I have become great friends."

"It's worth his while to become a great friend of yours," said Henry flatly. "This will finish me in America. Can't you give me at least the material for an advance article about the diary, so that I won't seem to have been shut out of a whole new development?"

"No," said Roger judicially. "Though I see your point, that would not be fair to MacLean. I think it's a bit grasping of you, Henry, to want to have the diary as well as all the other stuff I gave you."

He laughed softly. He always enjoyed fencing with Henry, it was so easy to put him down. Now he was flushing again and looking pettish, instead of shouting that the diary was worth all that other bull that Roger had handed him from time to time. Roger felt suddenly free and powerful, as he had done

123

long ago when he had realized one day that at last he was a match for his Nanny. It did not really matter what he said to Henry, nor what Henry's arguments were. Roger was going to do this thing in his own way. He had never intended to allow a discussion with Henry to develop, and this one would not have happened only for that queer little shock he had got on seeing Rosa at his door. Her similarity to Flora worried him still. She could have used that against him if she had realized its power. If she had had any skill in argument, who knows but that she might now have worn him down at last and made him let Henry read the diary. But she had said her say in the only way of which she was capable, and like all of his children, except Julia, she was short of the necessary amount of fighting spirit. This made things easy for Roger. He stood up and said:

"It's no use talking about it any more. I'm sorry you're not pleased, but then I have always found it is impossible to please everyone."

He brought them out on to the landing as if they had been acquaintances who had come to touch him unsuccessfully for a loan. And he felt the same unequal mixture of malaise and satisfaction that one experiences on these occasions—sorry to have had to be so firmly putting-off and still pleased at having succeeded in standing his ground, After all, it should not mean so much to Henry. He was reasonably well paid by the university, and Rosa had never been used to much comfort. Henry had never mentioned money, so it could not be that he was afraid of losing financially. And if what he wanted was prestige, Roger could not in conscience help him to acquire it at second-hand.

Still one thought remained to make him uneasy. Before going down to lunch he visited John again and this time he found him awake.

"I'm going out with Mark directly after lunch," he said. "I'll give you the key to my room. Just be sure that no one goes in there while I'm out."

"Not even Julia?"

"Of course not Julia. She might tidy. No one at all. By the way, how are you?"

"*Much* better. I've been asleep."

124

"I know. You look much better. Enjoy your day in bed."

"I might sleep again in the afternoon."

"I'll tell them not to disturb you."

At lunch he laid down the law about it.

"No noise upstairs this afternoon, please. Julia, you see to it that they all stay downstairs. John needs as much sleep as he can get."

"What about Louis?" Nellie asked, bridling.

"Louis can sleep too, if he likes."

Nellie could not quite make this out, though she suspected that there was something nasty in it somewhere. Roddy and Edward, busily dousing their food with bottled sauce, sniggered to each other hollowly, in a new way that they had learned recently. They often did this at the cinema at the more tense moments of the film, and they felt sufficiently rewarded for their hours of practice by the nervous titters that fluttered down to them from the galleries above. Teresa looked at them in disgust and said:

"Roger, do you think you could ban that noise?"

Roger said:

"I was about to say that that sound is never to be made in this house again. Hooliganism, and worse. Why don't you two get some useful work to do? And talking of noise, Teresa, you can't practise this afternoon either. It would keep John awake."

Teresa's face went white. She laid down her knife and fork, side by side, as if she were laying them in the grave. Roddy and Edward watched her with snakes' eyes from across the table.

"I must practise," she said. "I had only an hour this morning."

"An hour is enough," said Roger. "An hour is not bad at all."

"An hour is worse than useless," said Teresa rigidly. "It's only the preliminary, and if nothing comes after it, it's maddening."

Her lips tightened and turned downwards.

"I must have three hours this afternoon, at the very least."

"No," said Roger sharply. "John must sleep."

"And what about Louis?" said Nellie. "It's that awful flute he can't stand. It goes through his head like a knife, he

125

says. He told me to tell you that if he hears it at all while he's in bed, he'll do something desperate."

"What, I wonder?" said Roger acidly. "It would be almost worth while to see Louis do something desperate. But you can't practise this afternoon, Teresa, because John is ill and he wants to sleep. That's all there is to be said about it. The subject is closed."

"Not while I'm here to open it again," said Teresa. "John was asleep all the morning. He can't sleep all the afternoon again, like a dog. And Louis told me that *he* never sleeps, though I must say I don't believe a word of that."

"Listen to her! Listen to her!" Poor Nellie, as usual, lost her powers of speech when her anger had risen beyond a certain temperature. She had to sit back gasping and raging wordlessly while those Mallons, or indeed any of them that had the Mallon drop in them, seemed to derive fresh energy and power of articulation from their rage. Julia joined in on Teresa's side, but though he had never taken on both Julia and Teresa together before, today Roger was able for them. He would not give an inch, not so much as one half-hour was Teresa to have this afternoon.

"And if you do practise while I'm out, in spite of what I've said," Roger thundered, enjoying the reverberations of his own voice, "I'll find out about it. John will tell me."

"And Louis," Nellie bleated.

Roger swung around to gaze at her, as if he were training a big gun on her. Then he turned back to Teresa again, ignoring Nellie as if she were not worth shooting at. In that short space of time, Teresa's expression had quite changed. Suddenly she was calm, almost humorous, though she was breathing quickly still.

"Since you insist on it, Roger dear," she said sweetly, "of course I wouldn't dream of practising this afternoon. Besides, I shall be busy at something else. You have helped me to make up my mind."

"Yes, yes, find something else to do," said Roger, uneasy now as he remembered the valuable place that Teresa occupied in his life, not only for manœuvring but also for entertainment purposes. She had never allowed him to mould and direct her, as John had done, but she had always given value by her

126

independence, even when it was exasperating as it was now.

It was a good thing that he was going out, he thought, as he heard Mark moving about in the hall. It was so much better to go right out of the house, honourably escorted, than just to go upstairs as he usually did after these battles. That always had a slight air of retreat about it, perhaps because he was too conscious of the ridiculous appearance, from the back, of a man going upstairs.

He certainly looked immensely dignified when he was ready. He took a grey silk scarf from a drawer in the hall. That went well with his dark overcoat. He had a special kind of soft black velour hat, very hard to obtain, and he took his gold-mounted walking-stick which was nearly as old as himself and which still looked so opulent. He valued that stick as a third leg nowadays, though originally he had only used it for swank. Out of the tail of his eye, he saw Mark admiring him in the hall glass. Indeed, he did look very *distingué*. But he was careful not to strut, all the same. That would have spoiled it all.

Indoors, he had hardly realized that it was such a beautiful, clear, sunny day. The chestnuts and limes along Washington Road dropped a glorious heady scent all around him, so that he felt a spring in his step.

"Can we walk?" he asked Mark, sniffing the air. "Is it far?"

"Quite near," said Mark, delighted with the sparkle in Roger's eye.

How much better John knew Roger than himself did after all, and how right he had been about the necessity for taking him out. Mark would never have thought of such a bold plan himself, for he hated to interfere in other people's affairs. This was largely cowardice, he could see plainly now. He laughed aloud as he remembered his own agony this morning, hours of it, before he could bring himself to tell his father about the decision that he had made.

"What's the joke?" Roger asked. "Or is it just good humour?"

"It's a joke, all right," said Mark. "I was thinking of my interview with my father this morning, in which I told him that I had taken a flat of my own and would be leaving home for good."

127

"What did he say?"

"I was terrified beforehand, sweating and shaking. When I had managed to get it out, he said: 'Ah, yes. Don't trouble to run to me with every little thing, my dear boy. But of course I'm always at your service if you need me.' And he sniggered and sniggered all the time I was going out of the room."

"Very satisfactory," said Roger. "Now we'll forget him."

9

Teresa went to some trouble not to be dramatic about her personal affairs, but she did not often succeed. In spite of her, an air of drama crept into almost everything that she did, giving her most ordinary actions an extra drive and significance to which they were not intrinsically entitled. This came about partly because all of her movements were so complete, so neat and exact that they gave a distinct impression of having been rehearsed. Teresa was absolutely honest. She never deliberately heightened the tension, as she would have been well able to do, in order to further her own ends, and yet she sensed all too clearly the antagonism that she provoked in many good, ordinary people. Try as she would she could not help suffering from the knowledge.

It seemed to her therefore a marvellous thing that Mark did not distrust her. His kind usually thought that she was affecting superiority, or pretending to be odd in order to get attention. Instead he just took her as she was, listened to her patiently and had even appeared to accept her advice as being disinterested. This was why she felt so sure of her welcome when she called on him, two days after Roger's afternoon out.

His flat was on the second floor. She ran all the way up the stairs and arrived at his door breathing easily. Running never gave her any trouble. She had chosen the early afternoon, though she had no idea what his habits were. He seemed genuinely pleased to see her.

"What were you doing?" she asked him at once.

"Being king of the castle. And getting accustomed to sitting in a drawing-room. I've just realized that I had been spending all my time in my bedroom. I keep wondering why there is no bed."

"I've spent most of my life in my bedroom too."

They looked at each other with sudden amusement.

"It's a bond," said Teresa. She gazed around the little drawing-room. "This is heaven. If I had this, I'd practise all day long. But perhaps there are rules about noise?"

"I was told nothing about them, at any rate."

"There are rules about noise in our house," said Teresa, sitting bolt upright on the sofa, giving off sparks of fury. "Since the day you took Roger out, I haven't been allowed to practise. It's Louis's little head can't stand it."

"What about practising somewhere else? You could come here. I'd be out for a lot of the time, but if I were at home you could use the bedroom."

"Thank you, Mark. What a lovely thing to say. But I'm going to take more positive measures. Perhaps it's a good thing that I have had to come to a decision. Aldo and I are going to be married at once."

Mark felt himself shrivel up small.

"There's no point in waiting," Teresa was saying. "The snag is that we can't be married in Dublin."

"Why not?"

"Now, Mark, have sense. Imagine Nellie and her boys at my wedding. You can see, it just wouldn't do at all."

Suddenly Mark came to life.

"But are you sure that you know enough about Aldo to marry him?" he asked earnestly. "Italians have not got the same moral code as Irish people. The men don't behave like Irishmen: they all have mistresses, and the wives are quite complacent about it. They say it's a compliment to themselves, that a man who is so popular with women should have chosen them. You'd hate that, Teresa."

Teresa was astonished at the urgency with which Mark said all this. She had indeed noticed that he talked faster to her than to anyone else, stammering in his eagerness to get the words out. She did not laugh now, though it was a near thing.

"No, no," she said kindly. "That's the Spaniards, not the Italians. Oh, I know the Italians are not angels either, but Aldo's family is connected with the Papal Court, so they have to behave. Besides, one must not generalize." She gave a long sigh of contentment. "Think of it! We'll have a villa on the

130

Pincio, and half of a *palazzo* in the town, all to ourselves!
Imagine coming downstairs in the morning and not finding
Nellie there, nor Louis, nor those awful pledges of their
affection!"

"You don't have to marry Aldo and go all the way to Rome
to get away from them."

"Now, Mark, don't be nasty. Aldo is wonderful. Have you
never met him?"

"I've seen him at Roger's often, but I've never spoken to
him."

"Well, come along and meet him now, in a few minutes.
But first I want to arrange something with you."

She stopped, and looked at Mark so long and earnestly that
he felt as if the blood had dried in his veins and that he would
never move again. Teresa was frightened of what she was
going to ask, not only because it was so bold in itself but also
because she saw suddenly and clearly how final was the blow
she was about to inflict on Mark. In that pause, she reviewed
at lightning speed the trap in which she was caught. Mark
represented her only possibility of escape so far as she could
see. The fact that he was in love with her was an appalling
complication, one which she should have foreseen. Still, that
was Mark's misfortune, not hers, if you looked at it objectively. Teresa had never been able properly to attend to all the
people who were in love with her from time to time. With an
effort she managed at last to begin:

"Mark, I want you to come to Paris with me. Aldo and I
are to be married there, a week from today."

"Why Paris?"

"For respectability."

"Explain, please."

Mark was shocked at the harshness of his own voice. He
tried to achieve at least a pleasanter facial expression, but he
knew that he did not succeed. Teresa did not seem to be
offended, however. She gathered herself together most carefully, almost as if she were pleased that some outside pressure
was forcing her to be exact.

"If we were married in Dublin, there would have to be a
reception, paid for by Aldo, of course. The press would have
to report it and photograph it and describe the clothes and all,

131

because Aldo's family is news. His parents would have to come from Rome. They'd probably bring a Cardinal with them to perform the marriage. The Cardinal would have to be brought to see the President. It would all be absolutely and utterly awful, and it would take months to arrange. By the time it would be over, I should be in the bug-house. That finishes Dublin. Now about Paris. No one knows or cares what happens in Paris, there's so much going on there all the time. It's like a huge railway junction, Aldo says. We'll be married in Notre-Dame, at eight o'clock in the morning. We've spent the last two days talking about it. Aldo has fixed it all. He knows everybody. And as it happens, his parents were married in Paris thirty years ago, just the same way, to avoid fuss. So they can't object."

"Do they know about this?"

"They know about me, but not that we're going to be married in this way."

"And you're under twenty-one. Roger will never agree."

"It's nothing to do with Roger. Julia is the only one that matters and she has given her consent. Oh, Mark, I can't stay in that house a moment longer."

"Why doesn't Julia go with you? She'd be the right person."

"No, no. It's to look almost like an elopement. The priest in Notre-Dame wouldn't marry us without Julia's consent or perhaps it might have been the real thing. Or perhaps not. I think I would have told Julia in any case. But she can't leave the house for as much as a day. Remember, she does all the cooking. I won't be missed. She'll say I'm staying with a friend. No one will even ask what friend, they'll be so glad I'm gone. Please say you'll come with me, just as far as Paris. I haven't got any girl friends or I might have asked one of them instead. I've never been outside of Ireland in my life. I'll be afraid, every step of the way, if I have to go alone. And besides I do want to have one Irish representative at my wedding."

"Would it be proper for me to go with you?"

"Quite proper, Aldo says——"

Mark leaped to his feet, positively bellowing:

"Did Aldo suggest all this?"

"No, no. It was my own idea." Teresa pulled at his coat-sleeve and made him sit down beside her on the sofa. "I'm

132

sorry, Mark. When I began to ask you, I didn't know you'd mind so much. I'll go alone. I shouldn't have asked you."

Mark could not look at her, for fear of seeing her disappointment. He leaned back in the corner of the sofa and shut his eyes. The unconscious cruelty of her request made him almost weep with pity for himself. And yet it was an academic pity, detached because of its very depth, as if not himself but some other man were the object of it.

Before Teresa had come, he had been thinking about her so strongly that it seemed to him almost as if he had caused her by pressure of his will to appear at his door. Still with his damnable habit of self-restraint he had looked at her as calmly as if she had been the bread-man. She would never have guessed that his imagination had already placed her in charge of this very flat, had even put an apron on her and set her to cook bacon and eggs in the kitchen. The bold stroke of leaving his father's house had given him an appetite for bold strokes. In spite of his wish to please, he never felt in the least inferior. It had been his considered intention to snap Teresa from under Aldo's nose, but in his innocence he had not realized how far their attachment to each other had already developed. Now with grinding intensity he proceeded to think out the course that he must follow. It took only a moment, a black, dead moment during which the colours of the whole world dimmed and faded, like an old, once-beautiful picture. He would have made Teresa happy, not just in spurts but in every moment of her life. This would have been his study, and because he was clever he would have succeeded. What she would have given him in return was too marvellous to contemplate—the vision of herself in every mood and circumstances of her daily life. He thought of some of these now—Teresa reading, Teresa brushing her hair, Teresa asleep, Teresa playing the flute, Teresa listening to music. Then he had to stop, shut it all out, pull down a blind against these heart-rending little pictures which made him want to lie down here on the floor of his new drawing-room and die, because he would never see them except in imagination.

So he said, very softly:

"Of course I'll help you, Teresa. You must never ask things like this except from people who love you. It's too dangerous."

133

He was able to look at her now, and this steadied his nerves, because the reality of Teresa was far less disturbing than the terrible abstract pictures of her had been.

"You'll really come to Paris with me?"

"Yes."

She was on her feet at once.

"Come along and we'll tell Aldo. He'll be at the Marechiaro at three o'clock. He loves coffee bars—I think because all the people look a little yellow, like himself."

Every step of the way to the Marechiaro, Mark hated Aldo. By the time they were pushing past all the people standing at the counter, he was bored with him as well. Why could he not have married another Italian aristocrat instead of walking off with Mark's Teresa, causing all these complications? He remembered the superior way in which Aldo always stood about in Mallon's drawing-room, waiting for Teresa, rarely condescending to sit down, as if the Mallons were not good enough for him. But then uneasily he remembered too that Aldo when he came often slipped down to the kitchen to talk to Julia. Coming in late one evening, Mark had seen him, through the lighted basement window, sitting on the kitchen table swinging his legs, laughing with his head thrown back and all his marvellous white teeth glittering like a lighthouse. He was a huge man, with a massive head and broad straight shoulders which increased his appearance of arrogance.

"There he is," said Teresa.

Mark looked at her, and his resentment against Aldo began slowly to trickle away. A picture from an old book of Irish fairy tales came before him, of Aongus Og, the god of love, about whose head there flew continuously a cloud of singing birds. Teresa seemed now to be listening intently to the music of those invisible birds. Mark watching her would have seen the slightest reservation if one had existed. So he was completely disarmed, and bound even more closely to do whatever she told him.

Aldo had seen them at once. They sat at a small table in the dimness at the very back of the coffee bar. The chairs had spindly legs which whined in desperation whenever Aldo moved. He seemed to be finding it hard to keep still. He stood up to shake hands with Mark, towering over him.

134

"Now we can talk," he said. "I have been wanting to talk to you always, but we only meet at Mallon's and there you can't talk, you can only listen."

He arranged two chairs for them, and then he lifted his chin one inch, waved the forefinger of his right hand in a gesture inherited from a Roman emperor and said apparently to no one in particular:

"Two more coffees, please."

Immediately an elegant young woman put a cup of coffee each in front of Mark and Teresa. Mark looked enviously at Aldo and said:

"I'd have to beat her to make her do that."

To his astonishment Aldo looked a little embarrassed.

"I shouldn't do it that way, I know," he said. "She is not the kind of girl who should be spoken to in that way."

His tone made it clear that he believed in the existence of a kind of girl who could be spoken to in that way.

"Now," said Aldo, "has Teresa told you our plan?"

"Yes. I would do more than that for Teresa."

In spite of him, his voice trembled a little. Teresa looked down at the table. Mark felt Aldo's enormous penetrating eyes probing about in his brain, digging out interesting little items like his love for Teresa, his determination to serve her, as if they were archaeological finds, of small significance, inspecting them closely and laying them back again. The strange thing was that Mark did not resent this. By a perverse trick of the mind, he had taken a great liking to Aldo. It was not only that he had to admit that Aldo was really good enough to have charge of Teresa. As well as that, for himself he found that Aldo had a special attraction. He could not yet tell the reason for it, but he guessed that it was not merely a superficial charm which had captivated him. This man was as clever as himself, and in addition he had an air of sophistication, of confidence, which was complementary to Mark's own groundless fear of the world. In any case, he thought sadly, he had always known that he would never be able to catch Teresa. Only someone over-life-sized, like Aldo, would be a match for her. It was not that there was any ill will in Teresa, but only that whoever lived with her would have to be twice as agile as is normally necessary.

135

Aldo had two Aer Lingus tickets twitching impatiently in his hand.

"These are for Wednesday's five o'clock plane to Paris. I'll be at Le Bourget, waiting for you. Teresa can stay with my cousin Maria. Maria will come to the wedding too, and be a witness. She's the only one of my Paris cousins that I would trust to keep quiet about it. I have fixed you up at the Crillon. I hope you won't find it too noisy. Where do you usually stay in Paris?"

"At a students' hostel off the Boule Miche," said Mark.

"Well, this time it will have to be the Crillon, I'm afraid. I've arranged it now. It's a good address. That's important because Maria will tell all the families every detail later on. How she will enjoy that, you have no idea! They'll give us a meal after the wedding. Then Teresa and I will go to Madrid by air. I have never been in Spain. I want to find out how they have been getting on since the Romans left."

"Not too well, I hear," said Mark solemnly.

Aldo looked at him with delight.

"And you'll come to see us, to stay with us, every time you are in Italy. Remember, every single time."

"I have never been to Italy in my life," said Mark calmly, studying the effect of this.

Aldo put down his cup slowly and looked at him in amazement.

"You have never been to Italy? Never at all?"

"Never at all."

"Not to see the Pope? Not to Florence?"

"No."

"But you have been to Paris?"

"Often."

"When did you inherit your own money?" Aldo demanded sharply.

Mark answered as if he were answering a lawyer in Court.

"In January it was. But I've been going to Paris since I was sixteen."

"In January? You should have gone to Italy at once, at once!"

"But I'm at College," said Mark mildly.

"Ah, yes. That explains it. There will be holidays, though.

You must not lose any more time. I'll tell you what you will do. After the wedding, you will be half of the way to Italy. Instead of coming home you can go on to Rome at once. I'll get your tickets in Paris. Rome is wonderful. Even the railway station. At night it looks like a huge mausoleum in which the bodies of the dead have taken to trotting about with suitcases."

"I can see I'm going to love that. But I must do examinations at the College in a few weeks' time."

"Always the same in Ireland," said Aldo impatiently. "Examinations, examinations, always examinations. So you must come home and show the professors that you know as much as they do. But then there will be nothing to stop you?"

"Nothing."

"Then you'll come to us in Rome, and you'll see what sort of a *padrona di casa* is Teresa."

During the next few days, Mark saw a great deal of Teresa. Every afternoon she came with small quantities of her clothes and other possessions, and packed them into two suitcases which Aldo had left at Mark's flat for her, before going to Paris to make final arrangements for the wedding. Teresa kept her flute at the flat too, and she always practised an hour or two. Then she would sit for a while and talk to Mark, looking so much at rest in her arm-chair that it seemed to him impossible that she would so soon be gone from him. Each day he found out more about her sharp, direct mind, and each day made his agony at the prospect of losing her more acute. It was no use to tell himself that one cannot lose something which one has never had. And though he found several things to criticize in her, that was no help either. Just as she was he loved her, even though he could see that she was callous in spending so much time with him when she must have known quite well the condition of his feelings. Also her attitude towards Roger angered him. He wanted her to tell Roger what she was going to do, but she would not. She did not agree that she owed anything to Roger as the head of the family.

"Julia and I have always remained a separate family," she said. "We have kept our own standards. You can see that even on the outside. We don't dress in big woolly things, nor make remarks about our food. We go to bed and get up at reasonable times. Roger is used to that now."

"But he'll be hurt if you just go off without saying a word."

"No, he won't be hurt, or at least not much. Remember, if he had not banned my practice, I might not be going so soon at all."

"That was Louis."

"No, it was Roger. Louis has always hated my music, but Roger never gave in to him before."

"Perhaps Roger knows that Louis is really ill this time."

"No. He says Louis is malingering."

"Then why did he do it?" When Teresa did not answer, he said again: "I say, why did he let Louis have his way now when he would not before?"

"I think it's because of John. He was always more considerate of John than of Louis."

Teresa knew that she was on dangerous ground now. Her views of Roger and Roger's value were very different from Mark's, and already in her short life she had observed how easy it is to strike the first, most far-reaching blow to a friendship. Even if Mark were to contradict every word she would say against Roger, still a tiny spore of the poison might remain in his mind to inhibit his relations with Roger and perhaps to grow into the doubt and distrust which is the most deadly enemy of all friendships. She knew well, though not at first hand, what miseries are suffered by sensitive, uncertain people like Mark, how their own wish to love is their worst enemy, how too easily and generously bestowing their love in unworthy places, gradually they learn bitterly to distrust even their most proved friends. Unscrupulous as she was in many respects, Teresa quite simply feared the eventual vengeance of God if she were careless of Mark's sensibilities. It would be a real case of scandalizing one of these little ones, and remorse for it would haunt the rest of her life. So she let the silence develop and hoped that Mark would move on to some other subject.

Mark was thinking about John, whom he had not seen for a full week, since the evening on which he had become suddenly ill. John had sent him messages to say that he did not want to be visited. He was in a depressed state of mind, he said, and he said that he did not wish to communicate his depression to his friends.

"How is John?" Mark asked abruptly.

"Roger sees him," said Teresa. "I don't. He says John was very well on the morning of the day that I was told not to practise. Roger was out with you that afternoon, do you remember? When he saw John again in the evening he was very ill—or so he said—and he has been the same since then."

"What's the matter with him?"

"Indigestion, depression, headaches, all the things you get from leading a disorderly life, eating only what you fancy instead of what's good for you, giving way to your emotions, possibly drinking quantities of stout at too early an age. Maybe even making the most of his opportunities in other ways, too, for all we know."

"You certainly have got a low opinion of him. Has a doctor seen him?"

"Oh, yes. Roger got the doctor. He said John was to stay in bed and have the best of everything, just like Louis. No disturbances nor anxieties. It's a great life. Julia has two trays for every meal now instead of one. Do you wonder why I choose this moment to sail off and leave her? Why I don't stay at home and carry trays? It would only prolong the situation, that's why. I'll get Julia out of that. She'll come and visit us in Rome, and she'll never go back to that house again. Aldo says that's the best way, to ease her out of it gradually. Even though Julia doesn't exactly hug her chains, she has grown roots there, and she's quite attached to Roger."

"But what will become of Roger? Surely it would be wrong for Julia to leave him to the mercy of Louis and Nellie?"

Teresa cocked a cynical eye at him.

"Roger is not so helpless. He'll get on all right. You have just abandoned your own parents, remember, so you should understand that it can sometimes be necessary."

"That's different. My father really is the limit."

Still Teresa restrained herself, though the tirade that rose up within her very nearly burst its way out into the open. All she said was:

"I must look after Julia. She's not as young as she used to be. Her health won't stand up to that maid-of-all-work life for ever. Aldo's family has packets of money, all made out of canned food factories, and jam factories. He's going to give me an annual income which I'll hand on to Julia."

"Has she agreed to this?"

"No, of course not."

"Perhaps she won't leave Roger?"

"If she won't, I have another plan. When I start having babies, I'll set up a howl for her, and she'll come to live with me and Aldo in Rome. She won't resist that, you'll see."

"No, she won't be able to resist that."

He changed the subject then, lest she might say any more things of that kind, and knock him quite off his precarious balance.

Aldo going away had told Mark that his main function as Teresa's escort was to ensure that she would not panic at the last moment and fail to take the plane to Paris at all.

"I wish I did not have to ask you to do this for me," he said. "There are many girls that I could ask to bring her to the plane, but she would not obey a girl."

"Teresa told me that it was her own idea that I should go with her, not yours," said Mark, suddenly snappish.

"Yes, it was her idea, but I approved of it. You see what a difficulty I am in. 'Conte Aldo d'Uberti flies to Paris'; it will be in the *Evening Herald*. If Teresa is with me, that will be in the *Herald* too. You can see that this would be bad for Teresa. Always I think only of what would be best for Teresa. If the situation were reversed, I would do the same for you."

"Perhaps I wouldn't trust you."

"You would be wrong. And in any case, I trust you."

Aldo was not in the least offended, and Mark found that it was impossible to hate him as he should have done.

Sure enough, on Wednesday morning, Teresa refused to go. It was a day of warm grey, blowing mist, heavy with the feel of grass and flowers spending themselves in growth, a day to drift and reflect and take the least possible action. She came at the time that they had arranged, for even in her distress she was incapable of being late or of breaking an appointment. She sat on the window seat, her teeth chattering and her eyes flashing angrily.

"Julia has refused to come to the airport," she said. "I asked her, and she said no, it was better to have no fuss. I

140

didn't ask her to make a fuss. I only asked her to come to the airport so that she would be the last person that I would see in Ireland. She's like the rest of them. There's to be no feeling, no emotion. Chin up, stiff upper lip. Teresa is going off to Rome. What's all the fuss about? Don't touch her. Keep your hands off her, or she might weaken, she might cry, like David crying for Jonathan, or Absolom's father crying for Absolom. David should have kept a stiff upper lip, but he didn't, he made a show of himself. It's all supposed to make life easier. Oh, Mark, it makes it five hundred times harder! I can't go. I should never have promised. They're all so unbelievably earnest about not being earnest. No one ever tells the truth. Whenever by chance they express an honest emotion, they must create an alibi immediately by putting a cynical sting in its tail, lest anyone listening might think that they were innocent or holy or good. Trample down nature at all costs, that's their principle. Leave a tight, narrow little passage free in case God wants to squeeze through, a little passage that can be closed up at a moment's notice if it shows the smallest sign of widening. Develop yourself and be damned to everyone else, they say, and so they never develop, they harden and dry up and freeze solid. And Julia is affected by it at last. I thought she had kept herself free of it, but she's like them now, from living with them."

"Perhaps she was afraid to come to the airport, for fear that she would find it too painful," Mark suggested.

"What harm if she found it painful?" Teresa demanded. "That is my whole point. At least it would be a clean, honest emotion. And yet I don't want it to be painful for her. She has had such a horrible life that I can't bring myself to go off now and leave her, if it will make things worse."

"But you told me that she had agreed that you should go."

"Yes, but now she was so cold, I can't be sure that she has not changed her mind. Or worse still, that she has succeeded in hardening herself because I am going, in making herself insensitive so that she will suffer less. And if that is so, it would be wrong to leave her."

Here was Mark's chance but he did not take it. Instead he went to the telephone and talked to Julia for half an hour, and persuaded her at last to abandon the Mallons and come

141

and spend the rest of the day with Teresa. They had a meal at Jammet's and presently in her pleasure at seeing her mother being served instead of serving, Teresa became less agitated.

Julia never took her eyes off Teresa as long as she was with them. At three o'clock they collected the baggage and presently took a taxi to the airport. The mist had cleared, and it was a soft, luminous afternoon. Mark was hardly aware of it, for by now he was conscious only of an interior blankness, a suspension of the faculties of observation such as one experiences at a funeral. Repeatedly he suppressed the notion that he should not have been given this task at all, because in principle he knew that a man must be prepared to lay down his life for his friend. Just before they left her, some words of Julia's recalled him sharply to consciousness.

"Look after Teresa. There's no one I would trust with her so much as you."

He kept his temper, but while they walked across to the plane, turning every moment to wave to Julia on the balcony above, a thundering fire blazed in his brain. If he were six inches taller, they would not trust him, he thought. If they knew what was going on in his head, they would not trust him. Aldo and Julia despised him. Teresa was dead safe with him, because he was only five-eighths of a man. For a good two minutes, a bold little devil took possession of him as he thought of the many ways in which he could have betrayed their trust. In her emotional state of the last few days Teresa had been fair game, a sitting bird. But he had made not the slightest attempt to influence her. Instead he had helped considerably towards hardening her determination to marry Aldo. He had laughed at her provincial notion that Rome was too far away, that there was a certain risk in marrying a man of another race. He had proved that he was indeed a man to be trusted, and now he had to pay for it.

A well-meaning air hostess saw to it that they could sit side by side. Mark had feared even to put a hand on Teresa's arm and guide her up the steps, lest the ravening wolf inside him might leap upon her and eat her up. Now he had to endure several hours of nearness to her, close enough to be enveloped in the scent of her hair and her clothes. Looking through the window at the curve of Dublin Bay and the smooth sea beyond, it occurred to him that a good solution now would be if the plane were suddenly to dive into that cool, pale water, down among the rocks and weed showing so fantastically clearly on the sea-bed. But it was no use hoping for that, and besides the thought of death created a revulsion in him in spite of his misery.

Teresa was silent almost for the whole journey. After one or two attempts at starting an impersonal conversation, Mark gave up the effort and let her alone. Then gradually it was borne in upon him that she was tired of him, that she would be glad to see the last of him. Try as he would, he could not rid himself of this idea, though he had no evidence whatever to support it. Thus he found himself quite unable to communicate with her, and in silence they journeyed all the way to Paris.

Teresa was tired of Mark, of his patience and devotion and tedious, wearying uprightness. She hated herself for these sentiments but she could by no means control them. If she had been looking to him to help her to escape from Aldo how notably he would have failed her! Day after day he had urged her on, had assured her that she was doing rightly, until her head was in a whirl of doubt. The fact that she was sure about Aldo had nothing to do with the case. Mark should have argued against him, tried to prejudice her against him and get her for herself. Stimulated by the need to make a fight for Aldo, Teresa would have been put at ease. But Mark agreed too often with her judgements, except about Roger.

It was curious that he was so independent about Roger. It was not just an ordinary friendship, developed naturally and sustained by accidental affinities. Mark had an air of having decided in favour of Roger, for a known reason. Teresa remembered that he was thought to have read that damned diary that all the fuss was about, and that was probably behind the disruption of their hellish but once barely tolerable household.

As for the rest of them, Teresa smelt money in the air. Usually when Louis retired to bed there was money somewhere in the reason for it. John was up to something too, perhaps even expecting the police to call. How glad she was to be getting away from them, leaving them to rot, as the Victorian phrase used to say so expressively. She was glad too that she had successfully resisted the temptation to complain to Mark about Roger. That would have been really wicked, and so would have been the other temptation to put in a good word for Frances. Feeling remote and godlike above the clouds, she had actually considered doing this. Just in time she had remembered that she was really very fond of Mark though he was so worthy, and that she wished him far better than Frances for a wife.

At this point Teresa paused, shocked at her own nastiness. She panicked for a moment then, in fear that she would not change. But Aldo had assured her that she would, and he had seemed so certain of it that she had believed him. Now suddenly with all her strength she wanted him, because she could not bear herself for a moment longer. When they landed at Le Bourget, he was the first person that she saw.

10

For three days John had lain in bed almost without moving. The room was in semi-darkness, for he kept the faded curtains drawn close. Julia had attempted to open them but he had prevented her, while being careful to be polite, because she was in charge of his food. When Nellie, breaking her vow not to visit him, had suggested letting in some fresh air, he shot her out of the room with vituperation and oaths. Then he lay back feeling that he had cut his last life-line. Nellie, God help her, had at least an inbred conviction that she owed her children a duty of maternal love. This was a commodity which could be useful once in a way. John felt so deeply sunk in depression now that he could almost envisage a time when he would be glad of a kind word from Nellie.

He was quite certain that he did not want her now, however. He tried to suspend all thought, as he had read somewhere that it was possible to do, but he did not succeed. Memories kept looming up inside his brain, growing and growing until everything around them was black. Then his eyes would fill with tears of self-pity and humiliation, the vision would clear and he would have a quarter of an hour of relative calm before it all started again.

When he had read the diary this had begun, and of course as a consequence the interview with Henry had not gone at all as he had planned. His calm, weary, all-knowing air had deserted him, so that instead of being always one jump ahead of Henry his judgement had been faulty, he had made a fatal mistake and had ended by being made to look a juvenile fool.

What he had read in the diary had upset him. The mechanics of it had been dead easy. He knew they would be, when Roger handed him the key to his room. That was an opportunity beyond his wildest hopes. But he was not really surprised, for he had noticed lately that he was lucky in all of his undertakings however dubious. He knew that some of the credit must go to his own intelligence; since it is an accepted fact that accident-prone people cause to a large extent their own misfortunes, therefore the converse must be true. It was the sort of logic that he liked, and he was pleased to notice that he was becoming practised in this kind of reasoning. The entertainment was endless, once you got a good start.

There was a clear view from Roger's window to the front gate, so that if by chance the old man had returned early there would have been plenty of time for John to get back into his own room. He did not have to waste time in searching for the diary. There it was as MacLean had left it, on the small table near the window. Having locked the door, John sat down in MacLean's chair and studied its exact position before putting a finger on it. This was the sort of precaution that a less intelligent man might have omitted, thus laying himself wide open to detection. Then in full realization of the awfulness of what he was doing, he turned the pages back to the beginning.

He could not at once start to read. The fact that Roger did not want him to know the contents of the diary was not the impressive point. What really made him pause was the knowledge that this was going to be his last chance to see into Roger's mind. If he did not succeed in understanding him now, his only remaining hope was gone. He greatly feared that it was through his own stupidity that he found Roger's philosophy lacking in some essential. There was a part missing, a door shut which he could not open. He hoped that in the diary he would find the key. Roger need never know about it, but all of their future conversations would be illuminated for John by a new light, which would show the last of the pattern fitting neatly into place. More than once John had almost pinpointed the missing link. It was something to do with the reconciliation between Roger's tenet that there must be personal development before all, and his other principle that man has a duty to consecrate himself to the fulfilment of a single expressed project for the good of mankind in general, decided upon in youth and never relinquished until death. Sebastian, Roger's great creation, had been the archetype of all this,

146

Sebastian spending himself endlessly in disseminating his philosophy in all its detail, forcing an unwilling audience to listen, indifferent to whether or not he influenced them to changing their way of life so long as his point was made. For the life of him John could not see how Roger's two principles could be compatible. Now he hoped that at last all would be made clear.

Hours later he sat back in his chair and gazed hopelessly into space. Roger was a fraud, a great big fraud and nothing else. He had no philosophy at all. He had simply been amusing himself at John's expense, playing on his ignorance, his gullibility. Remembering long philosophical discourses from Roger, to which he had listened in wide-eyed wonder, John now wriggled with humiliation. It was laughable, the idea of Roger discoursing on how one should live, while all the time he was concealing a murk the size of an elephant in his past. Now especially his principle that man should learn to stand alone was laughable.

John had not paid much attention to the parts of the diary that concerned the development of Sebastian and the other characters in Roger's books. It was only by skipping quickly over these that he had managed to come to the end of the personal story in the time before Roger might be expected back. He had read the books long ago, of course. Roger had presented them all to him with solemnity on his sixteenth birthday. Because he was too young he had found them extremely dull, except for the dirty bits, and though he had had to read them then so as to be able to talk to Roger about them he had never been able to bring himself to reopen them since. He was much ashamed of having found Meticulism such a bore in itself, but of course he had never admitted to anyone that this had been his reaction.

What interested him now in the diary was the story of his own grandmother Flora, of her rival Sybil and of her tragic end. He thought that Roger came very badly out of it. Where Mark had seen high drama dominated by a rock-like figure and told in terms worthy of a Greek tragedy, John saw a sordid, obvious, slightly ridiculous little story, and the maunderings of an indeterminate selfish character. Savagely he resented all this. Until now he had not known how much

147

he admired Roger and depended upon him. Now deprived of him, he was left dangling in space. What could be more ridiculous than a philosopher, a leader of souls, who could not decide between his wife and his lady friend? It was true that Roger did not say in the diary that he had cohabited with Sybil after his marriage, but such a weak vessel as he might have made use of his opportunities. And anyway Flora must have thought he did or she would surely not have taken it all so hard. John was very much interested in speculations of this kind, though they were outside his experience. He could see that Flora would certainly have the same point of view.

He lay awake until four o'clock in the morning, thinking about it. This was not surprising, for he had slept for a large part of every day since retiring to bed. Still he was impressed with the drama of hearing the aged grandfather clock in the hall beat out the hours and half-hours while he lay staring into the blackness, imagining the slender, melancholy ghost of Flora rambling aimlessly unseen about the house. But he was afraid to pity her too much, lest she might appear to him, looking for sympathy.

Early the next afternoon he got up and dressed, announced that he was better and walked out of the house into the sunshine. It made him blink. He had forgotten that it was May. The chestnuts were in full leaf. He went from shadow to shadow, blind as a bat in the dusk. He had not washed, because in a vague way he felt that there was a certain danger of washing off the mood of resolution which had possessed him in bed. As he came near to Henry's house, he met Rosa hurrying along looking anxious as she always did when she was going out shopping. He walked past her with his eyes down, pretending not to see her; though he liked poor Rosa as well as he liked anyone, he was afraid that a conversation with her would break the continuity of his resolve, so that he would not be able to bring himself to visit Henry at all. He knew that Rosa stopped and turned, and looked after him when he had passed her, but as she did not call out, he took no notice.

Henry's house was in Melbourne Road, several turnings away from Washington Road. It was red-brick also, but it was more fortunate than Roger's house in having no basement.

John always looked at the front garden with great curiosity, like a farmer at the Zoo, for it was planted with flowers and shrubs and had a green lawn which Henry mowed with his own hand every Saturday. All very *bourgeois*, thought John, especially the regularity. But the flowers were pleasing, and he would like to have stroked the short grass which looked as if it would be warm as a cat's fur in the sunshine. To do this would have been an active compliment however, so he had to omit it, and walk past ferociously as if he saw nothing to right or left on his way to the front door.

Henry opened the door himself, as John had known he would. He was not lecturing these days, and their daily woman only came in the mornings. The children were at afternoon school. John prided himself on being able to remember details like that. He had come at this hour because he had been so sure that he would find Henry alone.

Henry displayed another *bourgeois* characteristic in that his formal manners were falsely good. He opened the door wide and said, as if he loved him:

"Ah, John. Come in. I'm glad you're well again."

John slouched into the hall. He refused to be parted from his overcoat. For one thing, he could see through the open drawing-room door that there was no fire in the grate, and besides he might want to get away quickly. A strange thing was that as he followed Henry into the drawing-room he found something formidable in the little fat waddling body which had always until now seemed merely ridiculous. He needed time to let this impression settle down before opening the subject of his business, so he was glad to see that Henry was prepared to make conversation.

"It's good that you're up and about so soon. I was afraid that you would be out of action for the exams."

"When do they begin?"

"Yours are next week. I hope you've been reading in bed. It's quite a good place to work. I remember when I was a student, my digs were so cold that I often went to bed at seven and did all my reading there. It's hard to remember stuff you have learned in a state of bodily discomfort, I found. Professor Dennis was talking about you the other day. He says you have a future in history."

149

"Did he, indeed? I wonder how he discovered it."

"He had his reasons. He said that you don't see history merely as a series of facts, but as an inevitable development brought about by the changing philosophies of the times."

"What a lot of big words Professor Dennis knows!"

Henry was not offended. He smiled genially as if John had said something witty.

"Oh, yes, he's very much interested in you. He thinks you'll go far."

John looked up through narrowed eyelids. He was sitting slumped down in his chair, a most unresponsive recipient of this spate of compliments.

"Now, why should Henry be making up to me?" he thought to himself.

Like a flash came the answer:

"Because he thinks I may help him to get a look at the diary!"

He hauled himself upright and stared at Henry without expression. He decided to create a little atmosphere by asking:

"Are we alone in the house?"

Henry looked startled as he answered:

"Yes, as a matter of fact we are. Why?"

"Good. I'm just out of bed. I came here directly, specially to see you."

"That was nice of you," said Henry. "Was there something on your mind?"

"I have just read Roger's diary."

John almost hissed the words. Then he leaned back and waited for them to sink in.

The impact on Henry was obvious. The look of artificial geniality left him, and was replaced by an expression of bewildered sorrow. He did not lift his head to catch John's eye. In fact he was staggered at the young man's impertinence, but John mistook his reaction for one of frustrated curiosity and greed. He decided to go slowly.

"I found it very interesting."

"No doubt."

This was not promising. Still John went on:

"So would you, if you were to get a look at it."

150

This time Henry did look at him, and now John mistook the spark of anger for one of interest.

"But Roger has refused to show me the diary. I have actually asked him, you know, and so has Rosa. Do you remember Mark Roche advised me to ask him directly? But for some reason that I can't fathom he has decided to close down on me."

"You might find out what is in it, all the same. There's more ways of killing a cat than choking him with butter."

Henry looked at John in amazement, and asked, in a soft tone almost clean of expression:

"Are you offering to tell me what is in the diary?"

Now that the moment was upon him John wished that it could have been postponed a little longer. Still there was nothing to be done now except to close his eyes and affecting nonchalance to plunge:

"Yes, for a consideration—to coin a phrase."

Henry stood up and began to trot about, pad-pad-pad on his little feet. This unnerved John still further. He began to sweat and to feel weak. It was not that he despised Henry less, but he just had a feeling that Henry had by some unfair method managed to get on top of the situation. He was irritated with him, as an actor might be at finding himself playing opposite another who does not know his lines.

Henry paused somewhere behind John's back and said:

"Let me get this clear. Did Roger show you his diary?"

"No, but I read it just the same."

"And you think I should find it interesting?"

John perked up.

"It's fascinating. I had no idea that Roger was like that."

"Did you make notes?"

"No. But that wasn't necessary. I remember every word."

Henry came around and sat down again, which was a relief. He seemed to be cogitating profoundly, as well he might. John was silent, appreciating Henry's dilemma. He felt that it would be a mistake to hurry him. Presently Henry sighed and said:

"And what is it that you want in return for this?"

"A hundred pounds. I thought fifty first," said John naïvely, "but when I had read it I realized that it was worth double that."

151

His eyes glowed at the thought. Henry had not moved. John wondered for a moment if he had misjudged his capacity to pay. There were two ways of looking at it: Henry lived in a rather poor way, because he was poor and could afford no better, or else Henry living in a poor way was able to save money. It was annoying not to know which was the truth. Certainly the mention of a hundred pounds seemed not to have given him even a moment's shock.

"Or even a hundred and fifty," said John tentatively.

"Wait a moment," said Henry. "We haven't reached that stage yet. You must give me some idea of what you have to sell."

So it was working. John could hardly believe his ears. He sat up and dropped his pose of slackness, becoming business-like and exact.

"As I see it, there are two sides to the diary," he said. "One of them deals with Roger's books. That's the one that MacLean is transcribing. It's marked off with blue pencil in the manuscript. Interspersed with it is the story of Roger's private life. That's always surrounded by brackets, which seems to suggest that MacLean is not going to be allowed to publish it. So you can have that."

"But I'm more interested in the part about the books."

"MacLean has all the stuff about the books written out. Roger is evidently going to let him have it all, as a continuous story. Don't you see," said John patiently, "you can't prevent MacLean from getting the literary part of the diary, short of murdering him and stealing his papers when he has finished the job."

"And you would not recommend that?"

John thought this a joke in bad taste.

"In any case, the personal story will be far more interesting to the general public. Anything about Roger will be news. You'll make your fortune out of it, if you sell it in the right places."

He saw at once that this was indelicate, and therefore a mistake. Henry's expression had changed, though with what significance John could not yet be sure. He was standing up again, whatever that might portend, tapping the fingers of his left hand on the mantelshelf, opening and closing the fingers of his right hand nervously. His voice was calm enough however, almost careless as he said:

"I wonder if you're talking about Roger's old mistress Sybil Burns. It's interesting if he mentioned her in his diary. She must be a very old lady now, well over eighty, I should think, and living on her memories, as they say. Everyone knew about her long ago, but it's such an old story that I suppose it has begun to be forgotten. She was a widow with some children. Her news value is not very high. I'm sorry that you were so shocked, as I can see you must have been. It was very naughty of Roger, but people excused him because he was an artist. I expect there was a more liberal spirit abroad in those days."

John felt a spate of rage flow through him at the suggestion that he had been shocked, and at the idea that he was narrow-minded, an idea put forward by fat, soft, suburban Henry, with his garden lawn mowed on Saturdays and his three-piece drawing-room suite. A sharp knowing laugh released some of the tension so that he was able to say:

"How typical of that generation to be indulgent with Bohemians. Sybil hasn't much news value, as you say, but Roger has. You can knock Roger off his pedestal with one flip of your finger, if you want to."

Suddenly John did not care any longer about the money. He could see that everything was going against him, and though he might have been able to recover even now, he found that he wanted more than anything to wipe the pitying smirk off Henry's face. He realized all at once his full hatred of Henry, and he found that the indulgence of lowering him was worth every penny of that hypothetical hundred and fifty pounds.

"You think you know all about Roger?" His voice was shrill but he could not control it. "You think you know all about Sybil? Did you know that her children are Roger's? Did you know that he still lived with her after he was married, and that when his wife found out about it she began to drink and take drugs? Until she died of them? Did you know that? How would you feel if Rosa took to drinking secretly, nipping out for gins at odd hours of the day until she was a dypso-maniac? And all because of you? There's literary value in that story too, I can tell you. Anyone with half an eye can see now why Roger gave up writing. Bad conscience, that was it."

Higher and higher his voice rose while hysterical words poured out of his dry, panting throat. Since he had mentioned Rosa's name there was a note of terror too, for Henry was advancing slowly on him, no longer a figure of fun but like a bitter moon-faced god of vengeance. With astonishing strength he seized John by the collar saying softly:

"I don't feel in the least tempted to choke you, but how I long to throw you out of my house!"

With no more words, he rushed him to the door, opened it effortlessly, shot through the hall and towards the open hall door. Here John, who had been collared before, twitched himself expertly free and ran like a hare for the gate. The crowning humiliation was that Henry chased him right out on to the road, shouting something about police.

With difficulty John dragged himself home and crawled back into bed, where he lay motionless with every muscle aching. He could not bring himself to think of Henry, not even to curse him. Himself he blamed most bitterly. It was hard to believe that a clever man could have acted as stupidly as he had done. He longed for Mark, but he had disappeared several days ago without warning. Teresa was gone somewhere too, so that he was denied even the entertainment of her flute practise. Then he remembered that she had been forbidden to practise so that he could sleep. It was likely that she was somewhere about, mute and raging. On the whole it would be better if she did not visit him.

He needed visitors, so that he should not be alone with his despised self. Memories of Henry kept slipping into his brain and having to be forcibly ejected. He wondered if wisdom and judgment would come to him with years. He had certainly misjudged Henry utterly. Disliking him for his superiority of position and education, he could see now that he had rationalized his dislike by treating him like a fool, and a dishonest fool. Events had proved both of his judgements to be wrong. When he remembered how much Henry now knew about him, John thought of murder and suicide, but these were daydreams too, like that fantastic picture of Henry paying him a hundred and

154

fifty pounds for information about the diary. Always when he came back to this John buried his face in the pillow and wept.

During the evening he heard a tapping on the panels of the door with a finger-nail, an infuriating habit of Louis. He had a typical knock at the front door too, for he scorned to carry a latch-key and he had learned somewhere that a gentleman never uses the basement door. He said that he liked to let people know in advance that it was he who was there, so that they could hurry to let him in. It never occurred to him that if he were to change the character of his knock sometimes, he would not always have to knock twice.

John made him wait now, too, staring at the ceiling until the second little scratching tap set his teeth on edge. As if he were on the point of death he moaned a resigned:

"Come in."

Louis scrabbled at the door until he got it open and then slipped in and shut it quickly behind him, turning quite around to do so. He was wearing Nellie's woollen dressing-gown, which was warmer than his own, and a pair of elderly mules which had once been Roger's. He had tucked the ends of his pyjamas into the tops of his socks, to prevent the draught from blowing up the legs. Impeded by the flapping of the mules he came slowly across and looked down at John.

"Why are you in bed?" he asked querulously. "I heard you've been in bed for days and days. Your mother said three days ago that she thought you were better: you got up and went out, and when you came back you just got into bed again. Why?"

"Because I'm ill."

"So am I. And we can't both be ill. Your mother says one of us will have to get up."

"Why?"

"She says Julia is beginning to grumble. I don't see why Julia should grumble. She has hardly anything to do. There's Teresa gone off to stay with a friend of hers. That's one less in the house. It should more than make up for having an extra person in bed. But she's lazy, I suppose, and after all the years of living here free she's beginning to think she owns the place."

John knew that this was grossly unfair, but he had a policy

155

of never defending one member of the family against the complaints of another. He closed his eyes and made no reply. Louis poked him with his finger.

"Don't close your eyes when I'm talking to you."

"I can't keep them open."

"Why not? I say why not?"

John recognized that Louis was feeling powerful now, because he was upright while John was supine. He wondered if it would be worth while drawing himself up into a sitting position but he decided against it. He directed a long, baleful look at Louis and then closed his eyes again.

"Because I'm ill," he said. "That's why."

"What way are you ill? I say, what way are you ill?"

"Lots of ways."

"Tell me one way."

"My head is buzzing," said John desperately.

"So is mine," said Louis. "Do your fingers buzz too?"

"Yes."

"And when you look at the light do you see spots, coming and going?"

"Yes, yes."

"Have you pains?"

"All over."

"In your bones or in your muscles?"

"Both."

"So have I," said Louis in gloomy satisfaction. "And it never seems to get any better, whatever it is. And shocking headaches, no one will believe how bad they are. I've had them all my life. They got me glasses when I was seven and things got a bit better, but then they made me read and read until I was nearly blind. Terrible headaches. I know in advance when I'm going to get them, but that doesn't help one bit. I often laugh to myself when I hear someone say that they have a headache. If they had one like mine, I say to myself that they could talk, I say then they could talk. Do you have a headache?"

"Yes."

"You're only imagining it," said Louis. "I can tell when a person has a headache."

He rambled over to the table. John was relieved until he

156

saw that Louis was poking around among the books. He picked up *Athalie* and said:

"Were you reading this?"

"Yes."

"Is it on your course at the College? I say is it on your course at the College?"

"I heard you the first time, and the answer is no."

"Then you're not to waste time in reading it. You're not in the College to get a liberal education. You're there to get a Degree."

"It's hard to avoid getting the liberal education as well."

"I didn't say you were to avoid it. Impertinence. I said it was not to be your main object." Louis came over and gazed down at him so that John shut his eyes again.

"I'm afraid the trouble with you is laziness," said Louis. "You just please yourself in what you read. So I'm going to take this book away with me, and you'll have one less temptation."

Goaded into fury by this, John sat up straight and said sharply:

"If you take that book, I'll tell Roger!"

"No need to be nasty," said Louis with dignity.

He walked across and replaced the book on the table. He touched one or two of the other books, but he did not read their names. Then he said in a melancholy tone:

"It's lucky for you to be able to read in bed. It must be wonderful for passing the time. I wish I could, but I know I'd get a headache in five minutes. I say five minutes of reading would be enough to give me a headache."

He looked in the direction of the door and John watched him, not daring to breathe, in hopes that he was about to go. But he came flapping across to the bed again to ask plaintively:

"When are you going to get up? I say, *when* are you going to get up?"

"When I feel well enough."

"When will that be?"

"How should I know? But perhaps it will be soon."

"Yes, make it soon, like a good boy. I wouldn't hurry you, only for Julia. You know how inconsiderate she is, to everyone except Teresa. It was mean of her to let Teresa off visiting just now, when she would have been so useful to us at home. But of course Teresa can do no wrong. There's only one good thing about Teresa being gone and that is that her damned flute is gone with her. When she comes back I'm going to tell her once and for all that she'll have to give it up and start doing something for her living, like everyone else in the house. It's no use putting a premium on laziness. Teresa is full of rude health, just like her father, well able to be up early every morning and out to work. But of course people never appreciate their health until they lose it, I say they never appreciate their health until they lose it."

He rambled towards the door again and this time he opened it. Standing in the aperture he said, raising his voice a semitone:

"And remember to visit me when you get up. I lie in bed all day long and no one comes to see me except Roger and Nellie. I took the trouble to come and see you, I say I took the trouble to come and see you. So you can do the same for me when you get up. That's not much to expect. And now here I am standing in the draught talking to you when I should be in bed. It's a very bad thing to stand in draughts."

He shut the door abruptly. John said to himself, aloud:

"I say it's a very bad thing to stand in draughts."

Louis's visit had been a nightmare. There was no escaping the similarity between their cases. It seemed in a certain way just that they should have a mission to torment each other. He was reminded of Dante's description, in his passage through the Inferno, of the tormenting of the Archbishop Ruggieri by Conte Ugolino. He recalled that though the Archbishop had appeared to be the greater offender, still Conte Ugolino had been there to bear him awful company in hell. Frozen together in one bed of ice, Ugolino for ever gnawed with his teeth at Ruggieri's skull, only pausing to describe the reason for it to Dante, in faultless three-line verses of melodious Tuscan, before returning with renewed vigour to his task. John remembered the opening words:

> . . . *Tu vuoi ch'io rinnovelli*
> *disperato dolor che il cor mi preme,*
> *gia pur pensando, pria ch'io ne favelli.*

Pur pensando, thought John, the idea of becoming more and

158

more like Louis as time went on was terrifying. Quickly he crushed down this unpalatable thought. He could never become like Louis. He had much more education. Louis had a surprising amount of knowledge gathered from his resented reading, but it was not indexed nor disciplined in any way. Formal education was a great safeguard. It was what was lacking in his two elder brothers, whom it had been impossible to persuade to put in the necessary time at school. John had rather liked school, partly because it was so different from home. He had discovered there that a life of idleness did not suit him, that he enjoyed learning for the personal satisfaction that it gave him.

Yet Louis had accused him of idleness. The trouble was that Louis was confusing the issue by staying in bed himself, making it impossible for John to take a few days' rest, even when he needed it. Unless he broke his leg, he thought bitterly, no one would believe that he was ill at all. Even then they would probably want to see the X-ray.

He went cold at the thought of going to College and meeting Henry. There was no denying that he had made an utter ass of himself with Henry. He wondered if there was any hope that Henry would be taken ill and die. He looked very healthy, and university people usually live to be quite old. Then he remembered with sudden joy that with no lectures to give, Henry would not be likely to be about the College much.

He began to plan meeting Sullivan. He half-closed his eyes, practising the remote, withdrawn, weary tone in which he would tell Sullivan that fatigue, mental and physical fatigue, had kept him in bed for several days. Bed, he would say, is the ideal place for meditation. But first he would find out what had become of Mark. He had no right to disappear like that without saying where he was going. He would look for Mark in and around the College first, and if he failed to find him, he would try his flat. Mark had become accessible, now that he had a place of his own. Of course formerly it had been possible to speak to him on the telephone but only after running the gauntlet, what with parlourmaids and that old bowsey his father and whatnot. And if by chance John were to run into Henry, he would glare upon him and go surly by, like the lion in the Capitol.

When Teresa had been gone for a week, Roger began to worry about her. He might have thought of her before, but he was having such a stimulating time with MacLean that he hardly had room in his head for anyone else. The rest of the household seemed to have retreated like a wave of the sea, leaving those two high and dry, absorbed in each other so that day after day they were able to progress uninterrupted with the work of editing the diary.

At first it was a pleasant change not to have Teresa there. Her personality was prickly, and it could be felt through closed doors and thick walls. Some of it even hung about in the air after she was gone, so that it would not have been surprising if a few notes of a ghostly cadenza had floated inconsequently down the stairs from her room. But presently Roger found that some familiar part of himself was missing. It was the same sense of loss that he knew he would suffer if he were to shave off his beard.

All the others were surprisingly docile, or at least reticent about their doings. Louis was in bed all day, as quiet as a mouse in a nest behind a kitchen wall, afraid to move lest someone might call the cat. Nellie sat cagily in the drawing-room for most of the day, afraid to go down to the kitchen lest Julia might make her cook something for Louis, and afraid to go up to see Louis lest he might send her down to the kitchen for one of the little snacks that he loved—tea and fingers of toast, or coffee and a chocolate biscuit, or soup in a breakfast cup. He had most unfortunately got hold of a women's magazine which had an article on how to tempt the invalid. There were suggestions about Benger's Food, and Horlick's Malted Milk, and egg flips, and it was stressed that everything

160

should be served with a clean tray-cloth, and a few flowers, if possible, to show the invalid that you did not grudge him his stay in bed. In a low querulous voice he would read these out to Nellie, so that she found that her only chance of escape was to lie doggo for long spells.

In the middle of the week John had got up for the second time, and though he did not look in the least well, this time he did not go back to bed again. He spent most of his days out, and he had given up dropping into Roger's room as he had always done. No doubt he was huffy about not having been allowed to read the diary, but Roger intended simply to let him cool off. That was always the best way with young people's tantrums.

Roddy and Edward were surprisingly missing this week too. They went out early every morning, being called for in a large car by one of their friends, and not returning until the evenings. Roger's guess was that they were planning intensively to rob a bank.

Julia was taking advantage of the unusual calm to spring-clean the basement. Roger went down at five o'clock and stood about in the kitchen, and pointed out one or two pockets of dust which she might have missed. She did not seem very grateful. In fact she looked as if she were preoccupied with something else altogether. This strengthened his suspicion that there was something unusual in Teresa's absence. He panicked for a moment, and stuck out his beard at Julia as he demanded:

"Where is Teresa?"

"Gone off with a friend."

"What friend?"

"Now Roger, don't fuss me just when I'm busy. Teresa has lots of friends. Why shouldn't she go off and stay with one of them for a few days?"

"It's a week. When is she coming back?"

"I'm not sure."

"Where did you go that afternoon that you went out to see her off?"

"I went and saw her off."

"Where?"

"Let me alone," said Julia desperately. He was shocked to see tears in her eyes. "It's bad enough without having to
161

put up with this inquisition as well. She's not a criminal."

"No," said Roger gently, "but she's my favourite grand-daughter and I'd like to be sure that all is well with her."

Julia looked at him angrily, as if he were taking an unfair advantage. Then she turned away and said:

"She was married early this week, to Aldo d'Uberti, in Paris. I saw her off at Dublin airport. She has written me a description of the wedding. They've gone to Madrid now."

Roger felt a little sick.

"Aldo d'Uberti? The big, quiet fellow who used to take her out?"

"Yes."

"And what do we know about him?" Roger had begun to recover. "He may be some fly-by-night, for all we can tell. This was not the way to do things. Can he look after her? Can he feed her, even?"

"It's all right," said Julia. "He's a millionaire, in lire any-way. His family is descended from the Caesars, or maybe from Claudius. I had a very nice letter from his mother."

"In English?"

"Perfect English. She'll look after Teresa, all right. She said so."

After a pause Roger said:

"Teresa should have got some new clothes."

"She had enough," said Julia shortly. Then she softened this by adding: "She doesn't care much about that sort of thing. She knows quite well that it doesn't matter a hang what she wore at her wedding. The clothes she had were nice."

"Still if I had known she was going I would perhaps have been able to give her something."

Julia looked at him with sudden interest. Then she said energetically:

"If you have any money, for heaven's sake give it to Mary. That child has room in her head for only one idea. All day long she moans and groans about how much ashamed she's going to be at marrying her Paddy without a wedding break-fast. It's no use arguing with her. I told her the church cere-mony was the important part, that the other is only a conven-tion, that lots of people can't have these things and they must put up with it, but she won't be consoled. I must say that

Paddy is very patient with her. He offered to pay for everything himself, but she won't have that either."

"How much would she need?"

"Fifty pounds would go a long way," said Julia, gazing at him speculatively. "Have you got some money?"

"I might have ways of getting it."

Julia remembering the two books of Japanese drawings did not press him, though she was sorely tempted to mention the gas bill. However, that to Roger would have been merely sordid, and might have spoiled his present rather healthy frame of mind. She had great practice in holding her tongue, and after all she had to give credit to Roger for having missed Teresa at all.

He still hung about the kitchen, watching her gather up her cloths and dusters, and presently when she began to prepare the evening meal he pulled a chair out from the table and sat down. She observed this with some irritation. She was so much accustomed to being alone that she placed very little value on companionship. Especially since Teresa went away, she had subsided into a kind of daze every time that she found herself alone, and she resented Roger's interference with what was becoming a rather pleasant habit. Still looking at him now out of the corners of her eyes, she felt almost sorry for him. She knew better than to offer him sympathy, of course, because he always reacted sardonically to any whisper of humanity in his children's relations with him. Paradoxically he felt quite free to speak warmly and humanly to them, if he felt like it.

"I wonder what Roddy and Edward are up to?" Roger said. "I've never known them to remain friendly with each other for so long."

"They have discovered a system for betting," said Julia, "a new one that's sure to work."

"How do you always know that sort of thing?"

"Edward told me. They have made quite a lot of money in the last few days."

"Did he give you some?"

"Of course not."

"I thought they looked shiftier than usual this last couple of weeks," said Roger after a pause, "but I imagined something

163

different from betting. Where did they get the money to begin with? Or did they do it on credit?"

"Who would give them credit, for heaven's sake! They got the money from that Conroy man with the Chrysler—I stopped Edward from telling me all about it, but he did insist on leaving a bundle of leaflets there in case I wanted to have a flutter with the housekeeping money. They're in the drawer of the table."

Roger opened the drawer and took out a folder entitled "The Turf Control System". Inside there was a heading: "How does the TURF CONTROL SYSTEM OPERATE on YOUR BEHALF?" Then came the answer: "The TURF CONTROL SYSTEM possesses special facilities for operating the CONTROL METHOD. These facilities are not available to the general public. But our fee is ONE POUND ONLY for our CONTROLLER'S CONSIDERED ADVICE. If our champion fails by some VERY REMOTE CHANCE to show SUBSTANTIAL PROFIT on a LEVEL STAKE, we will forward his NEXT FOUR SPECIALS free of ANY FURTHER CHARGE.

"Kindly reply as soon as possible, and FINALLY, don't be afraid to BET LIKE A MAN!"

Below, in red type, these words appeared:

"Stop Press! The CONTROLLER does it again!

" 'Sinbad' won 8/1. 'Katmandu' won 11/2. NO LOSERS!

"WHAT A WIZARD! ! !"

Roger laid the papers back in the drawer and remarked:

"How little these things change with the years. Though I think the grammar and syntax are slightly better than they were in my youth. And they address you nowadays as 'Dear Sir' instead of 'Dear Fellow Sportsman'. A little of the flavour is gone. The boys have made money, you say?"

"Yes."

"What a mess they are, Julia."

"A great mess."

"It was no use trying to teach them. They were work-shy. They would not learn anything. Julia, do you know what I thought of on the night that MacLean came to dinner? I wondered if they were a little mad. What do you think?"

"Not mad, just stupid," said Julia calmly. "There's no crime in being stupid. There's a place in the world for stupid

164

people. There must be, because God made them as they are. They do all the ordinary, everyday work for the clever people and they get mighty small thanks for it, only contempt and sneers, and sometimes pity, if they're lucky. But Roddy and Edward were always given to understand that they were to blame in some way, as if they could have got to work before they were born and improved the quality of their brain cells. Mary and Frances got off lighter, being girls. They were not expected to be clever. They both do work that is well within their capacity. But the boys are like the unjust steward: to dig they are not able, to beg they are ashamed. So there is nothing for them to do except to drift gradually into shady occupations."

She stopped because she saw that Roger was not listening.

"A betting system!" he said. "Could stupidity go further? I always said that John was the only one of those three that was worth anything."

By a miracle of repression, Julia's reply to this was only: "Time will tell."

Roger sat on with her until five minutes before it would be time to start carrying trays up to the dining-room. He observed this with the exactitude of long practice, because since he had no intention of putting his hand to such a menial task it was important that he should give a nice consideration to Julia's feelings. Watching him, Julia reflected that as he grew older he was less well able to control the mean calculating glances which he gave in the direction of the clock as the time for a meal approached. She was still surprised at herself for being able to see things like this so clearly, though it had always been so. Once she had wondered how people could be so careless, until she had realized that they imagined themselves protected from view by the bony structure of their heads. To Julia, their thoughts were almost as clear as if they had run up a flag with the wording of them printed in huge letters for all to see. She was able to reply with her customary restraint when Roger stood up and said:

"I must see how far MacLean has got, before he goes away. I'm afraid I've been neglecting him today."

It happened that Mark, arriving back that very afternoon from Paris, had gone at once to see Roger and had found that

165

he was not in his room. His disappointment was so great that he felt only a huge blackness as he looked slowly around the room. Everything was in its accustomed place—the chairs and tables heaped with the same books and papers, the piles of books on the floor, Roger's empty wing-backed arm-chair turned away from the empty hearth, the inlaid bed with its old embroidered silk quilt, and MacLean diligent at his post in front of the open diary. Slowly Mark was closing the door when MacLean called out to him in a deep voice full of resentment:

"Hey! Did you see me? You're not a Mallon! And you're not getting away with that. Come back here and say hello."

Mark came in and closed the door.

"Hello," he said. "I overlooked you."

"No," said MacLean. "You didn't overlook me. You're like all the others—you don't really believe in me. I feel like a damned leprechaun. Even Roger doesn't believe I'm real. I'm always expecting that he'll poke me to make sure. Here I am day after day after day and no one takes any notice of me. I smell coffee, but no one brings me coffee. I had to find my own way to the bathroom. And even there I was rapped out of it by son Louis who told me that the people in dressing-gowns have the first rights to the one up here and that there was another downstairs."

"They treat everyone like one of the family," said Mark.

"It irks sometimes," said MacLean. "The families of great men have a bad time. They're badgered all their lives, till they don't know where to turn. Father's concentration on himself makes him self-important, selfish, tyrannical, unable to see anyone's difficulties or anyone's point of view but his own. You get it exaggerated in the case of Mallon because his wife was not there to counteract his effects. And he's always about the house. If he were a politician he'd have to go out some-times. I was talking to Mulligan about this the other day, and he agreed he never saw a worse case than this household."

"Mulligan?" Mark asked.

He did not welcome this outspoken discussion of his friends, but he was quite unable to prevent it.

"Paddy Mulligan. Small man with a bowler hat. Very nice, sincere little chap, engaged to the girl Mary."

166

"Yes, yes, I know him," said Mark hurriedly, lest MacLean should think it necessary to acquaint him of the size of Mulligan's shirts and socks.

"Mulligan says this household always reminds him of another family that he knows where the father is an expert breeder of boxer dogs. Any time you go in there, he says, the daughters are up to their elbows in Puppilac and Fibis, mixing huge vats of fodder for the pups so that they all smell like nursing mothers. He says they're all getting a boxer look about them too, that puts the boys off. Mulligan is a very amusing fellow. And good-hearted. He can hardly wait to get his girl out of here."

Mark was dumbfounded. Accepting John's estimate of Mulligan he had hardly given him a glance in all the months that he had known him. Now he was not so effete as to fail in appreciation of Mulligan's down-to-earth parallel, though he should have resented the forceful criticism of Roger.

MacLean laid down his pen, evidently glad of the relief from work afforded him by Mark's interruption.

"It's an extraordinary thing that Mallon should have such a conventionally-minded grand-daughter," he said. "Poor Mulligan is in a terrible difficulty, He told me all about it. The girl won't marry him until she has enough money for a middle-class wedding-breakfast. Have you ever heard anything so extraordinary?"

"I know about that," said Mark. "John told me. But I thought she would soon be talked out of it."

"No. She has dug her toes in. There's something fine about it, in a way. It's her pride, poor girl. Mallon only laughs at her. I put it to him that if he sold the diary to Holland's he'd have the price of fifty wedding breakfasts. I thought he'd throw me out. When I get home I'll have to go in by the back door. Holland is saying some hard things about me, I hear from my wife."

Though Mark had not intended it, presently they were in the midst of a discussion about the probable effects of the publication of the diary. MacLean admitted that a philosopher who preached control and resignation in the enormous terms of Roger's books would probably look a little ridiculous at first when it was discovered that he had by no means taken his own advice. But that would be only at the beginning and it would pass, leaving a residue of sympathy and understanding for Roger, who had distilled this great and lasting philosophy from the very stuff of his own weakness. MacLean could only answer for America, he said, and there the fresh, untouched truth would have an universal appeal, which would give a new lease of life not only to Roger's books but also the the commentaries which had expressed and elucidated his philosophy.

Mark said he was afraid that Roger's praise of Flora, because of the astonishing degree of conviction that it carried, would make his feeling for Sybil seem false by contrast, like something that he had assumed to deceive Sybil so that he could make use of her. In fact it seemed to Mark that an impartial reader of the diary might very well dismiss Roger as a cynic, instead of as the tortured, conscience-ridden giant that he was.

"You underestimate the general reader," said MacLean. "It's a great mistake to imagine that there are not thousands and thousands of people in the world who can appreciate subtleties and distinctions and delicacies at least as well as you can yourself. If Roger would let us publish the diary as it stands, every educated reader would see quite well that there was a development in his mind as well as in his heart from Sybil to Flora, culminating and flowering in his books. They would see his remaining attachment to Sybil as nostalgic, like the attachment that people sometimes retain to habits and places in which they were once happy in a simple way. As for the uneducated readers, they would be bogged down in the first analytical disquisition in the diary on the mentality of Sebastian, and they wouldn't be able to read on as far as the problem of Sybil and Flora. It's all quite simple to me. I just can't see why Roger holds it back like this."

"One point you can be quite sure of", said Mark, "is that money doesn't come into the question at all. And I know he's not thinking of his own reputation, either, but of Flora."

"And Sybil?"

"I think he hates Sybil now."

"I dream about it at nights," said MacLean restlessly. "I see the book bound and jacketed, ready to be opened by the whole world. I can feel the stiff crackle as I lift the cover for the first time. It's giving me ulcers. It's giving me angina. And the money does come into it. Money—a lot of money, mind you—would do Mallon a power of good. He might even begin to write again. A low diet gives people queer ideas. That's what's wrong with Mallon. Look at those mystics that went off into the desert and ate nothing but flies. We know how to treat artists in America. Give them enough to live on and they'll go on producing the stuff just the same. Look at Bach. Look at Vivaldi. There's no harm in having money, even if you have to have a patron."

"Roger would probably be an ascetic no matter where he lived," said Mark cautiously.

"He might, indeed. Mallon conforms to pattern, all right," said MacLean, summing up. "All great literary figures are much the same, just as all professors of psychology are a bit cracked. You have to learn to handle them. When you do, it's not so bad. But you've got to recognize that there will always be a certain point beyond which they won't understand any ordinary values. Remember the way that Mallon turned on you the other day?"

Mark remembered with a little shock that Roger had turned on him because he had suspected that he was discussing him with Henry O'Brien. The recollection made it impossible for him to say another word. He went over and stood looking out of the window. He was quite unaware of the chasm which had opened suddenly between himself and MacLean, who presently shrugged as one well accustomed and resigned to oddities and went on with his work.

They were thus placed when Roger came into the room some time later. He took it for granted that they were waiting impatiently for him, and he made quite lengthy apologies and explanations for his absence before turning to Mark at last to say:

"Where have you been? Surely it is you who should explain, not me."

"In Paris," said Mark in a depressed tone, remembering it.

"You don't appear to have enjoyed it. Did you see Teresa there? It seems that she went to Paris too. Everyone went to Paris," said Roger heavily, "without telling me a thing about it. I wonder why."

"Yes, I saw Teresa," said Mark.

"Then perhaps you saw d'Uberti also. They've been married, did you know?"

"Teresa told me."

"But she didn't tell me."

There is nothing like a beard for concealing changes of expression. It was only now that Mark noticed that Roger had become quite agitated, had perhaps even been so before coming into the room. Where formerly he had looked ageless, now he looked old, with the quivering helplessness of age which no matter how pitiable it is can often be slightly undignified. Mark hated to see it. He was immensely relieved when gradually Roger's manner returned more nearly to normal as he said:

"All these girls getting married should tell me about it. No one else can do a thing for them. Why do they suddenly become independent? First Teresa goes without a word to Italy, and heaven knows when she will come back. After having lived in my house for so many years she might at least have said good-bye. I was always good to her. I paid for her music lessons. I bought her a flute, and I had to sell four books and my father's repeater watch to pay for it. I have kept herself and her mother for nearly twenty years in my house. These are facts, full under the nose of any intelligent person. I don't talk of filial gratitude because I know that that is a myth invented by parents who have gone mad. If it were ever to exist, it would be as a trimming, an extra embellishment. Teresa's keeping secret her marriage and her going away was a positive action, taken against me. It was not merely neglect. Why did she do it? Perhaps you know."

Mark felt himself cringe at Roger's stuck-out beard. He saw MacLean look up alertly, obviously expecting that he was again going to be attacked. He managed to keep his expression impassive as he said:

"No, I don't know why she didn't tell you. Perhaps she thought it would be easier just to go off without a word."

"Easier? Easier?" The beard quivered. "That is an idea from a cheap novel. I'll write it down among my clichés. Easier to walk off and leave your family, make a clean break, let them take it or leave it. Perfidious, I call it. Calculatedly perfidious!"

170

Then he left off staring at Mark, who took this as a sign that he had finished with him for the moment. He wanted to weep at the notion of having supplied an item for the book of clichés, but there was also something funny in Roger's failure to understand how terrifying an argument or a discussion with himself could be. Roger and Teresa in an argument would have been a battle of tigers.

Mark wondered if Roger had really forgotten his conversation with Teresa, in which he had forbidden her to practise for an indefinite time to come. If he had, it seemed to show that he had never known what an immense part of Teresa's mind was occupied by music. And if he did not know this, he did not know Teresa at all. But Mark remembered so many times during the last winter when Roger had called Teresa in to his room to play for himself and Mark and John, that it was incredible that he should have been entirely unconscious of her dedication.

It was no longer possible for Mark to ignore a strange trick that Roger had, of observing a fact as an isolated phenomenon, apparently feeling no obligation to take action nor even to draw a conclusion from it. In everything that touched himself he seemed to be able to seal off that movement of his mind which ordinary people regard as the most important: the feeling of the necessity to make progress. Mark became quite excited now as he came near to expressing something which had for so long eluded him. He had not yet got it quite right, but even from the point at which he had arrived it was becoming possible to see why Roger had written nothing for so long. That remained the most puzzling aspect of his life. Mark would not believe that the creative force could ever die a natural death, though it might perhaps be strangled. Even in this he did not believe, but rather that if it were forced down in one form it would soon manifest itself in another, like a neurotic disease which successively produces varying symptoms.

It was often evident that in large matters Roger failed to link cause and effect, because of the disconnected nature of his own mind. Perhaps this could happen in more concrete and compact cases too as in the departure of Teresa, but Mark could not prevent a little wisp of doubt, like the beginning of a

171

fog, from creeping across his vision of Roger. Hurriedly he sought for ways of escape for Roger, of proof that it need not be conscious lying. A man who habitually dramatizes himself slips gradually from his own natural skin into that of his creation, so smoothly that he may never notice the change. The only difference is that he gets new power and confidence in his role, and is now better able to convince himself and his audience of its truth. So a minor weakness may become a vast deception in time. If one must blame, it need only be for the minor weakness. The rest is a natural growth.

Now his concern was that Roger's vision of himself should not be disturbed. This seemed to him very important, in the same way as it would be wrong suddenly to awaken a sleep-walker. Though the causes of it were false, Roger's agitation was genuine enough. He was walking up and down the room, between the bed and the window. His steps were not measured as they usually were. Each time that a foot touched the ground, the knee bent or sagged a little, giving an impression of greater hurry. The late sunlight lay in broad gold bars on the floor, so that the room had acquired a dusty, closed, overfull feeling. Roger darted from light to shadow and back again like a man running through a forest. MacLean had given up all pretence of work, to watch him. He tried to signal to Mark with his eyebrows that something queer was happening, but the young fool was blankly absorbed in his own thoughts and would not look at him.

"There's a Biblical precedent for it," said Roger, panting a little. "I wish I could remember what it was. 'Cast out the bond-woman and her son'? No, that can't be it. The Prodigal eating the husks that the swine left in the trough? That's not it. Can't either of you help me?" They shook their heads. "Ignorance of the young. I'll remember it later. Perhaps it's a principle of justice, that if the chosen heir rejects the inheritance it should be passed on to the less worthy heir. Anyway, it doesn't matter a damn. I have something that I had always meant for Teresa when she would be getting married, and now I'll give it to Mary, that's all. Though I don't value gratitude, no, I don't value gratitude, I may get more of it from Mary than I would ever get from Teresa."

It seemed to Mark that he pronounced her name, each time,

as if she were dead. The low booming note of Julia's supper gong floated up from below just then, like a death bell. Roger stopped walking up and down and looked quickly from one of them to the other.

"Here in this room I have Flora's diamond ring, that was once my own mother's. I gave it to Flora when we were engaged to be married. Its commercial value is more than a hundred pounds. Its personal value to me was inestimable until I began to think of its commercial value. Can you understand that? And yet it must be that I do value it, because now I find myself quite put out at the idea of parting with it. I know that to keep it would be pure materialism. It's nothing in itself but a little chip of rock, cleverly polished and rather pretty. My mother loved it, and so did Flora, but it absorbed nothing of them. My imagination supplies its whole value. I won't forget its owners when it's gone. I haven't looked at it for five years. Cut away. Break away. Stand alone. Rings are a symbol of bondage; they are the links in the convict's chain, the dog's collar, the ring in the bull's nose. I Roger take thee Flora and chain thee up from this day forth, to do the cooking, to mind the children, to mend the socks. No, that is blasphemous. And it wasn't like that with Flora anyway. I don't want to look at the ring. There is no need for me to look at it. Mark, go to the bookcase drawer there behind you. Yes, that is the one. Now open it." Roger turned his back and shut his eyes, like a child playing a game. "A flat ivory box. Take it out." He whirled around. "Take it out, man! What are you waiting for?"

"There is no ivory box," said Mark gently.

"Of course there is. You must be blind. Look again. To the left. Here, let me look."

He pushed Mark aside with an uncivil shoulder and began to scrabble in the drawer. He paused for a second and then he drew the drawer right out and emptied the contents on to the bed. There were old notebooks, paper clips, sealing wax, tacks and nails, small door-knobs, a foot rule, several paper-knives and a large quantity of pencil parings. These scattered all over the quilt while Roger rummaged through them. Mark saw among the rest of the rubbish a small lettered bronze plaque which said: "No visitors please". He wondered what its history might

173

be. An ivory box of the kind that Roger had described would have been immediately visible.

MacLean spoke unexpectedly:

"Try the other drawer. Perhaps that's where it is."

Roger turned to stare at him.

Then he reached for the second drawer and spilled its contents on top of those of the first one. This time he did not rummage. He stood holding the heavy drawer and staring down at the littered bed. After a moment he said under his breath:

"Dear Fellow Sportsman."

Slowly and carefully he replaced the empty drawer in the bookcase. Without looking at Mark and MacLean who now stood side by side as if they were facing a common danger, Roger walked to the room door and opened it. Leaving it wide open, he went out on to the landing. Then they heard him running. They rushed for the door and were in time to see him scuttle down the stairs, with a clutching hand sliding unevenly along the banisters. They were able to move so much faster than he was that they were right behind him when he reached the foot of the stairs. He darted across to the dining-room door which stood open, since the family was not yet assembled for supper. While Roger paused on the threshold, Mark heard the voices of Roddy and Edward raised in one of their perennial raucous arguments, which no one but themselves understood:

"I did not!"

"You did, so!"

"Liar!"

"Liar yourself!"

"I did not!",

"You did, so!"

MacLean and Mark came right up behind Roger, so that each of them looked over one of his shoulders into the room. They were all there, John and Mary and Frances, Paddy Mulligan, Nellie, and Julia who had the detached appearance of a waiter at a public dinner. Roger did not raise his voice. Mark realized at once that he could not even if he had wished to do so. He spoke huskily, slowly, lifting each word out as if it were something heavy that he had to lift from a box. Mark saw John's face turn a sickly greenish-yellow. He saw Julia

174

take a step forward and then pause uncertainly. He saw Nellie bridle, preparatory to taking her usual dreary offence. Frances and Mary opened their mouths stupidly, and absolutely without comprehension. Mulligan nipped quickly around the table to take the elbow of Mary in support. What Roger said softly was:

"Dear Fellow Sportsmen!" He looked directly at Roddy and Edward and asked in a conversational tone:

"Which of you two young scoundrels stole my wife's diamond ring?"

Surprised into silence, they made no answer. Still looking at them with a gently inquiring expression, Roger gave a short sigh like a worried sleeper. Then Mark saw his knees slowly give way as if they were weary of carrying his weight. He slid quietly to the floor and lay in an ungainly heap across the threshold.

12

Roger was very light. Stocky little Mark was the one who carried him upstairs, refusing belligerently the half-hearted help that he was offered by the various ineffective Mallons. Julia ran ahead of him and cleared the bed of its absurd, pathetic collection of rubbish so that Mark could put Roger down. Only he and Julia and MacLean came into the room. Nellie had put on her nurse-face for a split second, but remembering that the patient was Roger she had hurriedly taken it off again. MacLean was sober and helpful. He got the name of Roger's doctor from Julia and was gone to the telephone in a flash. Julia said to Mark:

"It's that damned diary. And he was upset about Teresa's going without telling him."

"He would not have liked it either if she had told him that she was going."

Then they were unable to say any more in Roger's presence, even though he was unconscious. Inexperienced as they were, they had difficulty in getting him into bed. Julia had seen Nellie contemplate an offer of help and then change her mind. She knew that as long as she lived she would never forget this meanness of Nellie.

As soon as Roger was in bed, they stood one at either side and looked down at him. He did not seem distressed, though he was flushed and breathing quickly. His eyes were firmly shut. Mark felt suddenly tired and empty. There was nothing to be said. They remained quite motionless, absorbed in their own thoughts, waiting for MacLean to come back. It was Louis, however, who opened the door silently a few minutes later and slipped inside.

Louis was a new man. His eyes sparkled and shone. Though

he had come in so quietly they noticed at once that his step was firm. His hands were sharply thrust into the pockets of the woman's dressing-gown that he wore. Instead of being loose and indecisive, a tension had been set up around his eyes and mouth so that he looked aristocratic instead of decadent. He went straight across and gazed down with a judicial air at Roger. Then he glanced sharply at Mark with an eyebrow lifted high.

"A stroke, I think," he said. "Nellie has just told me. Has anyone sent for the doctor?"

"MacLean has gone to do it."

"Good. I'll go and dress. I'll be ready by the time he comes, but in case I'm not, hold on to him until I see him."

With a last penetrating survey of Roger he walked out of the room. Mark could not look at Julia. After all, Louis was her brother. His feelings were such as might give offence, if she were sensitive. But a moment later their eyes met in a long look of complete understanding.

"Did you ever see such a transformation?" said Julia softly. "I wish I could laugh." Her voice broke hysterically for a second and then she went on: "We'll have to watch out for him. I'm afraid he may elect himself the head of the household." She stretched a hand across the bed towards Mark, as if she wanted to touch him. "I'm sorry you should have this, Mark. You're not a member of the family at all. I forgot that."

"For the present purposes I am a member," said Mark.

MacLean came in then, looking back over his shoulder on to the landing with a slightly bewildered air.

"The doctor is on his way," he said. "I caught him at his rooms, just as he was about to go home." He went to look at Roger. "He hasn't moved?"

"No."

MacLean said abstractedly:

"How much of this is my doing, I wonder. I've been making him work too hard. I thought only of myself. It was like finding out suddenly that Shakespeare was still alive. You don't ask after his health. You just make a note of everything he says."

"Please don't blame yourself," said Julia, kind as usual.

177

"He has had family worries too. He liked working with you. He said it, every day."

"I would like to think so," said MacLean. "By the way, Mrs. O'Neill, have you another brother in the house?"

"Louis," said Julia, surprised.

"Yes, I know Louis," said MacLean with feeling. "It must be he that I met just now. He looks quite different. I just wondered—but of course there could not be two so much alike."

"Louis seems to have changed, right enough," said Julia. "We had him in here, all brisk and businesslike. I must say I would never have imagined such a metamorphosis possible."

A thought struck MacLean dumb. It also gave him a head-ache and a familiar sensation in the stomach which he knew presaged an attack of indigestion. He tried to control all speculation, in the hope that his stomach would be reassured, but his thoughts kept bounding ahead of him uncontrollably like a huge, well-conditioned, young dog.

Louis would perhaps be Roger's heir, if Roger were to die. The diary would be the most valuable asset, convertible into cash, among Roger's effects. Louis might now feel like selling it at once to MacLean. But, on the other hand, mean rabbitty little men are terrors for trying to get the best possible bargain. Louis might sell the diary to another firm. He might even make a special point of doing this, if by chance he had ob-served that MacLean held him in small respect. MacLean found himself quickly reviewing his few meetings with Louis, in an attempt to assess his position, and hoping to God that Louis had taken his superficial politeness at its face value. You never knew where you were with these Mallons. Even the least of them had a special insight which was denied to ordinary humans.

MacLean was deeply ashamed of these thoughts as he looked down at poor Roger's unconscious suffering. It was this shame that was setting up the conflict in his mind which was reflected in his stomach. He thought half-enviously of old Holland, who would, if he were here, already have invented an excuse to go out to Louis's room and there have struck a bargain with him. Before Louis would have his suspenders fixed on his shoulders, Holland would be slipping dollars into his pockets.

178

Louis would not think the less of him for this, MacLean knew, but still he could not bring himself to sneak away now and whisper hotly into his ear while Roger was still breathing. He was repelled as no good business man should be by Louis's obvious, rapid acceptance of the probability that Roger would die. It must have been that although Roger was so old, Louis had never speculated much on the change that would come about in his circumstances when he would be left in sole charge of himself. No doubt the freshness of this idea was what had roused him from his bed. Behind his new purposeful manner, little quivers of excitement could be seen, like the shimmer of an evaporating patch of oil on a hot road. It was an excitement of the same macabre sort that seems to grip the eager spectators of a motor accident, or a fire, or a dog-fight.

Rambling restlessly about the room, MacLean came almost with surprise upon the diary. It was open at the place, more than half-way through, where the extent of the injury that he had done to Flora was beginning to be plain to Roger. Nearly every line was surrounded by the square-ended brackets which indicated that the piece was to be passed over, and which MacLean had come to hate. He took a blank sheet of paper and folded it in two, and laid it between the pages of the diary to mark the place, before closing it. He wondered if he would ever open it again. His own notes and transcriptions from the diary were surely his own property, however, and he placed these carefully in a pile on a table near the door, as if to be ready for a quick getaway. At first he left the diary lying in its usual place, but presently he came back to it and removed it to one of the upper shelves of the tall bookcase between the windows.

When the doctor came a few minutes later, MacLean and Mark left him with Julia. He was a middle-aged, confident-looking man. As they left the room they heard him say to Julia:

"I thought this would happen some day soon."

Outside on the landing MacLean said softly:

"What next? Where do we go now?"

It was unthinkable that they should wait on the landing, where at any moment Louis might pop out of his room on top of them. Politeness suggested that they should join the rest of

179

the family, but it occurred to Mark that these had probably gone on with their supper. He knew that he would be angry if he were to find them eating, for he had an obscure feeling that it was more decent to go hungry on the day of a catastrophe. Besides, he feared that he and MacLean would be questioned uninhibitedly by Roddy and Edward, and even by John, as to Roger's condition and prospects of recovery, and that the absolute lack of personal interest and love of Roger in their attitude would be more than he could bear.

Quickly they decided to go to the kitchen. It was MacLean's idea.

"We'll boil a kettle," he said, "so as to be ready to make tea for Julia when the doctor goes."

It was a weak enough excuse for trespassing in a strange kitchen, but it served. They sat on the big table, swinging their legs and watching their alibi, the kettle on the gas, with no satisfaction.

Julia liked this doctor. He was kindly and generous, and he conveyed very clearly an understanding of the fact that a good part of his function was to protect the patient from annoyance.

"No visitors please," he said to Julia. "Make everyone keep out until I say that they can come in. You'll be able to do everything for him that's needed. There's no need for anyone else to come in here."

"What about me?" said Louis, who had appeared snapping at the doctor's heels like an ill-tempered little dog.

His manner was truculent. He had lost weight in bed, and his clothes hung loosely around him. He had not succeeded in finding his shoes, so he had put on a pair of Nellie's slippers. They were a dirty pale blue, and they fitted his slender little feet admirably. They did not make him look ridiculous. Nothing about him was ridiculous this evening, no more than a cannibal king in his barbaric regalia would appear ridiculous to his terrified captives. Louis's eyes were narrowed tightly with determination. The doctor paused for a moment before answering him. Then he said:

"One person only may visit Mr. Mallon. If you are prepared to take complete charge of him, making his bed, cleaning his room, bringing him his meals, giving him his medicines at the

180

proper times, then by all means do so. It would be a great charity."

"I'm a sick man myself," said Louis, shocked back momentarily to a whine. "I haven't been downstairs for weeks. I couldn't do all those things. I'd drop trays, to begin with."

"In that case it will have to be Mrs. O'Neill", said the doctor. "I think I should prefer it, in fact."

He turned firmly away from Louis, who hesitated as if he were going to insist on being a party to any instructions that were being given. In a moment, however, he appeared to decide that this would be dangerous, and he went out of the room leaving the door slightly open to show his continued interest. The doctor went across and shut it, and then came back without changing his expression to continue his conversation with Julia.

When they went downstairs a few minutes later, Louis was not to be seen, but as Julia was walking slowly back through the hall after she had let the doctor out, the dining-room door opened suddenly and there was Louis.

"Come in here, please," he said curtly.

He stood aside to let her pass in before him, and then he shut the door sharply. There was no one else in the room, The others had all gone across to the drawing-room, as they always did, leaving the remains of their meal and the used crockery on the table for Julia to remove. Tired beyond belief, Julia went absent-mindedly over to the table and took a slice of bread, buttered it with the butter-knife and began to eat it.

"Julia. Listen to me, if you please."

Louis was tapping with his forefinger on the table to get her attention. She looked at him without interest, and said:

"What is it? I'm listening."

"There are lots of things to be thought of," said Louis strongly. "First of all, money."

"We'll be all right for a few days. There's no need to think of it now."

"That's only one thing. I'm going to move Roger."

"You are not!"

Julia was surprised at herself for being able to put such force into the words.

"Yes, I am," said Louis calmly. "He can go into Teresa's

181

little room, now that she won't be wanting it. I hear she's gone off and married that Italian fellow that was hanging about here. Teresa's room will be very nice for Roger. The bed is smaller, easier to make. It's airier than his own room, because of having no balcony. It has a lot of advantages. Of course I don't mean he should be moved tonight. Tomorrow morning will do equally well. It's no use arguing. I've thought it all out."

"But why?" Julia asked wildly, casting about in her mind to discover a supporter inside the family. There was none. She went over them all. Mark and MacLean might not hurry to interfere in such an intimate family matter, but Julia intended to demand help from them if she needed it. If Teresa had been here she and Julia could have set up a barricade outside Roger's door and dared anyone to cross it. Louis was slanting his eyes venomously at her now, so that she was reminded of a weasel, or a rat. He was not going to be brushed aside easily, and she knew from experience that he would now be watching her narrowly for signs that she despised him. If he saw these signs, his determination would be redoubled. She longed for Aldo, or her own husband Hugh who was dead for nineteen years and two months, or for any big determined man who had no doubts about right or wrong and whose mere presence would have intimidated little Louis so that he would never even have begun on this horrible comedy.

"Why?" said Louis, and then on a higher note: "Why? I've just told you why. That room is too cluttered to be healthy. Roger will be much better off in Teresa's room. Tomorrow morning we'll move him in there. It's too late tonight."

"We can't move him without asking the doctor."

"I disagree. The best thing is to move him first. Then if the doctor objects to his being moved, he won't want him moved back again."

The logic of this was devastating. Julia said weakly:

"You don't move someone because the room is cluttered. That's a Mad Hatter solution. Wouldn't it be better to tidy up the clutter?"

"Nothing in Roger's room is to be touched by anyone except me," said Louis. "I intend to move in there myself. I'm not sleeping well. I'll sleep better in a room where I can be alone.

182

And I'm going to do some work in there. It's a good room to work in."

"What sort of work?"

"Writing, mostly. I have a lot of things in mind. For instance, I might write a biography of Roger. The materials for it are all in that room. I need a study of my own, but of course in this house I never got one. You and Roger and Teresa and John could have rooms of your own, but not me. Well, I'm tired of it and I'm not standing for it any more."

"We thought you liked to be with Nellie," said Julia without expression.

"Don't bring Nellie into this," said Louis with a little shriek. "I say don't bring Nellie into this."

"She'll hear you if you raise your voice," said Julia, now feeling towards Louis the first stirrings of sympathy for many years.

Still there could be no question of forgiving his preposterous attitude towards the helpless Roger. The slice of bread had given her a little energy, perhaps, for she was able to say:

"If you make any attempt to move Roger in the morning, I'll call the Guards."

"They won't come," said Louis calmly. "They never interfere in this kind of thing. It's ridiculous of you to think of such a thing. Now, don't get excited about it. It's a perfectly proper arrangement. Roddy and Edward will be able to carry him. He'll be quite comfortable."

"And what is Roger going to think of all this?" Julia asked desperately, almost in tears with the frustration of her attempts to communicate with Louis.

"Roger is unconscious."

"He won't be so tomorrow. In fact before he left the doctor said he was no longer unconscious, but asleep. Tomorrow, or anyway in a few days, he'll be up and walking around his room——"

The effect of this on Louis was terrible to see. Julia had begun to pile the cups and saucers together to bring them downstairs. Louis seized her right arm with both hands, sending several pieces of china shooting to the floor. His voice trembled and squeaked ludicrously.

"But he has got a stroke! I say he has got a stroke!"

"Yes, that is so. But the doctor says that the modern treatment is to get the patient out of bed as soon as possible. It helps the circulation. People are no longer kept in bed after strokes. He'll stay in his room for a few days and then he'll even be able to go downstairs."

Louis was listening to every word, watching her mouth move. From the oddity of the situation, the stream of her thought dried up. She felt painfully embarrassed for Louis, that his hideous little mind had been laid bare for anyone to see. She thought of reassuring him with a promise not to tell anyone what he had proposed, but when she was able to look at him, she saw that this would not be necessary. His eyes had glazed or dulled over, for they had already begun to look inwards again. Now he had the preoccupied appearance of a snail in the process of drawing in its horns. It was clear enough to Julia that he was telling himself that his experiment in looking outwards had been a failure, and that he should never have made the attempt. Desperately she tried to save him, for now she was tormented by little needle-sharp recollections of Louis when he was a boy, always too thin, with light fair hair and a high narrow forehead, and an odd, intellectual sense of humour. After their mother's death he had become a great reader. He had seemed always so safely occupied with a book that no one had noticed that his heart was shrivelling up.

It was a disaster that he had found out that Sybil and Roger had been living in sin, and had between them broken his mother's heart and caused her death. He was a clever little boy, and within the limits of his knowledge he had been able to understand a great deal of the situation. He had taken a violent dislike to Sybil on the one occasion that she had called at the house. Convinced that she was up to no good he had sneaked back to listen to her conversation with Roger and had heard her make her offer of marriage. Later that same evening he had had a fit of hysterics and had told the whole story to Julia. Between them they had decided to keep it secret from Rosa, and so far as Julia knew, Louis had never spoken to her about it. He seemed to have put the whole affair into an interior compartment of his mind, so long ago that the doors had rusted with age and were now immovable. Often in the last few weeks, since MacLean had been coming to the house and the excitement of the diary was in the air, Julia had

184

watched Louis and wondered why he never so much as sent her a look of understanding. She had received the impression that he was completely uninterested in the diary, though this was hard to understand. Surely it must have occurred to him that it might contain the history of his mother's death. Still she had been glad for Louis's sake that he had achieved such detachment. His dramatic reaction to Roger's illness had proved that he was far from being detached, however, but it also seemed to prove that he was still capable of being warmed back to life again. Though she saw quite clearly that her own carefully acquired integration would be endangered if he were to accept her offer of help, still she felt absolutely obliged to make it.

"Why don't you spend more time with me?" she said. "It's not good for you to be alone so much. It's quiet in the kitchen and there's the old arm-chair there. I'd like to have you with me. I really would."

At first she thought that he was silent because he was thinking about it rationally, but then she saw that his mouth was twisting and his eyes flashing with temper. Before he spoke, she had turned a little aside from him. Calmly she listened, and she knew now beyond question that she would never again be able to do anything for him.

"You would like to have me in the kitchen," said Louis softly. "I'm sure you would. For the first few days I should sit in that arm-chair you mentioned. But after that you'd have me wearing an apron, stirring pots on the stove, washing up the crockery, sweeping the floor, laying the tables. No doubt you would call it Occupational Therapy, but even if you did not, you would find me very useful. I don't need your amateur psychological treatment. If I were insane, I should prefer to be treated by an expert. And if I want company, I have Nellie. I say if I want company I have Nellie. You only want me because your daughter went away with that Italian. She used to be very useful about the place."

Julia felt her control slip a little, but she succeeded in saying:

"I'm not offering you amateur psychological treatment. I'm offering you peace, and company. I wouldn't ask you to help me unless you wanted to."

"So you had thought of it," said Louis triumphantly. "I
185

knew you had. Well, my answer is no, thanks. I'm a sick man I should be in bed, but always when I should be in bed, there's someone else in bed too, so I'm told that I should get up. Last week it was John. This week it's Roger. I never made the fuss about being ill that Roger made tonight. Well, I'm taking no more notice of other people's claims. I'm the father of a family and I must look after my health. I say I must look after my health. I don't feel well now. My legs feel queer, and my head, and my fingers are buzzing again."

"Louis, please don't go back to bed. I'm convinced that it is bad for you."

"You're convinced that it's bad for you, at any rate, to have to carry the trays. No, Julia, I have considered other people for long enough and the time has come when I must consider myself. You could get one of the girls to stay at home from work and help you."

But Julia was hardly listening now. She had suddenly realized that she had left Roger alone for too long. There was no time to sit down at the dining-room table and lay her head along her arms and cry for Teresa. When she began to move towards the door, Louis said suspiciously:

"Where are you going?"

"Up to Roger again. He shouldn't be alone for so long."

Her voice did not shake. Louis darted past her into the hall and up the stairs. She hurried after him, not knowing what he was contemplating. At the top of the stairs he paused and looked over at the shut door of Roger's room. But then he fluttered across to his own door, rattled at the handle until it opened and disappeared inside.

Roger was still asleep. Julia wondered how the doctor had known that he was no longer unconscious. He did not look very different from what he had been when she and Mark had got him into bed. He looked calmer, certainly, and his colour was not so high. Very quietly, she moved Roger's wing-backed arm-chair around until sitting in it she had an uninterrupted view of him. Then without any thought of the possible length of her vigil, she settled down to wait for him to awaken.

Down in the kitchen, MacLean was tired of waiting.

"That kettle will soon be boiled dry," he said to Mark. "Come along upstairs and we'll investigate."

They refilled the kettle and put it back on the gas, and went upstairs. The hall was deserted but a faint buzz of life came from behind the drawing-room door. MacLean looked into the dining-room.

"Well!" he said softly. "They decided to keep up their strength. Very wise. Four places unused—yours, mine, Julia's and Roger's."

He stalked across to the drawing-room door and opened it wide. Seven non-committal faces turned to look at him. John, who was the nearest to the door, half started out of his chair and then dropped back again. Suddenly disgusted with them all, Mark found that he could not bear to follow MacLean into the room. Without making any apology he turned away and went up to Roger's room. It was he who brought Julia tea and toast on a small tray from the kitchen. While he was engaged at this, he saw MacLean had put Frances and Mary to work clearing the dining-room table, brushing up the broken crockery and washing up. Mulligan was helping them, but there was no sign of the others. He was glad of this. Their utter unresourcefulness in a crisis had shown up their individual selfishness more clearly than anything else could ever do. He was quite determined not to become involved with them in any way, and he knew that he was in momentary danger of being questioned by any one of them about the cause of Roger's distress, and about the extraordinary accusation that he had made in the moment before he had fallen.

He was sitting with Julia in Roger's room when Henry O'Brien arrived. They had decided to interpret the doctor's instructions about visitors rather liberally, because to follow them absolutely would have been impracticable. Mark had just succeeded in persuading Julia to let him spend part of the night with Roger so that she could sleep. Henry was very agitated, but he kept his voice low:

"Mulligan telephoned me only ten minutes ago. It seems all this happened at six o'clock."

"I'm sorry," said Julia. "There was no point in telling you before now. I would have left it even later."

"I couldn't have come anyway, because Rosa is not well. I had to stay with her." Henry went across to look down at Roger. "He doesn't look too bad. Mulligan said he had a stroke."

In answer to Julia's look, Mark took Henry out on to the landing to tell him what had happened.

"He accused Roddy and Edward?" said Henry. "Not John?"

"Of course not John," said Mark. "It seems that the other two have been betting on a system, and I suppose they had to have some capital to begin with."

"Did they admit to having taken this ring, then?"

"There was no time. Roger fell almost at once. He hasn't moved since then. We're to call the doctor as soon as he wakes up. The doctor thinks there's no paralysis, but he says his speech may be affected——"

"Yes, yes," said Henry. "I gather that you're going to be here."

"Yes. I'm living alone now, so I can stay without any difficulty."

"Good," said Henry. Suddenly he was very agitated. "You're a sensible man, Roche." He turned his eyes downwards to avoid Mark's stare of surprise. "You know the young Mallons. There isn't one of them with an ounce of common sense or initiative or order. They're no use in any sort of an emergency."

Mark had been about to suggest that an exception might be made for John but he abandoned the idea. Henry was saying:

"When Roger begins to recover, you'll be with him a good deal. He's fond of you. He'll be satisfied in your company."

He paused. His expression was quite blank. He put his hands under his coat-tails at the back and began to rock gently from heel to toe. This activity which Mark had formerly found arrogant and offensive now clearly showed to him instead Henry's insecurity and uneasiness. Mark knew quite well that his own release from bondage had completely changed his point of view, which had formerly been entirely subjective. He delighted consciously in his new-found judgment, as a man cured of deafness might delight in picking up lighter and more distant sounds.

"What do you want me to do?" he asked.

"To protect Roger from scenes, I suppose," said Henry.

"From the Mallons? I don't think they'll come near him. They haven't even asked how he is. They're all down in the drawing-room now. The doctor routed Louis, Julia told me, by inviting him to take over the job of nursing Roger. John hates illness. He won't come near Roger until he knows he's well again. There won't be any scenes."

"You're forgetting about my wife," said Henry.

Mark was staggered. That newly-acquired judgment of which he had been so proud a moment ago was no use now. He felt hopelessly young and inadequate, and these feelings had for so long been coupled in his mind with fear that the first result of his shock was an almost complete return to his former miserable state. He made no answer because he could not. Fortunately Henry did not appear to expect one.

"I have never done anything harder than this in all my life," he said. "I'm sorry for you as well as for me. We must be rational. Personal feelings are not so important." Still Mark made no reply. Henry went on: "Roger is very fond of my wife, as far as he is fond of anyone. She is the only one of his descendants who has always treated him as a great man. She admires him without reserve, and rather unreasonably. She has not read all of his books. Philosophies and abstract ideas mean very little to her. I tell you this to help you to understand her difficulty. It is a serious one. She has noticed that Roger is enjoying teasing me about the diary. Rosa never teases anyone. Her sense of justice is offended by the very idea of it. But she has so accustomed herself to the notion that Roger is perfect that this obvious fact of his imperfection is something she can't bear. Since the evening when he attacked me in the drawing-room she has been worrying about it. Some time ago, she insisted that I come with her and ask Roger to let me see the wretched diary. It was horrible. After that I told her I would do nothing more about it."

"You think she may come now, while Roger is ill, and ask him again?"

"Yes. I wish I didn't have to tell anyone in the world these things. I know her very well after all the years, and I can see that she's trying to get up courage to do something that she thinks should be done but that is beyond her capacity. I'm sure she's going to demand that Roger give me the diary. I can't tell her not to, because I'm not supposed to notice that anything unusual is happening." A dreary, dead note came into

189

Henry's voice. "She's drinking, you see, little glasses of gin all day long, in hotels and pubs, and even at home. I stay with her as much as possible. That's my only way of preventing her. But I can't be with her always because she would notice."

"Shouldn't you get a doctor for her?" Mark asked.

"She may recover without that," said Henry. "This has happened before, and it passed off again. It was when one of the children was ill. But now you can see that she must not be allowed to visit Roger. She's working herself up to that point day by day. If she were to come here, she would hardly notice that Roger is ill. She drives herself on without mercy, and she would drive him in the same way. It would be equally bad for both of them. But I care more for its effect on Rosa than I do for Roger. That's the truth. One should hardly ever tell the exact truth."

"I wish people would always tell the truth," said Mark.

"No," said Henry emphatically. "There are many occasions when one should not tell the truth. For instance, I don't want Roger to see the truth about Rosa just now. If he asks for her you could say she has a bad cold. I may tell Julia something later on but there can be no purpose in adding this to her troubles at present." He had stopped rocking, but now he began again. "I've put you into an impossible situation. I should be able to ask John, keep it inside the family, but that is quite impossible."

Mark reassured him as best he could, and before he left the house Henry certainly seemed a little more confident. Mark went to the front door with him, and noticed that he did not seem even to consider going into the drawing-room. In fact he took special care to pass by the door quietly, as if he were anxious to avoid meeting the rest of the family.

13

At the end of a week, Roger was well enough to get up and
sit in his dressing-gown by the window. Peeking through the
open doorway when Julia went in and out with trays of food,
Louis was able to see that his beard was sunk on his chest
instead of being pointed at its old, arrogant angle. No visitors,
the doctor had said, and Louis hugged this injunction to himself as he pattered endlessly up and down his own bedroom
which now suddenly seemed so small. He would not himself
take possession of Teresa's room. That was even smaller. And
it had a cold, bare feel about it. Besides, it had retained a
miasma of Teresa, whom Louis had hated, and even in the
few minutes that he had spent there he had seemed to hear
her satirical, wicked voice in the air all around him, and the
ghostly toot of that blasted flute of hers. He seriously thought
of putting Nellie out of his own room to sleep in Teresa's, but
that would be easier said than done. Wives have rights, he
knew well, and besides Nellie had often proved to be his only
ally. Since Roger's illness he had become more dependent on
her than ever. She had even brought his meals, more than
once, and she saw to it that he got food as good as Roger
was getting.

Nellie brought him gossip from downstairs, too. Sometimes
this was comforting and sometimes it was not. It was good to
know, for instance, that Mary had at last agreed to allow
Paddy Mulligan to pay for their wedding breakfast and to
buy her some clothes. Nellie reported that he had converted
her by naming some aristocratic, even royal precedents in
which the lady had been honourably poor and unable to
provide for herself, and had not been too proud to accept gifts
of the necessities for her wedding. King Corphetua, said Paddy,

had had to buy every stitch for the beggar maid. No doubt Mary had seen too that with Roger's illness there was going to be no spare money lying around waiting to be spent on frills. Another good feature of Roger's illness was that it made a perfect excuse for the wedding being very quiet. This was a blessing, thought Louis, who found Paddy impossibly vulgar and had been shrinking from the prospect of spending a morning in *bourgeois* celebration in his company.

Frances was madly happy these days, Nellie reported, because Mark was in the house almost continually, only going home to sleep. Louis found Frances a bore, but this did not prevent him from hoping that Mark would have the sense to see that she was a Mallon, and to realize that Mallons were not to be picked up every day of the week. Even Paddy had been able to see that. Louis had often expounded on this point to Nellie when she had wanted to spend money on dressing the girls in commonplace fashion, waving their hair and so on. None of this was necessary for Mallons, said Louis. Nellie had conceded that this sort of thing was Louis's province, and she had learned her lesson well. Neither of the girls had ever had their hair waved, and the best part of it was that no one ever thought of ascribing Nellie's principles in these matters to Louis's teaching. Frances had come twice to visit Louis during the week and he had been struck by her appearance of exaltation, and especially by the fact that she seemed to have become impervious to his disapproving remarks. The effect of this on him had been so strong that his tone to her had quite changed, as if he were talking to a stranger.

Louis was very much put out to find that he could no longer lie contentedly in bed all day. This walking up and down was a new thing, but he could not help it. A feeling of restlessness pervaded the whole house, penetrating even into his bedroom which had formerly been an oasis of peace. All day he could hear people coming and going on the stairs and on the landing. The front door was continually being opened and shut. Draughts lifted the carpet by the door when anyone went in or out of Roger's room. Louis was quite worn out from the strain of speculating as to what was going on and being unable to ask questions. Especially he wanted to know about that strange thing that Roger had said just before getting the stroke:

"Which of you *two* scoundrels has stolen my wife's ring?"
Nellie had told him about this, but she said when he asked
her that since then no one had mentioned the matter. It was
one of the things that had prevented Louis from visiting Roger,
however briefly, until now. He might almost have enjoyed a
chat with his father about symptoms if he had not been afraid
that the subject of this ring would be brought up. Louis knew
nothing about a ring, but he thought with remarkable shrewdness that John might well have been included in Roger's
accusation. John had the face of a François Villon, in Louis's
judgment. He certainly was always extra careful of his pocket-
book, such as it was, when John was around. And heaven
alone knew what his sex-life was like, if he had any. Louis
preferred not to investigate that, for fear of what he might
uncover. He had noticed lately that John had been reading
novels of a new kind which was becoming popular, about
rather dreary people whose only claim to be interesting was
that their sex-life ran backwards instead of forwards. Louis
had snitched one or two of these and read them, but he had
found them dull enough.

Of all his children he disliked John the most. But there was
no denying that he was the only one of them all that had a
practical streak in him. It was he who had told Louis, only this
very afternoon, that MacLean had made a firm offer of twenty
thousand dollars for the complete diary. John had advised
Louis to take forcible possession of the diary and give it to
MacLean, but Louis could see plenty of difficulties in the way
of this. For instance, much as he wanted it, MacLean would
probably refuse to accept it without Roger's authorization.
Another point was that a better price might be got from someone else. The thing would have to be gone into carefully.

Louis had never been specially interested in having quantities of money until now. But his one brief taste of freedom,
when he had thought that Roger was going to die, had given
him an idea of what he was missing. He realized that money
undoubtedly buys freedom, and the word had given birth to a
cloudy little dream. Louis could see himself and Nellie alone
in a flat, cut clean away from all complications. Nellie would
do the housework and the cooking. He forgot for the moment
that she had done little or none of either since he had married

193

her. While she was busy at that, Louis would be free to range all over his little domain instead of being confined to one room in this awful barrack as he was at present. He had not told John any of this, naturally, since John was one of the things that was going to be cut clean off, but he had explained to him that nothing in life was as simple as it appeared at first sight. John looked contemptuous, but Louis was accustomed to this attitude from him and he took no notice.

Still he had found himself possessed by an unfamiliar excitement and desire for action when John was gone. It might be possible to see Roger and bring the conversation around to the diary, while keeping off the subject of the ring. He had put on his clothes, for he knew that it would be a mistake to visit Roger in his dressing-gown, and for two full hours he had been trotting up and down, up and down, trying to bring himself to the point of going out and knocking on Roger's door. He had had to cross the landing to the bathroom several times, because fear always manifested itself most inconveniently in Louis, so he knew that Roger was alone for the first time since the beginning of his illness. It was Julia's spell on duty, but Roger had sent her away. Louis had left his door ajar so as to hear their conversation.

"I'm quite well enough," said Roger. "There's no need for me to be watched all the time."

Julia said without expression, standing at the door:

"I'll be in the drawing-room. If you want me, just knock on the floor with your stick."

"Oh, very well," said Roger.

This was not very promising, thought Louis. Roger sounded distinctly grumpy. It took Louis a long time to forget it. It was five o'clock before he was able to open his door wide and slip across to listen at Roger's.

Maddeningly, there was someone else already inside. Furious at having wasted his nervous energy all the afternoon in bringing himself to an impossible pitch of courage, Louis's first impulse was to march boldly into the room and tell whoever was there that he wanted a private talk with Roger. He actually got as far as putting his hand on the door-handle, and then he noticed that the door was an inch ajar. He grasped at the fact that it was not now necessary to be abrupt. Very gently he

194

pushed the door. It opened without a sound, but still he found that he could not see into the room. He stared stupidly for a moment before he realized that someone had placed a draught screen just inside the door. It was an old one, very tall, covered with a reddish-brown canvas, and it had always been kept in one of those dim lumber-rooms in the basement. Louis's forehead wrinkled with vexation at the notion that it could have been brought upstairs and placed in position without his knowledge. It must have happened this morning, because last evening he had been able to see Roger, through the open doorway, sitting as usual in the wing-backed chair by the window.

Judging by the direction and the strength of his voice, he was sitting there now. His visitor was nearer to the door, possibly sitting on the bed. Louis opened the door wider, the better to hear them, and then with one of his quick, slick, slithering movements, he nipped around the edge of the door and placed himself between its leaf and the screen. His feet tingled with fright, so that he had a sensation of hardly touching the floor with them. Rapidly he began to compose excuses in case he were discovered: "I was on my way in to see Roger. I have a right to see my own father. Julia sees him. Mark sees him. I'll see him if I like," and so on and on. Meanwhile he knew that as long as he kept his hand on the knob of the door, he would look as if he were just going in. What a blessing, a blessing from heaven that screen was.

Then, all at once, his little white brain stopped chattering as he began to take in the significance of the conversation to which he was listening. Like someone trying hurriedly to recapture a lot of escaped chickens, he tried to recall the things that had been said while he had been in his preliminary state of agitation. Suddenly and independently of his other sensations, he experienced a moment of pure bliss as he realized that he was on the edge of overhearing something entirely private, words which would never have been uttered if the presence of a third party had been suspected. This to Louis was equivalent to the joy of a man who successfully indulges a private vice, while deceiving the world with the bland face of innocence. Louis's greatest hope was, of course, that sooner or later himself would be mentioned, and that thereby he would perhaps add to his excruciating little store some further knowledge of what Roger really thought of him.

Roger's visitor was Louis's own sister Rosa, who had always been Roger's pet. Louis could imagine her sitting on the edge of the bed with one foot stretched out and part of her hair coming down. There was always something trailing from Rosa. Her voice trailed too, never accenting, never emphasizing, but just drawing the words out one after the other as one might draw the contents of a bag of hopelessly tangled remnants of knitting wool.

It seemed that Rosa had arrived only a moment or two before Louis, for Roger had been saying:

"I'm very glad you've come. I wanted to see you. Are you well again?"

"Yes, yes, well again. I heard Henry telling Julia on the telephone, that I had a cold, but I hadn't a cold. I've been busy."

"You might have come when you knew I was ill. I know the doctor said I was to have no visitors, but that meant tiresome people like Louis. It was not meant for you."

Louis felt a tingle in his diaphragm this time, as if someone had suddenly punched him lightly, almost playfully there.

"Doctor?" said Rosa. "I didn't meet a doctor. I don't care for doctors at all. I'm glad to find you up and about, Father. John told me that I wouldn't be let in to see you. He told me not to come."

"He didn't understand."

Rosa went on as if Roger had not spoken:

"I have my key, and I just opened the door and walked up-stairs, so I didn't meet anyone who might have kept me out."

"No one would have kept you out."

"Oh, yes. John would have, if he had seen me. John didn't want me to come at all. He threatened all sorts of things, but of course I didn't let that stop me."

"John? Threatened? What do you mean?"

"Oh, nothing much. That's not very interesting. I don't mind threats; I have courage. Yes, I'm able for every situation."

Louis in his hiding-place felt another little shock run through him as he realized that Rosa, Roger's pet, who was not a bore like Louis, was now at this moment a little tipsy.

196

He remembered another conversation he had overheard a week ago, between Henry and Mark Roche. Henry had been asking Mark to keep Rosa out from Roger. Neither of them had been aware that Louis's door was a little open as it always was on general principles. In fact Henry had been quite outspoken, because Mark had misled him into thinking that the whole family was downstairs. Henry had said that Rosa had taken to drinking little nips of gin because she was worrying about Henry's being excluded from reading the diary. Louis could not work out exactly where John came into all of this, but he thought it distinctly fishy that John should be mentioned at all. No one named Roddy, or Edward, or the girls. John seemed to know a lot of things. John had known about MacLean's offer for the diary, for instance.

At the very back of Louis's mind an old, old memory stirred. It had been trying to wriggle back to liberty for weeks past, but Louis had always pressed it down ruthlessly into its dungeon again. Now, however, he gave it a little law, and in that one second it leaped out of its chains and rampaged all over the place until he thought his poor head would burst. He closed his eyes, feeling quite faint and sick, but he made not the smallest sound. And then Rosa said:

"Father, I came to tell you that I think you have done very, very wrong."

There was a little pause, and then Roger said lightly:

"In not giving my old diary to Henry to annotate, you mean?"

"That is only one of the ways in which you have done wrong. Very, very wrong."

She brought the words out slowly, and their drifting, weak sound gave a horrible impression that they were being spoken by someone long dead. Their dim echo trailed about in the air for some time after she had said them. Louis felt a shiver run like a delicate finger down his spine. Roger said:

"Rosa, I'm afraid you're not well."

"No, no," said Rosa. "It's you that is not well. I am very well. And I have courage to tell you these things, because your soul is in danger. I can see that, and I have courage now. Dutch courage, yes, but just as useful as the real thing."

"Where have you spent the day?" Roger asked heavily.

"I'll tell you that in a moment," said Rosa calmly, "because it comes into what brings me here at all."

"I'll call Julia. You've been drinking."

"Father, I'm surprised at you. This is my first visit to you since your illness. If you call Julia I won't tell you why I came."

"Well, tell me then," said Roger.

Louis noticed a strong tension in his voice, well controlled.

"You were nasty to Henry about the diary," said Rosa judicially. "There was no need to be nasty, but you were. Then you should have given the diary to that nice Mr. Mac-Lean who was so anxious to have it."

"I have let him see it," said Roger. "He's been working on it every day."

"Yes, but you've been cutting out bits. You should have given it all to him."

"That would have been impossible. You don't know what you're talking about."

"Oh, yes. I do know. You asked where I spent the day. I spent some of it with your old friend Sybil Burns. And she's the third thing you did wrong, though I suppose we should call her the first, really, don't you think?"

She seemed to wait for a reply to this. When Roger said nothing she went on:

"The wrong of Sybil is the oldest and the ugliest, as old and as ugly as Sybil herself. Father, she really is horrid. I can't think how you could have preferred her to Mother. Sybil is fat, too. Mother would never have got fat, if she had lived to be old, poor darling. I won't get fat when I'm old either, because I'm very like Mother. I know that, when I look in the glass. Though I was only three when she died, I remember her so well. I remember her brushing her hair, great long chestnut hair all waved from her plaits, falling down her back like waves of the sea."

"Stop!" said Roger quietly. "Don't say those things."

"I can see you are sorry for having been so bad to her," said Rosa. "That's a good thing, I'm sure it is. That will help you to understand why you should give the diary to Mr. MacLean. You can still do it, I'm sure you can."

"Do you mean that I should let the whole world read the

198

story of Sybil and Flora?" Roger stopped suddenly, and then went on in a completely different tone: "How do you know what is in the diary? You've never read it. How do you know?"

"I'll come to that presently," said Rosa. "Yes, I've been with Sybil. Fat, vulgar Sybil. She was very rude to me. But I was almost rude to her." Rosa gave a little crowing laugh at this thought. "She knew who I was at once. I didn't have to introduce myself. She said I was so like Mother."

"Yes, you are very like your mother," said Roger, half to himself, "very like in appearance, at least."

"You think it strange that I should know what is in the diary," said Rosa. "Well, Sybil knows too. Does that surprise you?"

"Rosa, why are you tormenting me?"

"For the good of your soul. Does it surprise you that Sybil knows what's in the diary?"

"Yes. How much does she know?"

"That it contains an account of your *affaire* with her. That it tells how you were inspired to write by Mother, and you couldn't write any more after her death because you were eaten up with remorse and self-disgust."

"That's not in the diary."

"Of course not, but a child could read between the lines. Have you anything to drink here?"

"No."

"I wish you had. I could go on better if I had a little drink."

"I wish you wouldn't go on. I'm not well. I had a stroke."

"You must hear the truth. You deceive yourself. It's no use trying to make excuses and get out of it. And I'm not well either. I said I was quite well but it's not really true. My head is hurting. I've had to think and think. I got so cross with Sybil, you'd hardly believe. I'll tell you what she's going to do. She told me. She's going to write her memoirs for an English Sunday paper. It's going to be all about you, naturally, because she hasn't any other memoirs. She's going to get five thousand pounds for them, but she won't have it all for herself. She's going to tell how she inspired you to write, how you used to sit together for hours and talk about Sebastian and MacGurk, and all those other characters in your books.

199

She's going to say how you worked out their symbolism and their development, and how it was through her that you learned the technique of filling up detail in your own special way, to show every aspect of the characters. She's going to say that if you were the father of Meticulism, she was the mother. She told me all that. I said awful things to her. I said I knew that when you were together you didn't spend the time in talking about Meticulism. I called her an old bitch." Rosa giggled hysterically. "I called her other things too, names I hardly knew that I knew. It was a good thing I did, because she got more and more angry. She knows lots of bad words and I'd say she's in practice, judging by the way they rolled out of her. She looked an old disgrace, over eighty years of age, with her jowls quivering, and shaking her fist at me, and saying all those rude words. I didn't mind as much as you'd think. In fact it only excited me, so that I was able to answer her back, and then she told me more and more. Father, she told me you are still giving her money. That was very wrong. You deprived your own children and grandchildren for her. I'm sure you thought you were obliged in conscience to do this, but she has three children who could look after her. Her eldest son is fifty-six. She told me. I thought it was ridiculous. And she told me the reason why she's going to sell her memoirs. Father, you're not saying anything. Don't you want to hear?"

"Yes, I want to hear."

Roger's voice was thin with pain. Louis was shocked at the change in him. He even contemplated interfering now and putting a stop to the whole affair but while he hesitated Rosa went on, dropping the words so fast and so softly that their consonants drifted away and were lost:

"Sybil knows you had a stroke. She's afraid she'll get no more money after you're dead. Her children are selfish. They don't give her anything. So she wants to make some money of her own. And she'll have three thousand pounds for this."

"A moment ago you said five."

"Three for Sybil, two for the person who gave her the idea and who will write it all down for her. She says she couldn't do it herself."

"Who is that person?"

"I'm coming to that in a moment. Don't hurry me, or I'll

get it all wrong. I've had to think and think. You have no idea. A funny thing was that Sybil seemed really to want to be known as your inspiration. You should see her. Inspiration!"

"I haven't seen her for a long time."

"I wish you could see her now. I wish that you could have had a vision, long ago, of Sybil as she is now. That would have been a very good thing. No, no. I don't want to be cruel. Please don't cry, Father. If you do I won't be able to tell you the rest. Don't you want to hear?"

"Yes, I want to hear."

Incredibly, Roger was crying. Louis felt a squeezing in his chest, a thin fleshless hand that squeezed and released and squeezed again, harder the second time. He gave a tiny moan, but neither of the people beyond the screen heard him. He controlled himself with difficulty to hear Rosa continue:

"She said she wants to be known in history as the woman who inspired Roger Mallon. I almost thought at first that she believed she was your inspiration. She was very earnest about it. And then I saw it was only jealousy of Mother, because she said that a strong, earthy woman like herself was better company for an artist than a miserable, worn out, effete one. I was surprised that she should have used those words. Very much surprised. They didn't seem to go with the rest of her vocabulary. I questioned her about that. I was clever. I can be very clever, when I like. I didn't ask her straight. I said that was all rubbish, and so she told me it couldn't be rubbish because she had got it all from someone who had been near to you all his life."

"Who? Who?"

"John! She was so glad to tell me that. John, she said, a literary man. He's going to be a journalist. He made all the arrangements for selling her story to the paper. He knows its Irish representative. Sybil has met him. She said he was a perfect gentleman. I wanted to laugh, she sounded so very backstairs, so very like Nellie. John is going to write it all down word for word, only correcting the syntax here and there, and for this Sybil will give him two-fifths of her takings. They're starting very soon, early next week. Sybil wants to get her word in first. She'll succeed in that much anyway, because no

201

matter how fast you are, it takes ages to print a whole book. But better late than never. Oh yes, and they're having the manuscript vetted—that's the word she used: vetted—by her son that is a lawyer, so that there won't be any legal actions. She thought of that herself, and she was proud of it, I could see. Have you anything to drink here?"

"No!"

This time it was an impassioned shout. Rosa said, very smoothly:

"I wish you had. I need something to drink. I could go on much better if I had something to drink. Don't you want to hear?" Roger made no reply, but she went on as if he had answered as usual. "I think I've told you nearly everything. If I had known about Sybil long ago, perhaps I could have helped you. I would have advised you to give her nothing. Though I hate John for the way he talked about Henry, still I must be fair. I'm grateful to him for telling me about Sybil."

Roger sounded almost like his old self as he thundered:

"John told you about Sybil? John told you what was in the diary?"

Louis shrank as he had always done at that note in Roger's voice, even when it was not directed at him. But Rosa said fretfully:

"Please don't shout, Father. I can't think when you shout. Yes, John told me. He hates Henry. I don't see why he should. Henry has always been good to him. You know, Father, John annoys all the professors at the College. He's so rude and overbearing, especially about anything literary. They say it's because he is your grandson, that he thinks he has inherited everything you know, everything you did, and that anything he does or learns himself is a sort of extra. Henry is always having to make excuses for him, telling them that he'll improve. Still I must be fair to John. Perhaps he doesn't know that he should be grateful. I hate, hate, hate anyone that is bad to Henry."

"Rosa, have I been bad to Henry?"

It was a cry from his very heart, but Rosa took no notice.

"Yes," she said. "You have. It's worse when you give people a lot of privileges and then suddenly take them away again. That's worse than if you never gave them privileges at all. And

Henry makes nothing of himself. He always says that the critic is the servant of the artist, not the judge. He says that some artists must have an interpreter. Henry was yours. People get tired of their interpreters, just as they get tired of their teachers. I can understand that. But still I can't bear it when people make little of Henry. John did that too. It makes me so miserable. You know, Father, I hate a drinking woman. So does everyone. Women look far more degraded than men when they drink. Why should that be, do you know? I wonder if many women drink? I'm sure lots of them do, because lots of women are very unhappy. Sometimes, I'm happy, but not today. You see, I can't go home until the children are in bed, and I get so tired. That's why I'm resting my feet like this. And I like being here with you, though I know you have done very wrong. At first I wished John hadn't told me about Sybil because it made me so miserable, but now I'm glad, because I've been able to tell you. I hope you're not angry. You should never be angry when you are told things like this for your own good."

She was chattering now, on a new, excited note which had more than a hint of hysteria in it.

"Father, I'd like if you would say something to me. I'd like that. I can't bear it when you won't speak. Just say you're not angry, and I'll go away. No one will know I have been here. You're so clever, you'll find a way to deal with all this. I know you will. There must be a way. Wicked people like John and Sybil always get what they deserve in the end. Now I wonder if I did right. Father, please tell me if I did right. My head is hurting. I don't want to hurt people. I want to be with Henry, and my own children. That's what I want. I wish Henry were here now."

Louis trembled with terror at the door, as Rosa's voice jerked on, so differently from the smooth dreamy trickle that it had been before. He began to wonder why Roger did not answer, why no sound came from inside the room but the sound of Rosa's voice. He imagined her plucking and pulling at the silk quilt in an effort to anchor herself to reality. He knew exactly how she felt, for he had often felt like this himself. It was fascinating to hear and follow the progress of her disintegration. He knew that he should walk into the room and create the diversion which would be the only chance of saving her. But he could not bring himself to do it. He thought of going downstairs for Julia. He need only say that he had heard Rosa's voice in Roger's room, and that he thought Julia should tell her that the doctor had said there were to be no visitors.

While he dithered and hesitated and justified and thought of ways of stopping every possible gap in his own defences, if he were accused, something new was happening beyond the screen. Roger was getting up out of his chair. Louis could hear little stumbling movements of his feet, little shuffles and the scrape of the chair pushed back. The rug that had covered his knees rustled to the floor. The book that he had been reading fell with a roll and a thump. Louis still could not bring himself to look into the room, but there was no need. From his years of practice he had learned to follow whole sequences of events by sound alone, like a blind man. He could hear Roger fumbling with his stick, that beautiful stick that Louis had always coveted. He could hear its soft sucking sound on the floor. Julia had put a rubber tip on it when she had brought it upstairs a few days ago. Louis half-turned, so as to be ready to flit out of the room if Roger were to come to the door. There was no need for him to go until Roger would be quite near the screen. Rosa gave a little shriek, and said:

"Father, Father! What are you doing? I'm sure you're not supposed to walk about. Please sit down again. You must be quiet."

"How can I be quiet?" Louis shrank away from the deadly venom in Roger's words. His voice rose. A dramatic note came into it, a note of genuine drama, thought Louis, who had for a moment suspected that it was spurious. Roger's words were measured in an academic, literary way which conveyed his pain more clearly than any everyday words could do. "How can I be quiet? I was calm, though no one could say that I live in a fool's paradise. You came in here and poured poison into me. You filled me full of bitter, bitter poison, so that my whole body has stiffened and hardened with it. John. That's the bitterest poison of all. John. Did it really happen as you said? Did John come in here, and read my old diary some time when I was out, and make such evil use of it? Did he go to Sybil and flatter her silly old head and make a fool of her, for two thousand pounds? Are all those things true?"

"Father, you're frightening me. I can't think."

"Are they true? Are they true, I say?"

"Yes, yes, of course they are true. How could I make up things like that? John came to me, too. He made an appointment to meet me at Trinity College and he took me into a bar somewhere near. I couldn't make out why he was telling me all those terrible things, but then he said he was angry with Henry, and I thought he wanted to upset Henry by upsetting me."

Louis recognized at once that Rosa had hit on the truth, in her strange wandering way, and he writhed with shame and disgust for his son. He knew John well enough to know that this revenge would satisfy him, and compensate for whatever slight he had suffered, or fancied he had suffered, from Henry.

Rosa was saying, talking very fast:

"You mustn't tell John I've been here. He threatened to tell the children all these horrible things if I came. He said he'd meet them on the way home from school. He said he'd hurt them. Now I'm afraid. I promised I wouldn't come, but then later I got courage and I thought I was doing right. Oh, what will I do now?"

She burst into noisy tears. Louis, rooted to the ground, heard Roger shout and thump on the floor many times with his stick, bellowing at the top of his voice for John, and Sybil, and the Irish representative of the paper that Rosa had named, threatening refutations and legal actions, banging up and down the room kicking savagely at the furniture as if it were human.

Louis heard Julia on the stairs. There was no time to get away. She hardly seemed to see him as she brushed past him through the open door and around the edge of the screen. Louis followed her, half-blinded by the emotions generated by the climax of the scene that he had overheard. Inside the room he blinked stupidly against the light. There was Julia, standing. There was Rosa, lying across the bed weeping. And there was Roger, perfectly still and staring in a surprised sort of way. A moment later, for the second time, he was stretched senseless on the floor at their feet.

This time it was Louis and Julia who got him on to his bed, but first Julia chased Rosa off it without ceremony. Then she made Louis help her to lift Roger. He weighed heavily, since

205

he was quite unconscious. It seemed to Louis that Julia left him an unequal share of the weight. He feared for his health, because he always avoided lifting heavy things, but when he emitted a little bleat about this to Julia, she chopped him off short in the most inconsiderate way. He had never seen the corners of her eyes narrow in that way before. As when the beam of a torch is narrowed its light is intensified, so now it seemed to Louis that Julia's glare was as long and bright as a stiletto. When she told him to telephone for the doctor, he scurried out of the room, not needing her called-out injunctions to be quick about it. He got the doctor on the telephone at once and was assured that he would be in the house in ten minutes. Scuttling up the stairs to tell Julia and receive her praise, he was passed by Rosa, still weeping uncontrollably. He made no effort to stop her, though he did consider it. He knew that she ought not to go out into the street like that. She could come into his room, or sit in the drawing-room, even, or wash her face in the bathroom. But whose responsibility would she be? That was the question. Louis was a sick man himself. He could not spend long in the company of an hysterical woman without being affected by it. Some people were able for that sort of thing, but not Louis. He was too sensitive, that was his trouble. A blessed saying of Nellie's swam into his mind: he had not got the constitution for it. Meanwhile, Rosa was groping along down the stairs to the hall. Louis held his breath. She was going along the hall, but she might still turn aside into the drawing-room,' or even change her mind and come back upstairs again. But she did not. He heard the front door open. Then he heard it close. With a rush he released the air from his bursting lungs, breathed in and out twice, rapidly, and shot upstairs to Roger's room, relieved of a great burden.

14

It took Roger a full week more to die. The doctor was furious about the whole business. He took Julia into the dining-room and questioned her for half an hour about what had happened, why his instructions had not been followed and in the name of Heaven, who had let Rosa in. No one could be blamed for that, of course, because it was clear that Rosa must have let herself in with her own key.

"But Louis was standing at the door when I came up," said Julia. "He may know something about it."

So they called in Louis and asked him, but it was no use. He looked as if he thought they might beat him, and he babbled a lot about having arrived at the door only a moment before Julia, which might or might not be true. When he had gone Julia said:

"I'm afraid he is not very reliable. I have no evidence whatever, but he had an air of having been there listening for quite a while. I don't know why I have that impression, but if he was there I'm afraid he is not going to tell us what happened."

"I'd give a lot to know," said the doctor. "I'm afraid your father won't survive this."

"My sister can't really be held responsible," said Julia distractedly. "She is easily upset, and she is very much attached to my father. The only possible thing would have been to keep her out altogether, but what was I to do? This afternoon my father said he wanted to be alone. I didn't think of standing guard outside his door, though that is what I should certainly have done if I had had any idea that this sort of thing was going to happen."

Julia was annoyed with herself after she had said this, for it was one of her private rules never to be wise after the event.

She had long ago decided that it was no use trying to change people after they had reached a certain age, and that therefore the only course was to follow the advice of Saint Francis and love them as they were, though love in the Mallon household was a term that could be used only academically. But now she had a frightening sense that all of her lifelong principles were letting her down, that a determined campaign against Louis's laziness and hypochondria might have been more Christian and more profitable to Louis than her attitude of *laissez-faire* had been. Since Louis had grown up, she had believed that the cure for him would have been regular, paid employment, however humble, and she had been impatient with his lofty attitude towards work which was not sufficiently honourable for a Mallon. Yet she had never remonstrated with him about it, and now she began to wonder if she should have done this. Though she had always reacted strongly against Roger's principle of detachment, still it seemed that it had insidiously influenced her, and that she had rationalized it into something that accorded with her own principles of charity. Now it seemed to her that what she had called charity had really been only a weak acceptance of other people's failings, instead of the burning, active, missionary zeal that it should have been. But as she went up to Roger's room after the doctor had gone away, she saw Louis's pale frightened face peering out at her from beyond the partly-opened door. In that moment she saw that it was the face of a hurt small boy of seven years, fixed in disillusionment, and far beyond the reach of any rough and ready amateur cure. She passed quickly into Roger's room, pretending that she had not seen him.

As if they had scented Roger's approaching death, all the people in the house suddenly became very quiet and watchful, like jungle animals. Though they had never been in the least helpful, now they had an air of having drawn back to an even safer distance, leaving everything to Julia. Nellie was the only one who said anything about it. She sat firmly in the drawing-room and announced that she had no intention of lifting a finger for Roger.

"Before I came to this house I had a bit of respect for myself," said Nellie. "He never did anything but laugh at me, as if the world wasn't full of people like me. He laughed at

Louis too, his own son. I wouldn't lift a finger for him. I couldn't bring myself to do it. Them that encouraged him in his badness can look after him now."

No one answered, but a few minutes later Frances and Mary left the drawing-room to clear the supper table, without being asked.

John was there, listening to his mother's yapping, with his chin sunk on his chest and his long, brown eyes blank. He had heard Julia tell the doctor that Rosa had been with Roger, and that she had had a fit of hysterics on his bed. He had also heard the doctor tell Julia that Roger was going to die. There was no secret about it. The dining-room door had been open and they had taken no trouble to lower their voices. Now John was sitting very still, but with every muscle tense, willing with all his might that his luck would hold and that Roger would die without regaining consciousness. It seemed that he had not spoken of the stolen ring again, and that he had placed the blame for its disappearance on Roddy and Edward. But if he were to recover sufficiently to start asking questions, it might happen that he would reach the truth. If he did not recover, John had no intention of wallowing in *bourgeois* confessions of guilt.

"Let him die, let him die," said John over and over, to that dim, grey-faced, spectral god who looked after his affairs and who had never so far let him down. Why should Roger wake up to ruin John when his fate was already decided? Far better for him to die now and be finished with it. Then John would have a fresh start; a whole new era would begin for him in which he fully intended always to act honourably by everyone, as he had done with that elderly belle Sybil. It was a sign of his new point of view that he intended to take only two-fifths from her, though in fact he would be doing all the work. If the sum had been smaller he might have been tempted to cheat her, but there was simply no end to two thousand pounds. As for the morality of publishing her memoirs at all, when the offer reached four figures, questions of morality disappeared, especially if one had been brought up as thin as John had. And Sybil's story had all happened so long ago that it would be like writing a biography of Henry the Eighth.

Only one thing troubled John, and that was that the paper

in which Sybil's memoirs were to appear had a cheap, sensational point of view. But he had decided that it would be childishly unprofessional to consider this. Later he would graduate into the heavies, as befitted a clever, educated artist. Just now, most desperately, John wanted money. He licked his lips with a quick little surreptitious lick at the thought of what one could get with it—clothes, shoes, books, girls, dances, drinks and above all, food—great quantities of lush, luscious food steeped and swimming in expensive sauces, not just a deceptive sauce covering unspeakable nothingness, as Julia was always so cleverly cooking for this household. Until now he had hardly known that he was perpetually hungry. He wondered if his brothers were too, but their hearts were cold, not like John's, and their bodies seemed to be powered by inferior diesel engines, with cold, slimy oil in their veins instead of blood. John hungered for six-egg omelettes, and great, dripping fillet steaks, and soups composed of kidneys and sheep's heads and the tails of oxen. For the prospect of these he would have sold every member of his family twice over, not to speak of old Sybil who was no better than she ought to be, and Roger who would only be paying justly for his youthful misdeeds.

It was Frances, of course, who saw Mark coming towards the front door. She was alone in the dining-room just then, and she let Mark into the house quietly and brought him in there to explain what had happened. While she spoke, she watched his face with such an anguished expression that for the first time he began to feel some sympathy with her. Until now he had always found her extraordinarily inept. He had never dreamed that she had been so much attached to Roger. For some time he had been uncomfortably aware of her devotion to himself. They often happened to be on the same bus in the evenings, and though he sat beside her from politeness, she was so rigid that their conversation had always been in trivialities. Now she showed a remarkable insight in reading his wishes. She advised him to go upstairs and make an immediate arrangement with Julia.

"You and John are the people that Roger likes best," said Frances, "but John is no use to him now. He seems to have gone to pieces in the last few days."

If John had gone to pieces, thought Mark as he followed

210

her advice, Frances had made a beginning at assembling herself. With a different upbringing and different clothes, he wondered if she need have been so very unattractive. Then he put her out of his mind and turned his full attention to Roger.

The fact that he was allowed to be with Roger for his last days seemed to Mark a kind of miracle. Julia brought in a sofa, and he half-slept on it at night at the foot of the bed. As if in compensation for their former carelessness, he and Julia made sure that Roger was never alone, and he had no visitors other than the doctor and a calm, assured, middle-aged Jesuit, for his old friend in that order was long dead.

In the first days, after he had revived a little, Roger groaned all day with the pain in his conscience. After that he began to talk, hour after hour, slowly going over and over the same points, trying to find out where he had gone wrong in his relationships with his family. A terrible, distorting light seemed to have been turned on for him, so that he saw himself as a great sinner from whom retribution was now demanded. He was not in the least consoled by the Jesuit's comment that his attitude could be a kind of inverted spiritual pride. Sybil's project of writing her memoirs was forcing him into handing over the complete diary to MacLean, and he was almost superstitiously impressed with the fact that it was Rosa who had pointed out his duty to him.

"If you want to know what Flora looked like, just look at Rosa," he said. "That is what she was like, on the outside. Rosa is a caricature of Flora, or a ghost of Flora, Flora without her cleverness, without her originality, without her sense of humour. She is like Flora just before she died. I have injured Rosa too. I saw the same look, the same look on her face. It was not only because of Henry that she looked like that. It was because she hated having discovered that I was such a traitor."

With his head bent so that his face was in shadow, Mark murmured some comforting remarks. Roger was lying on his back, as usual, staring at the ceiling. He listened attentively, and then said:

"Where is Rosa? What became of her after she left me?"

"Henry has got a good doctor for her. She is having some treatment."

211

"In hospital?"

"Yes. Henry says she'll be well again soon. He said you must not worry about her."

"Henry is a kindly, good, considerate man," said Roger heavily, "all the things that I never was."

Still he never would consent to see Henry, who came every day and waited for an hour to be summoned upstairs. And Roger could not bring himself to speak well of him.

"He'll probably write my biography after I am dead," he said sardonically another day. "Mark, I hope you'll never become a great man. Then you'll be safe from the biographers. They make a major misery out of every occasion on which their man didn't get his own way. They dig out injustices and misunderstandings, and make him look mean and petty and stupid, make him appear to have expected full indulgence from the world. Henry is an enthusiast for me; he'll write that damned biography *con amore*. I can see it at this moment. I can hear the reverent, hushed tone of it. I'll tell you something, if you promise not to tell Henry."

"I won't tell him."

"My parents called the doctor for me, when I got my first real inspiration for a story, at the age of seven. They made me stay in bed and gave me sedatives. It was a warning of what was to come. Henry writes about me as if I were not quite right in the head, as if I were a kind of inspired lunatic. No, that's not fair. He'll suffer, though, when the diary is published. But I can't help it. No just God would expect me to give my diary to Henry."

He talked about the diary a great deal, calculating what its effect would be on his own literary reputation. He always smirked a little to himself when he spoke of it, and Mark could see that after his first resistance had been so dramatically and painfully broken down, he was truly overjoyed that his masterpiece was going to be presented to the world, complete, after all.

"A bad effect may be that people will begin to think that my other books are autobiographical. They'll start an awful game of identifying me with Sebastian. Heaven knows where it will end. Look at what happened to poor old Joyce."

"But he started the game himself," Mark pointed out.

212

"Yes, yes, so he did."

Roger was silent for a long time while he thought about this. At last he sighed and said:

"What I most want is that Flora should be given her proper place. It would be intolerable if Sybil were to get the credit for me at the end of her life. And she may, you know. To many people it will seem almost *de rigueur* that my wife should be dull and my mistress witty and clever and exciting, instead of the reverse. Besides, the intellectual climate of today is all wrong for Flora. No one will believe in her innocence. Nowadays the vogue is all for toughness and subtlety. Innocence is thoroughly out of fashion."

"Not in Ireland," said Mark doubtfully.

"You think not? Well, perhaps you're right. Certainly the attitude will be very different in America. At home I'm rather hoping the published diary will be banned by the censorship board. My old associates will be very put out if it circulates freely here. It's distinctly rude to them in places. I'm sorry about that in a way, but I won't take out the references to them at this stage. I must do full justice and injustice to everyone."

As the days passed, Roger became more and more agitated, and his talk less consecutive. Mark made non-committal answers which Roger hardly seemed to hear. MacLean had been given the diary and had taken it away with him, bewildered at the sudden change in Roger's attitude but asking no questions.

"I feel that I stirred up a hornet's nest here," he said to Mark who arranged the business with him. "But I can't help feeling all the same that nothing matters so much as giving that diary to the world. The thought of it mouldering here after I'd gone away would have been enough to make me die young, I can tell you that straight. How is the old man?" he asked anxiously. "I'd like to thank him personally."

But he was not allowed to do this.

It was on the last day that he was able to speak that Roger mentioned John.

"John is my worst failure," he said, squeezing the words out painfully one by one. After a long pause he went on: "And yet I can't make out whether I injured or helped him more. I kept him away from his terrible mother. I taught him to read.

213

I even taught him to write. But I smothered all of his fine qualities in academics. He's spiritually worn out. He must recover from me. Then he'll have no more of these reactions. You know it was he who stole Flora's old diamond ring."

"Surely not," said Mark, startled.

"Yes, I think it was John," said Roger. "He sneaked in here and read the diary, too, probably on the day that we went to look at your new flat."

Wryly Mark remembered how John had persuaded him to take Roger out, for the good of his health, on that day. Roger was saying wearily:

"I don't know for certain about the ring, and I'm not going to try to find out. Mark, promise me you won't try to find out."

"Of course not. I'll never discuss it with anyone."

"Good boy. Never discuss John at all. Give him time. I was dissatisfied with John when I thought that he was honest and sober and hard-working. Now that I know more about him, I'm far more pleased with him. Isn't that extraordinary? I can see now that nowhere in this world could be found the paragon of whom I would have approved."

This was said with great bitterness, but after another silence Roger went on almost calmly: "My betrayal of Flora entitled every one of my descendants to betray me. In fact it put them under an obligation to betray me. Teresa knew that, but she couldn't bring herself to injure me, so she left my house."

"Teresa is happily married," said Mark. "I was at her wedding."

"I wish she were here now," said Roger restlessly. "I wish she could play for me, '*Che faro senza Eurydice*', or the Mozart flute and harp concerto. I wish she were here now."

"She'll come home soon."

"But I won't be here. All my life I preached detachment. Man was to lift himself up above all human attachments, cut himself free from his bonds, work for the spiritual advancement of mankind but let individual man go hang. It was all bull and balderdash. Individual man is what matters, and he shrivels up and dies for lack of love. If I could hold a pen I would write that down. Louis loves his horrible Nellie, but I took the good out of it for him by showing her up whenever I

214

could. To love and to be loved are the important things. It's like something from my book of clichés. No philosopher is needed to interpret that message. It's as simple and clear as it could be, and all the common, ordinary people knew it always; everyone knew it except the great Roger Mallon, an old spider, glutted with his own ego. Crush down all feeling, all emotion except my own. Watch everyone tirelessly for signs of weakness, and then expose them, show them up, make fools of them. That has been my life's work.''

Not another word would he say. Watching him as he lay there with his beard gloomily sunk on his chest, it occurred to Mark that Roger had liked the sound of his last words, and that he did not feel himself able to improve upon them. When later that evening he sank into a coma, and the doctor said that he would not revive again, Mark determined that no living person should ever hear what those last words had been. He remembered well that it was Roger's charity that had attracted him at first, long before he had met him. During the last painful day of Roger's life, he speculated endlessly as to how much of his personal failure Roger had really understood, whether he had fully realized the deadly injury that he had inflicted on each member of his household. It seemed to Mark that in naming John and Teresa, picking out the two among them who had best survived his blighting influence, Roger had shown that he did indeed understand.

Suddenly Mark wished with all his heart that it had been possible to convince Roger of the extent of Mark's own debt to him. And as he contemplated the change that had come about in his life under Roger's influence, gradually he began to wonder whether after all Roger had really been right in blaming himself so bitterly. Perhaps all of these people who were by nature commonplace—Louis and his children, Nellie, Rosa, Henry and even Julia—perhaps the searing touch of Roger's personality was in fact the one influence which had made their dreary lives a little exciting, which had exalted them for a while, even though it were only half an inch above the wet clay that was their natural habitat.

In the dawn of the morning Roger died, to the sound of fluttering, whistling, newly-awakened birds in the heavy-leafed summer trees of Washington Road. Mark and Julia

215

faced each other across his bed, overwhelmed by the indefinable dignity of death, which seemed to them both suddenly to have exposed its true character as a positive action rather than a passive assent. They were the only ones who shed any tears for him.

Having someone dead upstairs was not in the least like what the Mallons had imagined. They lowered their voices, to be sure, but not much, because the air of the house had become strangely lighter, and they could not prevent an overtone of relief, almost of happiness, from creeping into everything they said.

That was in the morning.

In the evening, when Mark came back to escort Roger's body to the church, he walked into the drawing-room and found them all quarrelling. He listened for a moment or two unobserved, and then went upstairs to be with Roger for the last time.

Louis was in the midst of the quarrel. It was about who should have Roger's collection of children's books. Nellie said that they should be sold.

"There's no one would read the like of them nowadays," she said with contempt. "And anyway, what did an old man want with a lot of children's books unless it was for his second childhood? God rest his soul," she added hurriedly.

Mary wanted them for her own children when she would have them. Paddy supported her stoutly in this. He had never seen the books, which were always kept in Roger's bedroom. What he was really supporting was the idea of his unborn children, an unexpected idea which for some reason filled him with a rather belligerent excitement.

Roddy and Edward wanted them to give to their friend who had been so good to them about the race-horses. He had children who tore up their books at the most shocking rate, and Roger's collection should keep them going for a good six months.

Frances wanted them just to have them. Passionately she wanted to have something of Roger's for herself, but she saw as soon as the others began to get interested that her chances were finished.

John wanted them to read again and again, to anchor him

216

to Roger from whom he had received the strange, uncomfortable creative gift that was for ever seething within him, and which he feared might at any moment slip underground and never be seen again.

In the end, Louis shouted them all down. He said that he was the head of the house now, and that they would all have to do as he said. He decreed that John was to have the books, and he pointed out that he was the only serious reader among them and the only one who seemed to have inherited some of Roger's literary gifts. Louis pitched into them with gusto. He felt powerful. He felt free. He was truly, now, the head of the family. Soon he would move into Roger's room. He would probably break a door through into his present room so that Nellie could come in and out. It would be quite as good as a flat—like a service flat, really, because Julia would still do the cooking and the cleaning. There would be much more money, on account of the diary, and it would come to him unless Roger had taken the trouble to alter his will. Louis was sure he had not done this, yes, he was sure Roger had not altered his will. And in that event the contents of the house would belong to Louis too, which was one reason why he could say who was to have the books.

Louis did not care a hang who had the books, really. The only thing he had wanted, he had got. At seven o'clock in the morning, before the coffin came, before even the nuns came to dress Roger up in his habit, Louis had slipped in and had taken Roger's gold-headed walking-stick that he had always, always wanted. He had put it away safely on top of the wardrobe in his own room. It would be at least a month before he would be able to use it, but during the time of waiting, it would be wonderful to know that it was there.

After the funeral was over, Mark visited the Mallons' house only once again. Everything looked just the same, but for him it was as if the roof had been stripped off and the jackdaws had begun to nest in the empty fireplaces, as he had seen once in a burnt-out house. The heart of the house was gone, and it had been replaced by something quite different. Mark sat for an hour in the grip of an icy paralysis, as if he were in the presence of Roger's ghost. He tried to explain some of this to Frances, who made some effort to dissuade him when he got

217

up to go, but he soon saw that it was no use. As he walked away from the house in the last of the daylight, he knew that the whole Mallon episode of his life was over.

He had to wait many years before he found someone in the least like Teresa.

POOLBEG

Dublin 4

Maeve Binchy

By the best selling author of
Light a Penny Candle and *Echoes*.

These four stories, set in the heart of Dublin's fashionable
Southside, focus on the dilemmas facing four ordinary
people. There is a society hostess who invites her
husband's mistress to dinner, a country girl lost in the big
city, a reformed drinker beset by temptations, and a
student grappling with the problem of an unplanned
pregnancy. With her intimate grasp of human feelings
and her uncanny ear for dialogue, Maeve Binchy lavishes
sympathy on all her characters, brave and foolish alike.

ISBN 0 905169 77 8   Rep of Irl IR£3.50
                                              UK£3.15

POOLBEG

The Lilac Bus

Maeve Binchy

By the best-selling author of
Light a Penny Candle and *Echoes*.

A collection of eight interwoven tales, brimming with wit
and laughter. The people who travel on the Lilac Bus
lead separate lives in Dublin during the week, but are
thrown together at weekends for the journey home to
Rathdoon. Their paths begin to cross in an unexpected
and intriguing way.... In these stories, Maeve Binchy
uses deft touches of irony and humour to point to the
goodness and folly of human nature.

ISBN 0 905169 78 6   Rep of Irl IR£3.50
                                           UK£3.15